A Frieze
of Girls

Sweetwater Fiction: Reintroductions
Edited by Charles Baxter and Keith Taylor

Rediscovering the lost literary classics of the
Great Lakes states.

OTHER TITLES IN THE SERIES:

Castle Nowhere: Lake-Country Sketches,
by Constance Fenimore Woolson
with a new introduction by Margot Livesey

ALSO OF INTEREST:

The Glass House: The Life of Theodore Roethke,
by Allan Seager
(University of Michigan Press, 1991)

A Frieze
of Girls

— ✳ —

memoirs as fiction
by Allan Seager

The University of Michigan Press
ANN ARBOR

A CIP catalog record for this book is available from the British Library.

Library of Congress Cataloging-in-Publication Data

Seager, Allan, 1906–1968
    A frieze of girls : memoirs as fiction / by Allan Seager.
        p. cm. — (Sweetwater fiction)
    ISBN 0-472-08957-9 (acid-free paper)
    1. Seager, Allan, 1906–1968—Childhood and youth. 2. Novelists,
American—20th century—Biography. 3. Michigan—Biography.
I. Title. II. Series.

PS3537.E123Z466 2004
813'.54—DC22
[B]   2003053360

"Dear Old Shrine, Our Hearts Round Thee Twine," "Actress with Red
Garters," "Miss Anglin's Bad Martini," and "The Drinking Contest" were
published in *Esquire Magazine*, and "The Joys of Sport at Oxford" in *Sports
Illustrated.* "Under the Big Magnolia Tree," "Powder River in the Old
Days," and "The Nicest Girl in Cook County" originally appeared in *The
New Yorker.* "The Cure" originally appeared in *Atlantic.*

Introduction

Charles Baxter

Imagine a writer who has suffered a series of setbacks: neglect, cultural isolation, poor sales, all the usual complaints writers have to contend with plus a few extra, such as tuberculosis. He is not by nature a cheerful type but decides to gather together certain of his stories as a coming-of-age potboiler in which his youth is presented as a series of comic trials whose hero is a sort of American Candide. He has a gift for constructing comic scenes, a gift that includes the perfect timing that such scenes require. The author presents his younger self in a charming manner: small-town boy makes good despite his many mistakes. This same author also serves as an amusing guide to his times—the era of Prohibition—and to his subject, the portrait of the artist as a young man in the Midwest. The book that he writes, *A Frieze of Girls*, he subtitles "memoirs as fiction," an ambiguous phrase with a faintly sinister overtone. It can mean that he is telling his story as if the narration followed the form of a novel. But perhaps it means that he is lying about his past, either the subject matter or the tone he brings to it. In either case the reader has been warned. Following its publication, the book briefly becomes a best-seller.

In one of those ironies of which life is so fond, *A Frieze of Girls* turns out to be the last book written by its author to be published during his lifetime. In its tone, it is unlike almost everything else he wrote.

I first read Allan Seager's memoir several years ago when a friend recommended it, cautioning me first that I would have to search for a copy, since it was out-of-print. Also, she said, the book had a series of emotional and stylistic "hairpin turns," a description she didn't bother to explain to me, although I felt I knew what she meant. In any case, I found a copy in the public library, and as I read it, I almost fell out of my chair with surprise and happiness. I loved the seemingly effortless and self-deprecating wit, the sentences built for speed, the retrospective wryness that permitted the narrator to comment on his younger self. Seager is a charmer. But I also thought—and every one of my rereadings of *A Frieze of Girls* confirms this—that the author was being somewhat duplicitous in the service of his art. The comedy falls into a particular subgenre, that of inadvertent stoicism covered over by modesty. It is a very, very rare tone to strike in American writing, and the model for it, distantly, might have been Stendhal, whom Seager had translated—*Memoirs d'un Touriste*. The narrator of this memoir is a tourist himself, and never more so than when he is squarely at home.

It is worth mentioning this to first-time readers of *A Frieze of Girls* because the charm and the wit in this book are so obvious that its depths might not be immediately apparent. One notable characteristic of many Midwestern writers is that they sometimes disavow complexity and then hide it where it won't show. Seager, a native of Michigan and a nearly lifelong resident of that state, practiced this sleight-of-hand assiduously in his memoir. We can all laugh at the foolishness of our youth, and if we live long enough we are usually expected to forgive ourselves for that foolishness. But sometimes we don't laugh, ever. Sometimes the lapses in behavior continue to feel dire. Sometimes the forgiveness comes hard, or with a conversion, as in Augustine.

There is no conversion in *A Frieze of Girls*, but its author *has* become a writer, almost without anyone else, including himself, knowing how he managed it. The story he has given us at the surface would seem inevitably to lead to another conclusion entirely: how the autobiographer became a plain ordinary guy, maybe a car salesman. But he didn't become that guy. He became the person who wrote this book, along with five novels, a volume of stories, a translation of Stendhal, and a biography of Theodore Roethke. It is as if we have been led by a charming and witty tour guide into a room that is not listed on the floor plan.

What *A Frieze of Girls* actually seems to be about is the familiar comedy of adolescent suffering. This is a high-wire act, and at times the comedy falls away, most notably in the third story, about a murder, and the central story, "The Old Man," about the narrator's grandfather, an abusive, cruel, and willful pioneer of sorts who fought at Gettysburg and cleared his land, raised his family, and died unloved and unmourned by everybody. It is a stunning portrait, starting with the old man's recollections of Gettysburg and moving down to the small detail of the scars left on the hands of the narrator's father, Arch, by the grandfather's whip, administered when the boy happened to plow uneven rows. This story is close to one that Seager subsequently tells about himself and the particular day he showed the manuscript of his first novel to his father (the man who was once whipped). His father's first words were, "What do you make it so thick for? Nobody will read it." Allan Seager did not complain. "But I said nothing," he tells us, because "by that time I knew what kind of people we were, I guess."

That hapless dismissal of pain in the shrug-of-the-shoulders, that heartbreakingly American "I guess," marks Seager's narrative as a painful set of disclaimers. Sometimes it hurts to watch, and that pain mixed with comedy is what gives *A Frieze of Girls* its distinction and, finally, its liberation from the category of a mere crowd-pleaser. In this book, Allan Seager was writing better than he knew. As a result, many of its scenes and individual sentences stick to the memory as if glued there.

Allan Seager was born in Adrian, Michigan, in 1906 and died a few miles away in Tecumseh in 1968. (Here I am relying on the excellent book-length study of Seager's work by Professor Stephen E. Connelly.) As the reader of *A Frieze of Girls* will discover, Seager spent part of his youth in Memphis before going on to the University of Michigan and then to Oriel College, as a Rhodes Scholar. While in England, he contracted tuberculosis and was sent to Trudeau Sanitarium in Saranac Lake, New York. After his recovery and another year at Oxford, he returned to the University of Michigan, where he taught for most of his adult life. He wrote stories, biographies, and novels, of which *Amos Berry*, published in 1953, is probably his best, the tale of a poet and his businessman father. Most of Seager's fiction has a somber cast, though it has flashes of pitch-dark wit—in this, it sometimes resembles the fiction of Wright Morris. Nevertheless, Seager had bad luck with sales—he seems to have had little or no instinct for self-promotion—and as he aged his view of the literary world and of lives in the Midwest grew progressively darker. *A Frieze of Girls* was conceived of during a bleak time, which probably gives its tone a peculiar nervous resonance.

The plot is as follows: Seager's protagonist, himself, is determined to become a man, as that role is defined by his particular era. Various complications ensue. In the America of Prohibition, manhood meant finding or making liquor of various kinds and then drinking it. A man would be able to hold his alcohol; in this respect, the young Seager is a champ. Such a man would also be able to charm and seduce those mysterious beings, women. Time and again, Seager tells the story of his baffled attempts to charm these elusive characters, all of whom insist on surprising him by becoming, under his inspection, real persons, complex human beings. The beautiful Marta van der Puyl is first seen wearing a red garter and last seen reading *The Decline of the West*. Another actress, Margaret Anglin, shows the narrator a thing or two about worldliness: in response to an earnest Midwestern fraternity brother who tells her, "You wouldn't want to run into a nude young man," she replies, with some asperity, "Why not?"

Then there is the drinking. The stories of drinking are funny but I persist in seeing a darkness around the edges of these accounts, as if, in being initiated into this mystery, the cast of characters is being ruined without quite realizing it. Perhaps we are all conscious now of certain features of alcoholism that Seager's generation chose to ignore. In any case, the reader notices how little enjoyment the drinker seems to have in his drinking—how much it seems like an ordeal to which the power of will must be deployed in order to lose control and to keep the appearance of control at the same time. The spectacle is a bit like that of Washington Irving's little men spied by Rip Van Winkle in the Hudson Valley before his long sleep: they bowl for sport, but they never smile. And so it is here.

There is also the comedy of the American and British clash of styles (my favorite moment coming near the end when Seager tries out some American rah-rah fight-talk on his British teammates), and the comedy of the American provincial arriving in Britain, a subject that had not lost much of its force from the time of Henry James. (It still hasn't; as I write, Americans are still barging into parts of the planet where they know little or nothing of the native culture. Complications *still* ensue.)

In bringing this wonderful book back into print, I believe the University of Michigan Press is doing the general reader a great service. Allan Seager was a writer of great gifts; Hugh Kenner thought so, as did Malcolm Cowley and Robert Penn Warren and Sherwood Anderson and Donald

Hall and many others. This may be Seager's *easiest* book, though, as I have suggested, any reader can sound its depths because, like one of Henry James' true artists, Seager could not write a potboiler without also creating a work of art. Certainly, of all Seager's books, it is the one that gives the most immediate pleasure. As a memoir, it gives a glimpse of an entire generation of American men whose struggles for dignity and maturity were, as often as not, both comical and dangerous simultaneously, as if they were on a road whose hairpin turns would force the driver to change direction in an instant. You hold your breath; you laugh; you see the embankment over which the car could plunge; and you are grateful that there is a virtuoso driver at the wheel.

Contents

Preface

A couple of years ago when she was smaller and a shade more credulous I told my younger daughter I had been a hunchback until I was twelve years old, a tiny cheery newsboy who "carried" the Adrian *Daily Telegram* summer and winter (leaving little pinkish footsteps in the snow where my ankles had chapped and bled). I said that I had an isinglass bubble sewed into the back of my mackinaw so that for a nickel people could lift the bubble and rub my hump for luck. I said that Dr. Stephenson, a kindly surgeon whose paper I always folded and stuck between the knob and the door, had operated on me free and straightened me up so I could be like other boys. I think I was trying to arouse her pity so I could use it to make her do something I wanted. Her pity, however, lay quite still and she said coldly "You're lying." She was right. I made it up. I excuse flights like these by insisting that the experience of fiction is part of her education.

But when I tell her that I know a girl who clerked in Cunningham's Drug Store who used to go with a guy named Sultan Shakmannoff, then an electrical engineer but once a circus rider and that this Shakmannoff on holidays at the lake where we used to catch bluegills would dance springily along the shore, singing hoarsely and wearing soft boots of black leather that came above his knees and had little turned-up toes, my daughter, who has been at this lake, looks at me coldly and says "You're lying again," although it is the simple truth. Sultan made the first shish kebab I ever ate, marinating the lamb in wine and herbs for a day before skewering it. I believe he was a Georgian.

I am not trying to establish my daughter's skepticism here, still less to spur the indignation of child-lovers everywhere by my treatment of her; rather I am trying to show that the feel of truth is very like the feel of fiction, especially when either is at all strange.

I am old enough to know that time makes fiction out of our memories. Some people, some events it pulls front and center. It stores others in the attic until we find some use for them. It discreetly buries a few forever. Can anyone remember his life accurately, objectively the way a camera and a tape would have recorded it? I doubt it. We all have to have a self we can live with and the operation of memory is artistic—selecting, suppressing, bending, touching up, turning our actions inside out so that we can have not necessarily a likable, merely a plausible identity. In this sense we are always true to ourselves, and if I say that the pieces in this book are autobiographical, they are so only in this way. They cover some episodes of my life from the age of sixteen to about twenty-five that I thought interesting. I really haven't the effrontery to think of them as The Education of a Young Man.

When I started to write them I was a little surprised to find most of them coming out funny and I was not the only one who thought so. (Legions of readers, legions.) I did not regard myself even young as a comic figure. A man likes to think of the years of his education as fruitful, adventurous, maybe exhausting but not funny. And I knew they had not been amusing at the time for, as I say later, I kept a kind of diary and in it I was always suffering. At last I could see that memory or perhaps the septenary cellular changes had contrived a later me, the one who was doing the writing, pompous, seedy, ept, and irascible, bronzed with experience whose past lay on his face like the scorings on a ham, and I could regard the caperings of the earlier version with the detachment that permits comedy. It is never funny when your own bag of groceries splits; when it is the other guy's, nearly always. And, green, I was another guy.

'Sociologists sweat to teach us that we are all faceless conformists, but I don't believe it. I think Americans, one by one, are a strange people. We seem to enjoy or suffer a greater variety of experience than others. It may be because we have stayed loose—we range upward, downward, and sideways in the jungle gym of our society as a matter of course. When I was a hunchback, I never expected to dance with Lady Astor or to plow with horses—yet I have done both. And the young Americans I have set down here, like Sara Egan, Arno Bevins, Marta van der Puyl, seem in retrospect stranger than I and they weren't even trying. I do not know what has become of them. Now, they may be stranger yet.

The English were different. Except for the church-robber, those I have recalled seemed to be types rather than individuals. *Pace* Dame Sitwell, the eccentric was rare. The weather may be a force here (they all try to stay out of it). Perhaps the age of the country and the clamps of a once-feudal society have worn away any new spines or shoots but I think it was chiefly types that I met, the young gentlemen of Oxford. Although the organization of the University is less anxious and offers much more intellectual freedom than any in this country, it is not the curricula that do the work. It is the weight of an old tradition *sifted* from the minds of servants, tailors, schoolmasters that extrudes them in the proper mold. By dozens of subtle hints Oxford men are taught that they must and will be the props and ornaments of the nation. Unconsciously they obey. I read about some of my contemporaries in the papers occasionally, people like Mr. Dingle Foot, M.P., or Sir John Gielgud.

I think this book got its start one day when Joseph Henry Jackson was giving me lunch at the Bohemian Club in San Francisco and asked, "If you think of your life at twenty, what comes back first?" The question was apropos; of what, I can't remember, but my answer contained the title of this book: "It was a kind of frieze of girls and long aimless car rides at night." A frivolous reply, perhaps, but true. Everyone, God knows, has his peculiar consignment of long sweaty troubles that lie in his memory as heavily as shame, dirty and unforgettable. I had my own, but somehow they weren't as prompt as the girls who leaped over them and came running back as fresh and lovely as in life.

* I *

Under the Big Magnolia Tree

*T*he high school I went to was three miles from where I lived. In my freshman year I used to ride my bike. It was a Gendron, black with the steering column silver, and delicate silver arrows on the frame. I am aware I am trying to make it sound good but it was really a second-rate bike. Whenever anyone asked me what kind it was and I said "A Gendron," they always said "A what?" I wanted a Dayton, all-copper frame, but a Dayton cost eight dollars more.

I used to make it to school in about fifteen minutes. As a Yankee in a Southern city, I had made few friends and none in my part of town, so I rode alone. There were no stop lights then. Traffic was thin. I knew all the hills I could coast down and I made pretty good time. I was a military courier on most of my trips. On a few I was a bicycle road-racer, a less interesting pretense because I had no competition. By the end of the year, I had worn out the road-racing and the courier dodge and I simply rode to school, going slower and slower, dawdling, trying to find something interesting along the way.

I found it all right. One hot fall morning in my second year I was trying to see how slowly I could ride, no hands, along a streetcar track without falling into the little rut that paralleled it when I saw this girl. She was walking and she walked like a colored laundress with a bundle on her head, erect, languid, graceful. My front wheel fell into the rut, then the hind wheel, and I was tipping over before I looked away from her. I caught myself, my foot stamping on the pavement. She glanced at me and I rode on furiously.

I carried an Ingersoll dollar watch then and I was so flustered I forgot to check the time. I looked at the clock when I got to school and I figured it must have been about twenty past eight. I remembered the place exactly, in front of a barber shop in what would now be called a shopping center on a street named Crosstown where two main streetcar lines intersected. The next morning at twenty past eight I was riding slowly out Crosstown, passing the barber shop, two hands, because you can ride slower that way. I didn't see her. I didn't see her for three days.

Central was a big high school with about fifteen hundred pupils and during that three days I didn't run into her once in the halls when classes changed. I knew mornings were my only chance because I was going out for football afternoons. At fifteen I was six foot one, and I weighed a hundred and forty-seven pounds, some of it muscle. I had an appetite like a boa constrictor and my notion of a little snack between meals was a quart of milk and a loaf of raisin bread. On Thanksgiving Day I ate one side off an eighteen-pound turkey, nonchalantly, hardly realizing what I was doing, and my mother cried when the guests had left and said it was obscene to eat that way. As a high-school sophomore, that was not my idea of obscenity and her tears made little impression. The point was, I couldn't seem to gain weight. I might have made a rickety end but I was slow on my feet so they played me at second-string center. As an end, if anybody had thrown me a pass, I might have caught it in some tense last quarter, gone galumphing down the field and made a touchdown in front of her. And if I did that, I felt I could merely walk up to her and say "Hi." Centers, however, are

buried under guards and tackles and have no opportunities.
I did what I could. I got into one of the early games
against a team from Tunica, Mississippi, because the regular
center tired in the heat which was around ninety-five. The
Tunica center was the kind of boy you see sometimes in
the country. He stood six feet seven inches tall and he
weighed two hundred and sixty pounds. I don't know if
his head came to a peak, but he wore what seemed to be
a little teeny helmet with the earpieces standing out at right
angles three inches above his ears and Army shoes with the
cleats nailed on. He was in his own way most of the time
and his only value was awe.

His coach must have told him to fall on the opposing
center as soon as he snapped the ball. He fell on me just
once. I felt as if I were squirting out like a tube of tooth-
paste. After that, when I snapped the ball I jumped back.
He crashed to earth steadfastly every time and I would run
up and stand on him, scanning the play as from a little
hill, and I made a couple of fancy tackles from behind.
At last the Tunica coach must have seen me abusing his
big boy because the referee put me out of the game for
dirty play. The game was being held in the Memphis
Chicks' ballpark and, when I trotted to the sidelines, two
thousand people roared with laughter. On Monday morning, I crept past her a little way beyond the barber shop,
watching her covertly, hoping she might give me a little
memorial laugh but she didn't.

The problem was to get to see her at all. I had run into
her once and overtaken her once in the halls at school
but no more. She was not in any of my classes so I judged
her to be a junior or a senior, and that was an added burden.
I bicycled slowly past her about three times a week, won-
dering if I dared steer into one of the rocking Crosstown
streetcars and come staggering away from my bent bike
with some spectacular bruises, but I had built up her seren-

ity to the point where I feared she would not notice even
blood. Fame was lending me no *savoir-faire* because I was
not famous; my name appeared under the heading "Substi-
tutes" once a week in the *Commercial Appeal* and I could
hardly swagger up to her with the confidence of a regular
halfback.

I quit going out for football and I quit riding to school.
The coach did not plead with me to keep on playing. I
don't think he noticed I was gone. Walking meant that
I had to start for school at least a half-hour earlier. This
rather pleased my mother than anything because I slept like
a bear in the winter and she had had trouble mornings
getting me on my feet, fed, and away. I saved up my allowance, bought a little alarm clock, and bounced out of bed
at seven o'clock sharp.

Afoot I could synchronize my movements with hers very
closely, and I did. I would make the corner of Crosstown
and Madison at eight o'clock and lurk around, gaping at
the store windows and waiting at the streetcar stop, never,
somewhat to the surprise of the regular patrons who eventually came to recognize me, boarding any car until I saw
her turn off Madison onto Crosstown. Then I would stalk
her, keeping about thirty feet behind, out Crosstown to
Union Avenue on the sidewalk. At Union there used to
be a vast vacant lot crossed by a diagonal path. Through
the tall weeds and under a clump of willow trees I would
sometimes move up as close as ten feet.

She never looked around or gave any sign of knowing
she was being followed. Skirts were short then. She wore
black silk stockings, and, on mature consideration, I think
she had one of the three most beautiful pairs of legs I ever
saw. I hoped, of course, she would turn her ankle or get
scared by a cottonmouth (I had never seen one inside the
city limits) or even bitten, what the hell, or drop a pencil
I could return to her, tipping my cap politely, but nothing
happened all winter and all spring. I just followed her.

I had not specially minded quitting football because I had one other possibility of getting famous enough to approach her with some confidence. I was a swimmer. I had won ten or a dozen sprint races the summer before, and among a small coterie of younger boys I was regarded as a champ. However, fame in Memphis did not come from winning fifty-yard races. It came from winning the annual ten-mile swim in the Mississippi River.

The participants would board the *Kate Adams*, a majestic old side-wheeler, at the foot of Beale Street and ride slowly ten miles up the river. Then they would gather on the round stern of the *Kate*, wearing black silk suits, their limbs glistening with olive oil. A gun cracked and they dove in. Back-watering a hundred yards away were a group of rowboats—one for each swimmer, who would head for his boat as fast as possible. Every time he breathed the swimmer would try to keep the stern of his boat in his eye (some had been given licks of red or green paint), and it was the rower's job to guide him down the river. Finding the main current of the Mississippi in a rowboat is not easy and, unless you kept in the current, you had little chance of placing in the race. I had heard of men whose rowers had blundered into the slack water near the Arkansas shore and the unhappy contestants had spent hours climbing over floating logs and inhaling long streamers of green slime.

The ten-mile swim was won monotonously every year by a timber-sawyer from the Wolf River bottoms named Willie Lewis. He used an English overarm side-stroke. He rode a crosscut saw all winter, he said, to strengthen his belly muscles for his scissors kick, and it certainly did. I had beaten Willie many times in short races and I believed I could beat him in the long one because I swam a crawl, a new and mysterious stroke then and even a mediocre crawl can beat a side-stroke. It was not that I feared losing the race. What kept me out of it was the silt. After a couple of hours in the river, silt would seep in under the swimmers' eyelids, about a teaspoonful for each lid. When they finished, their eyes were bugged out and swollen like a bullfrog's. I didn't like that and I made no plans to enter the race that year.

When summer came and school let out, I had, through some painfully casual sleuthing and by concocting false friendships with girls I didn't like, found out her name (which was Helen) and her age (which was eighteen), and I think she knew I had been following her. These were the only results of my sophomore year. At sixteen the discovery of her age depressed me profoundly and I came very near giving her up. She was old enough to go out with college men and probably did—horribly, lasciviously knowledgeable drunkards from Sewanee, Virginia, and Washington and Lee in twenty-one-inch bell-bottom trousers. I took up my summer job as lifeguard at the Municipal Pool glumly, occasionally fishing out children and fat ladies and acquiring an almost Mexican tan. It was an item on the sports page of the *Commercial Appeal* that revived my interest in fame and Helen.

It said that the Southeastern AAU Swimming Championships had been awarded to Memphis that summer. This meant some fairly big-time sprint races. I paid my dollar entry fee for the fifty- and the hundred-yard dashes and went into training. It didn't mean giving up anything. Unlike my enemies, the college men, I was a disgustingly clean youth. I didn't smoke and I didn't drink. All I did was swim miles and take in about a gallon of milk every day.

I won the fifty and took second in the hundred and, as the only Memphis swimmer to win any medals, my picture was in the paper four days running. "This ought to do it," I thought. The only flaw was that I hardly ever saw her at all.

The lifeguards at the pool sat on mushrooms of concrete

placed at the edge of the deep water with the shallow water behind them. Being a guard gave you a certain cachet, but only among the patrons of the pool. Forward young girls would sometimes reach up and pull at your toes if they stuck over the edge but you paid no attention to that even if they were pretty. One day, looking behind me, I happened to see her, alone, in a black suit, lying on the beach of sand that surrounded the pool. I peeked at her every two minutes for half an hour and at last, excited and despairing, I jumped down off my post, waded through the screaming children of the shallows, and walked up to her with a dry mouth and a pounding in my ears.

I said, "Hi, Helen."

She said, "Hah you, Allin. Sure is hot."

I fell down in the sand beside her. She said I sure was a good swimmer, winnin' all those races. I said "Thanks." She asked me if I were going to the Treadwell's dance, the first of the season. I said I was. There was more of this kind of talk for about ten minutes and at last, hating her, I think, because if she did not exist, I would not be in the agonizing position of trying to say something I didn't know how to (that she was fairer than the evening air, clad in the beauty of a thousand stars; I was reading poetry then) and perhaps in my hatred and frustration achieving a saturnine curtness she found not unattractive, I said, "I want a date with you."

Immediately she was lost in calculation. "Next week, Thursday? Nuh-uh. Friday? No, I'm going to Greenvul for the week end." She sat there and I glared at her beautiful legs while she bent her long fingers back, totting up the evenings she couldn't possibly see me. Finally she said brightly, "How about three weeks from next Friday?" I nodded, got up mutely and walked away, glad it was over.

I had plenty of seersucker suits but only one linen one

and I had that freshly laundered for the Treadwell's dance and wheedled Lorena, our colored cook, into ironing an extra-sharp crease in the pants while I stood over her. "Bear down, Lorena," I said.

Dances were surrounded by a stiff protocol then. If one was being given at a private house like the Treadwell's, a big Georgian mansion on the Parkway, one upstairs room was always cleared of furniture down to the bare floor for the crap game. No liquor was served. You brought your own and left it in your car. You did not go one inch off the dance floor with another man's girl unless you saw him passed out or, if he was ambulatory, you were willing to fight him. There was a slipshod understanding, tacit and not always sound, that if you could get a girl into a car at a dance, you could neck her. In theory, however, the high-flown theory of Southern gentility, inflamed with violence and antique pride, the only possible reason for being alone with a girl seemed to be rape.

A young man would hang sullenly at the edge of the dance floor keeping his eye on his young lady while she danced with a stag. If the stag wickedly started to lead her out to a car, the young man would wait, sometimes wrapping a handkerchief around his fist, and precisely as the stag's foot left the hardwood and was stepping over the threshold, the young man would belt him an awful one on the nose. Then, in deference to the parents of the girl who was giving the dance, the fight would continue under a nearby street light. There were always two or three of these *combats d'honneur* and sometimes Freddy Roth, a punchy local welterweight who had turned to bootlegging, would show up and irritably pound some high-school boy to a jelly for not buying enough gin.

It was the heyday of the Charleston but I never saw a whole roomful of people doing it, possibly out of some vague respect for the floor-joists. A dance would go along

at a sedate fox trot for two or three hours and then some
little Mississippi girl would start it and the other dancers
would make a ring around her and her partner and watch.
A pretty girl might loll and fidget away her adolescent
years in some hot little town on the Delta where there was
nothing but a store and the I.C. railroad. Then would come
a good cotton year and she would emerge with all the
energy of light from this shabby rustic chrysalis, hit all
the summer dances in Memphis, and wind up with a glorious debut at the Peabody Hotel in December.

I remember one of these tireless beauties named Georgia
Peacock, out of Clarksdale, one night, who did seventy-
three figures of the Charleston, wearing out five partners.
The wet spot would appear between the shoulders of his
linen jacket and by the time he was wet to the belt, he
was done. He would bow away on the beat and a second
partner would come in on the beat and all the time, in
front of these relays of weak men, halfbacks, wrestlers, and
basketball forwards, this lovely fragile girl, gently born,
who had never done a hand's turn in her life, would keep
up the wild intricate shuttling of her dance, her hair in her
eyes, knees and elbows flashing like gems, her tongue between her teeth at the hard ones, laughing and screaming
at the band to "hit it." The Mississippi girls were fabulous
and they scared the hell out of me.

Naturally I had only one purpose at the Treadwell's
dance. I saw her two minutes after I entered. She was getting a good rush. I waited until I had determined by the
frequency with which he cut in who her escort was because he was the one I was going to have to fight. He was
barely as tall as she was, an SAE from Sewanee, not that
his size made any difference. My intentions had crystallized
since I had spoken to her and I aimed to kiss her even if
her date was an All-Southern tackle, I cut in.

She said, "Hi."

I said, "Hi," and she renewed her humming, this time in my ear. We moved about ten feet before I felt the tap on my shoulder. I cut in on her twice more. The third time I said, "Let's go outside."

She said, "Nuh-uh."

Deliberately, according to plan, I said, "I want to kiss you."

She didn't even remove her cheek from mine and look at me. She said, "Later, honey. Not tonight."

I took this as seriously as an oath. The dance was over for me. I went upstairs, watched the crap game for a while, and went on home.

The next fortnight I passed in complicated negotiations about my date with her. My family did not own a car then and none of my few friends' families did either. Picking up girls in taxicabs was not *comme il faut* and it was somehow sinister. Taking a streetcar was cheap and walking girls anywhere was unthinkable. I had to find someone with a car. Nobody wants to go out on a double date unless he knews exactly what kind of evening it is going to be and that was one piece of information I couldn't give.

For lack of friends I was operating among my admirers, the swimming fans. Swimming has never been a high-class sport like golf or tennis and I sounded out some fairly shady characters. One of them suggested that just the three of us go down to his uncle's farm at Corinth, Mississippi, where his uncle, who made it, would give us a gallon of corn, and stay and stay.

At last, through the good offices of two mediators, I met Jackson Bolton. He was seventeen, fat as a pig, and his face was like a cheap red wallpaper pattern with acne. The natural isolation forced on him by his looks had made him pretty nasty but he had a Dodge touring car, owned it himself. It took me three evenings to worm a firm commitment out of him: I was to buy the gas and the gin. Gas was five

gallons to the dollar at the time. I said, "How much gin?"
"Pint for me," he said.

That was only a dollar. Admission to the East End Dance
Pavilion where everybody went would be another dollar.
I could see I might get out of it for as little as three dollars,
three and a half if she got hungry and I had to buy her a
couple of hamburgers.

When the evening came, it was wretchedly unnecessary
for me to shave. I stayed in the bathtub scrubbing so long
that my fingers shrank nearly to the bone. I soaked my
hair with Sta-Comb and it hardened, brittle and perfect.
I polished my shoes and pressed the laces after I had finished browbeating Lorena into leaning on my linen pants
until they could nearly stand alone on the creases. The last
thing, I cleaned my nails and pushed the cuticle back. These
were, of course, all magical acts. I sat down on the front
steps with my creases accurately set to wait feverishly for
Jack Bolton.

When hope was about gone, he came, only five minutes
late. I handed over the expense money and found that he
had already sampled the gin, which I thought was a foul
thing to do, somehow. We picked up our dates and went
to East End. To say she was beautiful is useless. Every time
I saw her she was so beautiful that I resented her because
she made me and everything round about seem awkward
and ugly. We danced and danced and I barely said a word,
resenting her. I knew nobody ever made any time on a
dance floor and I was waiting until the pavilion closed, when
Jack had promised—in fact, the whole deal hung on this—
that we would drive around afterward.

We had done about a mile of the driving around and we
were coming up a long hill on Madison Avenue where, at
the top, stood a big magnolia tree always full of sparrows.
I took a deep breath and said, "How about that kiss you
promised me?"

She turned to me coolly and said, "I'm ready."

I kissed her briefly. No lights flashed. Her arms did not steal around my neck. The sparrows did not leave the magnolia tree and form into a heart-shaped flock above the car, twittering. She had fulfilled a contract and I knew there was no longer any hope at all. I was simply too young to have the right technique. I don't think I was able to speak to her again except to say good night.

At my suggestion Jack and his date and I drove downtown to a joint called the Iron Gate and bought a half-pint of gin. I knew what was proper—you took the half-pint and bottoms-upped with it if you were a man. Anxious not to let Jack know this was my maiden effort but equally anxious to learn what gin tasted like first, I took out the cork, tipped it up, and touched my tongue to it. For fear Jack would think I was cheating, I said, "I want to find out about the alcohol." We had all heard about liquor made from wood alcohol that made you blind. I didn't like the taste, but Jack had pulled up under a street light so he and his date could watch. I held up the flat ugly little bottle and drank it all. Innocents can sometimes do this. I forced the resurgent boiling to stay down and gasped, "Gimme a cigarette." I was very drunk in a few minutes but I felt better.

The next day I knew I had jettisoned everything, renounced her, given her up, thrown her away. I grew, so I thought, cynical, made mean remarks to my sister. I drank gin on Saturday nights. I lost a swimming race to a guy I had beaten seven times before. I woke up every morning remembering to feel bad that day but I usually forgot about it. When I realized at last that I was too young and green even to go to hell for a woman, I did feel bad for a day or two.

One day toward the end of summer, I was downtown and I saw a flowerseller's stand in front of one of the department stores. He was selling magnificent full-blown red roses and the price on his card said fifty cents a dozen. They were the most beautiful roses I had ever seen and I could afford them. I had read enough to know how roses should be presented, in a long white box with the stems sticking out a hole in the end. I said, "You got any boxes to put them in?"

"Ain't got no boxes," he said.

I bought two dozen anyway and he wrapped the big bouquet in newspaper with a clip at the top. I had never given flowers to a girl before.

She lived in a ground-floor apartment on Madison Avenue near Crosstown. I took a Madison Avenue car just at the rush hour, carefully holding my bouquet high above the heads of the other people standing.

I got off at Crosstown and went over to her apartment. I went up on the porch and knocked at the screen door. She came, hot, without any make-up, but still grindingly beautiful. I held out this huge bundle of newspaper and said coolly, sardonically, "A slight token of my esteem."

"How come you brought me this?" she said.

"Tear the top of the paper," I commanded, holding onto the bottom, the stems, myself.

She tore away the newspaper wrapping and folded it down. No roses. Only two dozen bare stamens. All the petals had fallen off. That was why they were selling for fifty cents a dozen. The petals were a jumble of red at the bottom of the paper cornucopia I was holding. Before she had a chance to say anything, I dropped the whole mess on the floor and ran. God knows what she thought.

During the following winter Pavlova came to Memphis. I was getting cultural then and I went to see her. I knew nothing about ballet but I thought *Le Cygne* was very graceful. Coming out of the Lyric Theater in the crowd, I found it was snowing for a wonder and just ahead of me

I saw Helen. She was wearing a little black satin hat with a veil and with her was a long tall rawboned ugly guy who must have been ten years older than I. They turned up the street in the snowstorm and I followed as if she had a string on me until I caught myself, seeing how silly it was. She walked on erect, languid, graceful, carrying, like a colored washwoman's bundle, quite unconsciously, the load of all my fancy, the giant Tunica center with the imprint of my cleats in his back, the little gold medal representing the Southeastern fifty-yard championship, my virgin half-pint of bootleg gin, and the twenty-four red roses without petals. I never saw her again. I understand she married the big rawboned guy.

* II *

Powder River in the Old Days

*W*hen my children come home from the movies, where they have been watching Randolph Scott or John Wayne keep their vigil on our old frontiers, I like to tell them that I, too, was once a cowpuncher, and in one of the most select areas for that line of work—the Powder River country in Wyoming. I usually begin "Once upon a time, I became a cowpuncher through the machinations of a wicked uncle...." The fairy-tale beginning quiets them, and they find it plausible that I should have had a wicked uncle and never ask about him. They imagine him quite easily as the crooked-sheriff type with the broad-brimmed, flat-crowned hat, the string tie, the handlebar mustache. I know they do, because I asked them once, and I have never corrected this image, although it could hardly be more false. My real uncle wore Borsalino hats and used to send to Alexander & Oviatt's every six months for neckties and French lisle socks. He had a set of Shaw's plays and I believe he had read them. He was a childless banker, and the only reason I call him my wicked uncle is that when he died leaving a considerable fortune he left none of it to me.

I use the word *machinations* only to arouse my children's interest. Actually, there weren't any. When I was seventeen, he wrote me and asked if I would like to spend the summer at his home in Wyoming. My father and mother decided to let me, and as soon as school was out, I went.

The town where my uncle lived was so close to the Big Horn Mountains that you could not see them for the foothills. The country round about had gone through a cycle of cattle, sheep, and dry farming, and now it was devoting itself mainly to raising horses for cavalry remounts and entertaining the first dudes. It was an interesting town—I often saw English, French, and Italian officers come to buy horses—but what chiefly concerned me was the fact that it was thirty-eight hundred feet above sea level. I had never lived so high. I couldn't stay awake. I slept a solid twelve hours a night and, as a rule, I took a little nap from eleven in the morning until lunch. Lunch always knocked me out, and my siesta afterward lasted three or four hours. I was fairly alert until dinner, but the period between dinner and bedtime was a struggle.

My torpidity annoyed my aunt. Marooned on those bleak slopes, with only the snow and the cottonwood trees to look at most of the year, she yearned for society—not the picayune galas of church socials and the local Five Hundred Club but the impossibilities of Park Avenue, Le Touquet, Paris. Copies of *Vogue*, *Spur*, and *The Tatler* filled her magazine rack. I don't believe she wore a stitch of clothing that didn't come from, at worst, New York. She couldn't stand me yawning around the house. I represented a social opportunity. She wanted me to have engagements. She told me there were two boys she wanted me to meet; the first was Henry Blackadder, who came from a very nice family and was, she believed, a senior at Yale. I looked at her appalled. I was about to be a senior in high school. Then I reflected that when you got to be as old as she was, a difference of four or five years in men's ages was probably not appreciable, so I said nothing.

One afternoon she got out the Cadillac and took me to

pay a formal call on Henry Blackadder. She had an Indian
chauffeur named Frank Takes, which was short for Takes-
the-Gun. He never spoke on duty, but once I had come
across him washing the car and he turned out to be very
affable. When we reached the Blackadder house, I learned
that Henry was upstairs packing to go on a trip to Montana.
His mother thought it would be nice if I went upstairs to
help him. I went upstairs. Henry and I shook hands. I sat
mute on the bed while he folded his marvelous clothes and
laid them in his suitcases.

He said, "Spending the summer here, eh?"

I said, "Yes." Then I said, "You're a senior at Yale?"

He said, "In the fall."

That was it with Henry Blackadder.

The next boy my aunt took me to see was St. John
Creavy. She called him Sinjun and told me to be sure and
do the same. The Creavys lived on a ranch and on the way
out she told me about them. Frederick Creavy, St. John's
father, was really the Earl of Tynemouth, although he
didn't use the title in Wyoming. He had been a younger
brother, and he had come out to the States to make his own
way. To everyone's amusement, he had begun as a simple
English cowhand. He had prospered and had married a local
girl. Then a brother had died; then the Earl died and the
title had come to Fred. He had hired an English butler
but the butler couldn't bear it so far away from home, so
now the Creavys had only maids. I was to remember to
say "Lady Tynemouth" when I was introduced. St. John
was home from Jesus College, Cambridge, for the summer.

Lady Tynemouth was seated in a rattan chair on the
lawn beside the ranch house. She told me that St. John was
out at the stables. After a quarter of a mile's walk, I saw
him sitting on the top bar of a corral. His riding boots
gleamed in the sun, and as I went up to him, I saw that
he was wearing whipcord breeches. I muttered, "Your
mother sent me out here. My name is Allan Seager."

He said " 'dyoudo" and asked me if I rode, saying he needed a spare man for polo on a scratch team of dudes and cowhands he had got together. I thought I rode rather well. I had covered dozens of miles through the eroded gullies of my father's farm in Tennessee in a McClellan saddle on the back of a dapper little single-footer named Prince, but I knew what Creavy meant. He meant an English saddle. I said "No."

"Hmm. Toughers," he said.

After a while, I said "I'm glad to've met you."

He waved his hand, gave me a genial smile, and said "Cheers."

I went back to the ranch house.

After these failures, I was able to snug in for two or three days, but my aunt shook me out of it. She said she had found me a girl. Ordinarily this would have aroused me from any lethargy, but I was suspicious by then. "What's her name?" I asked.

"Hilda Berryman. She's Faustine Berryman's niece, and she just got here yesterday. It's all arranged. You're to have tea with her tomorrow."

I had never had tea with anyone. "How old is she?" I asked.

"Why, how would I know?" my aunt said. "I haven't seen her. She's just a young girl. Her aunt says she's lovely."

On the off chance that Miss Berryman might be as lovely as her aunt had said, I got up from my nap sharply at three the next afternoon. I bathed, shaved, and put on a whole suit of clothes. I received my aunt's last instructions, and I managed to duck the Cadillac, because Frank Takes-the-Gun was washing it again.

Hilda answered the door herself. I thought she *was* lovely, but I could see at first glance that she was hopelessly old. I was six feet one inch tall, and in a crowd I could slyly pass into groups of people twenty or even twenty-one. But with one or two people I never pretended, because under any kind of pressure my coordination was bad; I had only to approach certain pieces of furniture to see them go crashing to the floor. Following Hilda, I negotiated a passage through what seemed to be a forest of flimsy chairs and taborets and made the living-room sofa, where I crouched gingerly beside her, gathering myself for the cup of tea and its saucer. I was aware that she was talking brightly and I was grateful. I got the sugar and the lemon in the tea all right, and, having achieved a precarious stability, was ready to say something. I said, "Where do you go to college?"

Well, it was Smith. She had just come from Bar Harbor, and she had once danced with the Prince of Wales. When Siegfried Sassoon had come to Northampton to give a reading of his poetry, she had gone out afterward into a sort of garden, where she could be alone to review the experience, and Sassoon himself had come up, mopping his face and saying, "Good God, what a mob! D'you mind if I talk just to you?"

Trying to keep afloat on this wash of sophistication, I said I had been reading Chekhov. This was well received, and we passed on to the stories in recent issues of *Vanity Fair*. Her hair was bobbed, a rich chestnut. Her eyes seemed green and she smoked long cigarettes of a pinkish color. I was beginning to think her the most beautiful girl I had ever seen, and I nerved myself to the point of asking "What kind of perfume do you use?"

Her eyes changed focus and she said, "Black Narcissus. Why?"

"I think it's wonderful."

Now that she had noticed me, she said, "How's it come you've read Chekhov?"

"What do you mean?"

"You're so *young*." She smiled when she said it.

"I read Chekhov all the time," I said sullenly. Beautiful as she was, I knew I had to get out of there.

I walked back to my uncle's full of imaginings. My aunt pounced as I went in the door and asked, "How did you like her?"

"Wonderful," I said dreamily.

"When are you going to see her again?"

"I don't know," I said.

"You don't know? What do you mean you don't know? Didn't you even ask her?"

"Aunt Emily, she's twenty-one years old."

This struck a brief spark of comprehension from my aunt's flintlike determination. "A great hulking thing like you, anyone would take you for twenty-one," she said. "Now you just phone her and ask her to go to the dance up at Piney tomorrow night. We'll take you."

Piney was a store and a dance hall thirty miles up in the mountains. Everyone went to the dances—ranchers, townspeople, dudes, and cowhands—and usually there were two or three Indians, with pigtails and high black sugarloaf hats, looking solemnly in the windows. I would have liked nothing better than to drive the Cadillac up there with Hilda Berryman alone, if I had known how to drive, but I didn't want to appear chaperoned before all those eyes, local, Eastern, and Barbaric. I knew this was a crisis, but I said, "Uh-uh."

"Why not?"

I couldn't explain, so I made a helpless great leap back into childhood. I sort of glazed my eyes and said, "I don't want to."

She really let me have it then. She concocted a series of lavish visions of the happiness I was rejecting because I was too uncouth to appreciate it. If I had not been such a lout with Henry Blackadder and St. John Creavy, she would have staged (I don't know where) a string of jolly little bachelor parties for me—black tie, I gathered. She sketched out a marital future for me. I could just as well love a rich girl as a poor one, and she happened to know that the Berryman girl had money in her own right. She quoted with stunning accuracy, and somewhat less aptness, the passage from *Lear* about how sharper than a serpent's tooth it was to have a thankless child.

From my childhood retreat, I recognized this as a purely adult crisis; you waited it out and it would blow over. When she subsided into a gloomy mutter, I said, "I'm sorry, Aunt Emily," and went up to my room.

I was able to resume my estivation for a few days, drowsily pondering ways of getting to see Hilda Berryman alone, and then my uncle took a hand. He said to me, one night at dinner, "How'd you like to go up on Powder River?"

"Where's Powder River?" I asked.

Powder River was to the north and east, in the real cow country, he said; it was seven hundred miles long, a mile wide, and an inch deep. I would have a chance to see the Old West—there weren't any dudes up there, he said, laughing.

"Sounds good," I said. "When do we start?"

"You start tomorrow morning," my uncle said. "Some fellows are taking some horses up to Hargraves' place, up there. You can ride along with them, if you want."

"All right," I said.

He woke me in what seemed like the middle of the night, and we drove to a ranch house east of town where the horses were. It was just getting light when we arrived. I could see a corral with about eight horses in it, kicking and biting each other. Three more horses were saddled and tied up outside the corral. Sitting on two of them were two young men, their knees around their saddle horns, smoking cigarettes. The third horse, a little black one, was mine.

I had thought maybe we were going in a car; my uncle had said "ride." I was wearing a tweed cap, the jacket of one of my old suits, a pair of my uncle's blue jeans, and high laced boots. I looked more like a *fin-de-siècle* cyclist than a horseman. However, I had ridden horseback in Tennessee, and I approached my mount fearlessly.

My uncle introduced me to the two young men and went back to town. Their names were Jimmy Whitford and Pat Einsleben and they weren't much older than I was. They had finished high school in June and were picking up a little money cowpunching during the summer before going down to Laramie to the University. I didn't get on my horse at once, because I had heard there was something tricky about mounting Western horses, and I was hoping to see one of them do it first.

"We better get started," Jimmy said. He slid off his horse and let down the corral bars. A hush fell over the horses inside. For two or three seconds they stood perfectly still, trembling. Then they all burst out of the corral at once, and ran off over the countryside every which way. Jimmy had his reins in his left hand, and he put it on the horse's neck, his left foot in the stirrup, took the saddle horn in his right, and he was on. I untied the black horse and did the same. He was moving before I was seated. By then, Pat and Jimmy were off in the middle distance, rounding up the other horses.

They got them together and started them down the road, the three of us following at a slow trot. "How far is this place we're going?" I asked.

"Hargraves'? About ninety miles," Pat said. "We'll do it in two days."

I didn't know what a rate of forty-five miles a day meant. Since then, I have heard of cavalrymen killing their horses by doing fifty miles in a night, though they would have had a lot of equipment, while all I had was a package of sandwiches tied on behind.

I don't know whether the boys were playing a joke on me or not, but the little black horse was a pacer. I was glad, at first, because a pacer or a single-footer is easy to ride if you aren't going far, and I knew I couldn't sit a trot the way the cowpunchers did. However, if you are going to ride all day long, it is better to take the bang-bang-bang of a trot than to have one side of you pulled forward and the other back at every step.

For the first two hours, we were in fairly civilized ranching country. There were barbed-wire fences on both sides of the road, which kept the horses from darting off. They could go only forward or back. Occasionally one of them would wheel slyly and come charging straight at us, all flying mane and rolling eyeballs, but Jimmy and Pat would turn him and head him around. When we got to open country, the horses seemed to have used up their matutinal zip and they drove like sheep.

By then, the sun was up and shining in our eyes. Immediately around us were vast plains of sagebrush, with no trees except a few aspens and cottonwoods in the creek bottoms, and in the distance the long suave lines of the hills. It began to get hot, and we didn't talk much. When we did, Jimmy and Pat were very civil. They knew they had a dude, but they didn't refer to my costume or my horsemanship. When the sun had passed over our heads, they both took out bandanna handkerchiefs and tied them to shield the backs of their necks. I did the same with a clean white handkerchief. Pat asked, "How's the little black horse ride?"

The little black horse had begun to tear subtly at my abdominal muscles some time before, but I said, "Fine. Why?"

They looked at each other, bleak, deadpan. Then Pat said, "Ain't neither one of us ever rode him, that's all."

About seven o'clock that evening, we pulled into a whistle stop on the C.B.&Q. railroad. There were three trees, a water tower, some corrals, a general store, and a frame house adjoining it that had a HOTEL sign on it. Pat and Jimmy put the tired horses into the corrals, and fed and watered them. Then we all went to the store.

I walked wide between the legs, feeling as though I were still astride, but not a horse—maybe a boiler full of steam. My head was so hot I was sure I had a fever, and while the others were arranging with the proprietor, who was also the hotelkeeper, for beds and supper, I noticed a mirror behind a counter piled with bolts of yard goods, and went to look in it. I felt changed. The mirror had CHEW MAIL POUCH across it in frosted script, and, peering between the letters, I saw that my forehead and nose were dead white under the dust but my cheeks and the sides of my neck were a deep, sore red.

We went over to the hotel. Pat and Jimmy ate a couple of pounds of the local beef. I ate only a quart of vanilla ice cream, and went straight to bed. It got cold there at night, so there were plenty of blankets. Draped over an armchair in my room was a ratty old Paisley shawl with a hole in it, and there was a large piece of Brussels carpet on the floor. I laid both of these over the blankets on my bed and crawled in. When they called me, at four in the morning, the fever was gone and I felt better—at least until I climbed into the saddle.

Pat and Jimmy let the horses out of the corrals. A lone Indian, in moccasins and a blue serge suit, was sitting on one of the struts of the water tower. The horses broke out of the corral and tore off over the plain beyond the C.B.&Q. right of way. I saw the Indian laugh—a spectacle of some rarity. The horses, I had learned, had never had so much as a hackamore on them. We were taking them up to Hargraves' to be broken.

The second day was much like the first. The country didn't seem to change, except when I looked behind, toward the mountains. The foothills gradually shrank to a thin green line, and bursting into the air above them was the white massif of Cloud Peak. I had never been far enough away to see it before.

It was just getting dark when we reached Powder River. It was a raging torrent five hundred yards wide. Pat and Jimmy rode up to the bank and stared down at it glumly. "What's this about it's being an inch deep?" I asked.

"It is, usually. I never seen it like this. Ain't been no rains," Pat said.

"Must've had a heavy dew up the river," Jimmy said.

"I'm laughing," Pat said sourly.

He rode back a little way, got off, let out his cinch, and slid his saddle and blanket to the ground. Jimmy did the same. I got down and led my horse back there. "What you doing?" I asked.

"Going to sleep here tonight," Pat said. "The river ought to be down in the morning. We'll just have to turn the horses loose and catch 'em then."

We were standing in a gravelly patch of sagebrush. It would be cold with nothing over me but a saddle blanket, and, as stiff as I had been that morning, I didn't know whether I would ever rise again after a night lying on gravel and sharp chat. We had talked about snakes, too. "What about rattlesnakes?" I asked.

"Why, they don't just come up and bite you. You got to bother 'em," Jimmy said.

I thought simple trespass might be a bother to them, and I led my horse back to the riverbank. I knew I could make it across, but I didn't think the little black horse was in shape to swim very far. I was trying to see how deep the river was. A dead tree came bobbing past. Its roots caught on the bottom and it stood up straight for a second before it was swept along, so I gauged that the water was only four or five feet deep. I went back to Pat and Jimmy, who were gathering wood to make a fire, and asked, "How far is it to Hargraves' after you get across?"

"Can you *swim?*" they both said.

"Sure," I said, justifying civilization.

"We can't swim a lick," Pat said.

"Toughers," I said. "Guess you'll have to sleep here then."

I mounted and slid down the bank into the current. Pat called, "If you make it, it ain't but about a mile! Just keep on the road."

"Don't you worry! I'll make it!" I called back.

The little black horse took the current well. The water came up to my calves, then to my thighs, and we still had bottom. The horse instinctively faced upstream, but, pushed by the current, we crossed on a long downstream slant. When the water reached my armpits, I could feel him swimming, and I tried to hold his head up with the reins. Then I felt him touch bottom; he had had to swim only eighteen or twenty feet. In a minute, I rode up the far bank, dripping. I turned and waved to Pat and Jimmy, and yelled, "Come on! You can make it!"

I saw them talk a minute, and then they saddled up. They drove the tired mustangs into the river ahead of them, and the mustangs came out first and stood dripping and shuddering with their heads hanging down. I sat watching Pat and Jimmy's taut faces above the brown water with real enjoyment. They made it all right, and they talked about it the rest of the way to Hargraves'.

I was too tired and it was too dark for me to pay much attention to the ranch when we got there. Hargraves was a big man of forty who needed a shave. His wife had that weatherbeaten, male look women get when they have been lonely and overworked. There was no one else there. The kitchen had a clay floor that shone in the lamplight. Mrs. Hargraves fed us fat, thick bacon, beans, bread, and coffee, and we went to bed. The Hargraves hadn't expected me, so the three of us had to sleep in the same bed, but it didn't matter.

In the morning, I was sure everyone could hear me creak when I moved. Mrs. Hargraves silently fed us bacon, beans, and bread again. I thought that afterward we would have nothing to do but wait around until Pat's brother came to get us in a car. The horses we had ridden were part of the lot that was to be sold to Hargraves, provided he liked the look of them. My interest in horses was faint that day, but Hargraves wanted us to see this bunch, and the four of us went to the corral they were in to look at them. The others talked about hocks and fetlocks, while I, happy to be standing up, furtively clenched certain muscles to see if they still worked. Hargraves said he would start breaking the mustangs the next day. Later, he asked me if I had ever been on Powder River before, and when I said I hadn't, he took me to his artesian well. Water was flowing out of a four-inch pipe. Hargraves struck a match and held it to the mouth of the pipe, and I had before me the entertaining spectacle of fire and water coming from the same spout. The match lit a blue flame about a foot long that whistled straight out of the pipe, like a torch.

Then a little fat man with a gun on his hip came riding up. I hadn't seen a gun on anyone's hip since I came West. He got down and forthrightly told Hargraves he would have to dip all his cows.

"Why, for God's sake?" Hargraves asked.

"Tick," the little man said.

Hargraves said, "Man, I can't dip any cows. I let all my hands go for the summer."

The little man only shrugged. He got on his horse and went off down the road at a walk.

"Who's he?" I asked.

"Government man." Hargraves looked at us. "You got to stay and help me dip my cows. It won't take long."

My seat and thighs cried out almost audibly against this,

but I could see that a kind of unbrookable neighborliness was involved.

"How many you running now?" Pat asked.

"Two thousand head, maybe," Hargraves told him.

After a while, we had dinner, and then we all three mounted again. I stood in my stirrups; I had seen real cowpunchers do this. Hargraves said to Pat, "Mile over that hill, you'll see some aspens. There's a bunch of cows there." To Jimmy, he said, "Go down there in those bottoms. They'll be strung out." And to me, "Go straight up that coulee. There'll be a hundred and fifty, two hundred up there."

We rode a quarter of a mile down the lane together before we split up. I asked, "How do you drive cows?"

"Just get in behind 'em and holler," Pat said.

I rode up the coulee. I didn't know how far I'd have to go, but in ten minutes I saw my quarry—a couple of hundred whiteface cows grazing peacefully. I rode slowly through them, and when I had got behind them, I called, "Come on! Get up! Let's go!" in a quiet, coaxing voice. Then I shouted. Then I swore at them, riding nervously back and forth. Nothing happened except that a cow here and there glanced up curiously at me and then went on eating. My throat gave out. I waited and tried again. Not a cow moved. I was sitting there baffled when I heard the clippety-clip of a horse coming fast. Hargraves was on it. He shouted, "What in hell're you doing with them goddam cows? Bring 'em on down!"

"I can't," I said.

Hargraves yelled at them once, and they all lifted their heads and started down the coulee. I thought: They know him; but I doubted it even as I thought it. There was some trick to it.

I didn't find out what it was, though. Hargraves sent me

out again the next morning. I found my cows grazing in a swale. I rode around behind them and began to holler, and they all threw up their heads and started out of the swale at a trot. I got them down to the corral promptly, and Hargraves sent me out for another bunch.

I started these up almost casually, and then, about half-way back to the ranch house, they came to a big coulee. They trotted up to the edge and looked down into it. It was about two hundred feet deep—a long slope of sand. No cow wanted to try it. I shouted and cursed, but they wouldn't go down. I rode along the bank a little way but I couldn't see the end of it; we had to cross. I took my horse back a hundred yards, kicked him into a gallop, and rode straight at them, shouting, expecting them to scare. They parted to let me through, and I nearly pitched down the slope myself.

The beasts didn't awe me as they had the day before, but I didn't know what to do. I was sure that Powder River cowpokes must have been in worse predicaments, and I tried to think of something easy and careless—something *frontier*—that would start them down. They were still strung out in a long line along the edge of the coulee, bawling. I tried running at them on foot, yelling and waving my cap. They didn't even look around. I booted a couple of them in the tail. They gave me hurt looks. I picked a small one and charged her hind legs as I would a tackle, trying to make her stumble forward. It was like running full tilt into a wire fence. I bounced back and the cow mooed reproachfully. At last, I picked up a week-old calf and tossed it down the slope. It rolled over and over, and the mother followed it, bellowing. The others followed the mother and I had no more problems. That night, I asked Pat to show me how to roll a cigarette with one hand.

For three more days we rode the range. (I still rather like the phrase.) At last, we had all the cattle penned in the corrals, objecting. By government order, we had to immerse each one in a concrete vat full of a solution of warm water and nicotine sulphate to kill the ticks. The vat was about thirty feet long, eight feet deep, and the width of a cow. A chute of cottonwood logs ran up to one end of it, and a ramp led down into the fluid. Hargraves said we would begin with the bulls.

Hargraves himself cut out his head bull and drove him into the chute. He was one of those enormous Herefords, with long, down-sweeping horns and a back as broad as a sidewalk. He was wary, and he walked the length of the chute stiff-legged, showing the whites of his eyes. He came to the edge of the ramp and stopped. He looked the setup over and started to back up the chute in a stately fashion. Hargraves went behind him, slipped a four-by-four between the cottonwood logs and against two uprights, and stopped him. "Now, come along, sir. Come on, old fellow," he murmured warmly. "Nothing to scare you." The bull lifted his chin and breathed fast, but he did not move.

"Gimme that pitchfork," Hargraves said.

Pat handed it to him.

Hargraves thrust it between the logs and jabbed the bull in the ham. "Now, git along there, you old bastard," he shouted. The bull blew all his breath out roughly, and we could hear his horns knock against the wood.

"He ain't gonna move for that," Pat said.

"I know he ain't. I know what he will move for, though," Hargraves said, and he went into the barn.

He came back with a broomstick and a couple of dry-cell batteries. He had driven two nails into one end of the stick, and he wound some copper wire around the nails. He ran the wire up the stick, fixed a pushbutton to the wire, taped it down, and attached it to the batteries. He went up to the chute and touched the nails to the bull's flank. Then he pressed the button.

It may well have been the most magnificent sight I will ever see. The bull had room for a little run and he went down the chute as fast as he could go. He soared and, like Nijinsky, paused a moment against the blue sky, rampant, the sun glinting off his coppery flanks, one foreleg daintily bent, and his eyes as big and round as pool balls. Then he fell and the water choked his bellow. A tremendous splash rose and we all cheered.

Nothing exciting happened after that. The young bulls docilely followed the old one, and the cows the bulls.

The dipping took several days, and then Pat's brother came to get us in a car. The trip back to town took only four hours.

I got out of the car at my uncle's house. It was the middle of the afternoon, and my aunt saw me from the front porch. "Don't you come this way!" she called. "Go around to the back."

"What's the matter?" I said.

"Pah! Look at you."

I must have been pretty dirty. I hadn't shaved, or even bathed, except once in Powder River, and it was so muddy that I must have put on more than I took off. I went to get a bath and I heard my aunt telling Frank Takes-the-Gun to burn everything I had worn—everything. When I was clean, I put on some dude clothes and went out on the front porch. My uncle had come home. He was asking me what kind of time I'd had and I was telling him, when my aunt broke in, squinting at me. "What's the matter with you? You're fat."

I didn't believe that. I felt lean and rangy. Bacon, beans, and bread make a weary meal three times a day, and after the first day or so I had eaten only enough to keep going on. I went and looked in the mirror over the hall table. She was right. I wasn't lean at all. My face was as round as the moon, and my skin was tight and shiny. I looked pumped up.

I went back out on the porch. My uncle said offhandedly, "It's just that water."

"What do you mean? What water?" my aunt asked.

"The water they drink up there," he said. "It's full of gas. He'll deflate in a day or two."

I waited a few days until I went down. Then I felt like a cowpuncher. With my red hands and red neck, I looked rather like one, and I believed that a natural way to ingratiate myself with Hilda Berryman would be to call on her and tell her all about Powder River. There was a livery stable in town. Later, I would rent some horses, and she and I would go riding. I gave myself two hours of stern sartorial preparation.

My aunt caught me slipping out of the door and asked me where I was going. When I told her, she said, "You missed your chance there, all right, all right. Henry Blackadder's back from Montana."

I went on in spite of this. During the short nights on Powder River, lying three in the bed with the coyotes yowling, I had built up Hilda's beauty grain by grain until, if she had been mine to swap, I wouldn't have swapped her for Corinne Griffith or Norma Talmadge as Moonyeen.

When I saw her in the flesh, she held up very well. But it was her advantage every time we met, and I had to wrestle for twenty minutes with *The Forsyte Saga* (which I had not read) before I could get on to Powder River. I enlarged the lone Indian in the blue serge suit into a surly tribe of Sioux; I whipped the head off a rattlesnake with a quirt (which was quite true; he had been sunning himself on the log that served as the Hargraves' front stoop); and I posed as William S. Hart imperturbably guiding a stampede. Then I asked if she would go riding with me.

"Not here," she said, dismissing everything west of the Appalachians. "I ride only an English saddle."

I wasn't surprised at all. This was merely one more penalty for being too young. And since, when evening came, so would Henry Blackadder, I thought of getting away. Still, I had to plot my exit, make myself look good. I said that if she wouldn't ride with me, I would ride alone ("into the sunset" went unspoken); I said restlessly that I wanted to get back into my boots and jeans, implying that my present muscles made dude clothes constricting. In fact, I said, it had put me to quite a lot of trouble to get ready to see her.

She sniffed, smiling. "And you even shined your shoes, didn't you?" she said.

That ejected me. I wrote to her halfway through my senior year in high school, but I never mentioned Powder River to her again.

* III *

Game Chickens

*W*hen I finished high school in Memphis, it was in the middle of the year. The graduation exercises were held about the first of February and the next day I went out to look for a job. I intended to work for a year and a half, save all my money and go to Yale, or, if I could not get in, I was going to ship out to Hamburg, Germany, on a cattle boat. I cannot remember now why Hamburg seemed to be more important than Gravesend, Cherbourg, or Stockholm. I believed Yale to be a difficult college to enter so that I felt an alternate choice was necessary and I may have heard that a great many cattle boats went to Germany.

I particularly wanted a job in the office of one of the big cotton factors on Front Street facing the levee, a cobbled ramp that sloped down to the river. If you worked for a cotton factor, you wore very good clothes, which at that time meant four-button, no-padding-in-the-shoulder jackets and narrow trousers with sharp creases, and during working hours the suit would be covered with wisps of cotton lint. Inevitably you went to all the debutante parties, and many of your colleagues were young Englishmen from Liverpool, and this seemed to be a strange romantic fact. I tried all the offices on Front Street but I didn't get a job.

38

We were Yankees and I had no connections. I didn't get
a job anywhere else, either.

After looking for a week or so, I began to get discouraged.
I began to think I was no good. Although I had taken the
platitudes of the principal's address at graduation with a
grain of salt, I had unconsciously accepted more of their
message than I realized. I took to spending more and more
of my afternoons swimming at the YMCA to bolster up
my self-esteem. It was a small sixty-foot tank with a low
ceiling. When I took the water, my kick made a loud boom-
ing noise that made everybody stop and watch, and had
even drawn fat businessmen out of the barber shop and off
the rubbing tables. (It was not the way to kick, I found
out later, but I enjoyed the racket.) I swam a good deal
and I thought I was getting myself in shape for the outdoor racing season which began in June.

It was there that I met George L'Hommedieu. The first
time he told me his name, he called it "Lommadoo" and he
spelled it out immediately with a certain pride and then
said it was a nuisance as a name. I saw him come out of the
showers one afternoon. He was about twenty-four or -five,
with a good-enough build, but I knew he couldn't swim because he walked gingerly over the wet tiles as if they were
hot, and he tried the water with his toe before he climbed
down the ladder at the shallow end. The first day, he stood
timidly around up to his waist, patting the water as if he
wanted to make friends with it. Occasionally he screwed
up his face and lay down on his side in the water, straighten-
ing up immediately to cough, spit, and wipe his eyes. He
seemed to want to swim, but he knew nothing about it. As
I chugged by him, he seemed to admire the display, so I
volunteered to teach him, and in a week he could swim
the length of the pool. His arms looked stiff and brittle as
he did it, and he always swallowed quite a lot of water when
he tried to breathe, but anyone could tell it was a crawl

stroke he was attempting and not a nasty feminine side-
stroke. At the pool we became quite good friends.

He told me he was a graduate of the University of Illinois,
and this was a recommendation to me because any college
man was not only a Bachelor of Humane Letters or something; he also knew about liquor and women. When I saw
him in his clothes, I thought at first he worked for a cotton
factor; he dressed with the same elegance. I asked him, but
he said no, he worked for the Illinois Board & Filler Company. It seemed to be a dull name and I didn't inquire further. Although he was a Yankee like me and alone in
Memphis, he got around a good deal. He mentioned the
names of two or three debutantes, and I was sure he led
an exciting life. I was a little proud that I had taught him
to swim. He became a proxy through whom I could imagine
the conquest of the wild beautiful Mississippi girls who were
drawn up to Memphis from the river towns of the Delta
to "come out" every winter. Some were girls from towns
with the same names as theirs; I remember Elizabeth Banks,
from Banks, Mississippi, and I imagined God knows what
big white-pillared mansions, with the banjos strumming
in the evening, and white-wooled old Pompey with the
julep in the silver cup. I thought the Banks girl looked like
Corinne Griffith, and I hoped she was kind to George and
saved him some "no-cuts" at the dances. Actually, I can
see now that he was a lonely young man who probably
spent most of his evenings at the boardinghouse reading
magazines on the bed in his room.

He got me the job I had been looking for, and, while
working on it, I walked out of a room three minutes before a murder, maybe five minutes; anyhow, it was as close
as I have ever come. We were sitting on the edge of the
pool one afternoon and he asked me if I wanted a job. I
told him I did, and he said I could have his. He was quitting to work for a glass company up north, and his home

office had told him to find someone to replace him. The job was nothing, he said, very simple, very easy. I told him I was two months past my seventeenth birthday, and I had never had any business experience.

"That's all right. Don't worry. There's nothing to this job. Meet me here tomorrow, and I'll take you out to look the place over," he said.

The Memphis Branch of the Illinois Board & Filler Company was at the extreme north edge of town. Beyond it lay river-bottoms and gum-tree woods. When I first saw the place, I was troubled and frightened. It seemed tremendous, and George had explained on the way out that my title would be Manager. I doubted whether I could manage all this. Something would be sure to come up that I wouldn't know how to handle. There were several long, dingy, gray, two-story buildings made out of corrugated iron. They were laid out almost in the shape of a U. Between the ends of the U was a small corrugated-iron building painted a dull red. This was the office. It sat on a small patch of gritty, neat grass and there was a drooping tree beside it. We got out of George's Ford and went in.

It was an old office. The walls were made of pine boards, painted a mustard color, and bulging here and there. Against one wall stood an old-fashioned high stand-up desk. There was also a battered oak flat-top desk with a swivel chair, a rickety adding machine, a huge black safe with a rustic scene on the door, and a rusty little base-burner stove. Two rush-bottomed chairs with wire between the rungs stood in corners.

George knelt at once in front of the safe, and spun the knob around the dial forward and back. I could hear the tumblers clank faintly.

"This is a hell of a safe," George said as he swung the door open. He brought out a bottle of gin from the top shelf and stood aside to let me look in. "We keep coal in there.

Coal, gin, and stamps. They're the only valuables. No money comes through this office." In the main coffer of the safe was about a bushel of soft coal.

"What's the combination?" I asked. I thought it sounded businesslike.

"There isn't any. Just give 'er a whirl," he said.

I asked him what the Illinois Board & Filler Company made.

"Oh," he said as if he thought he had already told me. "Egg-case fillers. We sell fillers, and flats, and knocked-down cases."

This meant as little to me then as it does to you. George went into an adjoining room where the files and typewriter were, I learned later, and brought out, folded up and dusty, one of those crisscross things they put eggs in. Unfolded, it was a large square network of three dozen little squares. A case of eggs holds thirty dozen, hence there would be ten of these networks—fillers, in fact—five on each side. The wooden egg-case, made of $\frac{3}{16}''$ gum or $\frac{7}{32}''$ cottonwood, was sold in a bundle, the sides, the ends, and the top and bottom all bound together, and the dealer had to make a box out of it himself.

George passed me the gin bottle and said "Good luck." I thought he meant good luck with the gin, but afterward I was ashamed to realize he had been toasting my fortunes on the job. I did the genteel thing. I took as small a drink as I dared, coughed only once, and, by blinking rapidly, kept the tears from running down my face. Italians made the Memphis gin, a standard product that smelled like *Hearts and Flowers* perfume. I was glad it was not their "brandy," a liquid made of corn whisky, peach flavoring, and red pepper. George took several swallows with great ease while I watched admiringly.

He told me he had been authorized by the home office in Illinois to pay me a hundred and ten dollars a month. This seemed a large salary to me, but he explained apologetically that it was really small because there was so little to do most of the time, nothing but sit there all day long, and hope that freight agents from the railroad would stop in and talk. The reason they were freight agents was because they were affable fellows who could tell a good story, and he kept the gin in the safe for their entertainment. I could come to work the next day and he would stay with me two weeks to show me the ropes. Then he was going North.

As he said this, the screen door opened, and a thin, wizened, little man came in.

"Cathey, this is Mr. Seager. He's taking my place," George said.

Cathey rolled a twig from one side of his mouth to the other and said, in a high voice, "Uh-huh."

He would have been about five feet eight inches long if you had laid him out flat on a table and measured him, but he was only about five feet tall as he stood there, because he was all humped over into his pants pockets. He wore a large, fuzzy gray fedora hat covered with grease spots and wisps of cobweb. His shirt was blue and dirty, and he had on a pair of black trousers that shone down the thighs from the oily dirt that was ground into them. He was about thirty-five years old and he had a long, sagging face. As he stood there, the face did not change; he did not glance up from the floor; he looked like a man alone on a street corner.

"Cathey's the foreman. He knows about everything. If you want to know anything, ask him," George explained.

It seemed to me that I ought to acknowledge the introduction in some way. At seventeen, manners are not consideration for other people; they are a display you make to prove you have them. I stepped briskly forward with my hand stuck out, and said, "How are you, Mr. Cathey?"

He rolled his light eyes up at me and down again. He pulled a hand slowly out of his pocket and held it three inches in front of his thigh. I could take it if I wanted to. I took it, limp, thin, and moist, squeezed it once, and let it go. He put it back in his pocket. George went on talking to me about the job. Cathey stood looking at the floor, moving the twig by hand from one corner of his mouth to the other, then spitting, and, after a few minutes, he turned around and walked out of the office.

"Doesn't he ever talk?" I asked George.

"Who, Cathey? Sure he talks. He knows all about this place. He could run it all by himself. He can read and write."

After George had gone North and I had settled into the work, I found that there really was very little to do, just as he had said. The factory "ran" four months of the year. The rest of the time we shipped orders out of stock, and I kept bankers' hours.

I used to take a Poplar Avenue streetcar, pick up the morning mail, and board a Thomas Street car for the factory. The Thomas Street cars were the oldest in Memphis. They ran very slowly, rocking backward and forward, and it was nearly nine-thirty when I reached the office, which was at the end of the line.

It would take me about an hour to answer a letter or two (in longhand), and write up the orders and bills of lading. Cathey came in sometimes silently, sometimes saying " 'morning," picked up the orders and bills, and walked out. He and one colored man made up the orders, and before noon, I would see our ratty old Ford truck taking the cases and fillers down to the depot to be shipped. At twelve-thirty, I took the streetcar back downtown, had a malted milk and a sandwich, picked up the afternoon mail, and was trundled sedately back again. There was another hour's work and I was finished for the day. I had to stay there, though, because somebody might call up on the phone.

During the off season, there were only three people in this huge clump of buildings—Cathey, J.T. the Negro, and myself.

At first I spent some time exploring the place. The factory had made cottonseed oil during the war, but none had been made there since. The windows were thick with a gummy dust, almost opaque, and inside the light was dim. Lost festoons of old ragged cobwebs hung everywhere with lint and chips of wood caught in the loops. The floor was damp and, against the wall in heaps of dust and corners, some kind of pale weed sprouted. There were structures I took to be vats, blistered and rusty, and, wherever there was machinery, the lines of its curves, spokes, and joints were broken by the thick coating of grease someone had put on to preserve them. In some of the rooms there were metal bins full of moldly cottonseed hulls, and it was from these that the whole factory took its rank rubbery odor. Rats lived on the hulls.

The rats were monstrous and Cathey's terrier would never go inside the factory. They had lived there fattening on the greasy hulls so long unmolested that they were full of confidence, and they usually moved at a slow trot, shaking all over with their fat. They didn't seem to see, hear, or smell very much. You could walk up within a yard of one; then, at some point, he would become aware of you and slash like lightning at your ankle. I did this just once and then I let them alone.

Once, after a tour of these gloomy buildings, I was coming out of a doorway into the sunlight when I saw a chicken yard in front of me. I had not noticed it before. Chickens were just chickens to me and I was about to pass by when I saw they were not ordinary chickens.

I walked over to the fence and looked down at them. I had never actually seen any before, but I knew from pictures in the *National Geographic* that these were game chickens. "Them are game birds." I heard Cathey's high voice, and, turning, I found him at my elbow.

"What do you do with them?" I asked.

There was an accent of soft scorn in his voice. "Fight 'em."

I was young and ignorant, especially with people, and half-consciously but helplessly, I blurted out the obvious. "It's against the law, isn't it?"

It was as if he were overlooking a breach of etiquette. "I fight 'em Sunday mornings over there in the bottoms with the niggers."

"With gaffs?"

He spat over the fence, and a young cockerel jumped and fluttered. He swung his pale eyes at me deliberately and said, "Uh-huh." Maybe he thought he could tell what kind of a damn fool I was by looking at my face. He knew he was going to work with me, damn fool or not, and he hunched his shoulders and leaned over with his forearms crossed on a thin little fencepost, and resumed politely but without any polite inflections. "We git over there about ten o'clock Sunday morning, and we fight two, three mains for ten-dollar side bets." He spat again. "Make money."

The cocks stood high off the ground. They had long serpentine necks that gleamed in the sun. Some were a beautiful greenish black, others a reddish bronze, others a kind of dirty speckled gray. Everything had been bred off them but muscle. They stepped around stiff and alert, stopped, scratched, stopped, the neat reptilian heads turning slowly, blinking, one claw lifted, and then ran quickly on.

"They's good blood in them birds. *Im*ported. Those gray ones are Irish Grays. You know Paul Dickson down at Rosedale?"

"No. Who's he?" I said.

"Got a big place down there. He keeps a big string of game birds. I got 'em from him."

I would have liked to ask him more about cockfighting but I didn't want him to think I was any stupider than he did already. I said "Well, I better be getting back to the office," and just as I said it, before I had time to turn away, I saw him smile, a slow hoist of his sagging cheeks that let out his orange, broken teeth. He knew I had no work to do and I had been stupid again.

As spring came and the weather got warm, I tried to find things to do. I practiced typing about an hour a day, sitting on a tall three-legged stool. I was anxious to get ahead (of whom, I didn't stop to think), and I considered buying a book on poultry so that I might learn the business from the egg up. I tried conscientiously to envision the industry as a whole: the farmer, the wholesaler, the salesman, the manufacturer, and the Home Offices, but I was always stopped by a sort of sneaky thought that egg-case fillers were not very important. I know now that this was not a sneaky thought. It was a conviction that I was unwilling to recognize then, and it made me inefficient in the little work there was. I made mistakes steadily.

I had to keep a simple set of books on expenditures and payrolls. I knew they were simple, but within two weeks of my start I was three cents out, and I never did find that three cents. Once a month I took an inventory of the stock on hand, and one warm April day with a light breeze and the toadfrogs chirping and clunking in the bottoms behind the factory, I walked right past a whole warehouse full of fillers, and I showed a fifteen-hundred case loss on my inventory. Three days later, I had a special-delivery letter from the president of the company. It began conventionally enough—"Dear Mr. Seager"—and, opposite the salutation above the body of the letter was typed "*In re:* Monthly Inventory." It continued, "Yours of even date received and contents noted. Would say in reply" (and here the style blew up) "just what the hell are you doing down there, Allan?" Then he explained, more formally, my mistake.

The worst came a few weeks later, although I didn't hear about it for a long time. A letter came in canceling an order. The letterpaper was charred brown around the edges, and on it the customer said his whole establishment had burned up. I thought for half an hour about the shock and distress of having your business burn up, and then I sat down on my stool to compose a consoling reply. I wanted it to be warm, humane, and sympathetic; I felt that this would help the prestige of the I.B. & F. Co. I began, "I am terribly sorry to hear about your fire. Fire is so relentless and uncaring. . . ." There was a lot more like this, and it was not until six months later that Uncle Joe Thompson, the salesman, a shrewd old man with an Elk's tooth, brown vici kid shoes, and a wad of Peachy Plug always sleeping in his cheek, came in off the territory and said there was a fellow over in Marked Tree, Arkansas, thought I was crazy.

When the weather got hot in May, my attempts to improve grew more sporadic, and they withered completely in the summer, when the little iron office building used to take enough heat so it jumped up and down. Nobody came to visit the place then, not even the freight agents, and I sat stripped to the waist with my feet on the desk, reading *The Faerie Queene* and *The Adventures of Gargantua and Pantagruel*. The sweat used to run off my hands and forearms to my elbows, then drop off to the floor. There was always a puddle under my elbows. I got through both books during the hot weather. I had picked them because they were good and thick and would last me a long time. I did not want to be lugging books back and forth on the streetcar from the library.

Cathey spent a lot of his time sitting next to the cold boilers in the factory, some of it with the game chickens, and a little of it talking to me in the office. He never stayed long because it was too hot, and, after he saw the puddles under my chair, he would urge me to come sit by the boilers with him, but I thought it was the same as sitting down cellar and I had heard that would give you rheumatism. I got my name in the paper whenever I took part in a swimming race during the summer, and I think this made Cathey look more kindly on me. Anyhow, he became affable and, for him, talkative.

He had been a soldier in France during the war. I wanted to hear about his experiences. It went this way:

"Yeah, I shot a German."

"How?"

"Just shot him, that's all," and he would stare at me with his faint blue eyes.

Or he would answer, "Sure, I been to Paris."

"What was it like?"

"Well, it's bigger'n Meffis, more spread out."

"Was it a beautiful place?"

"It was all right."

The only thing touching his war experience that he seemed willing to discuss at length was the crudity of the French. They were a barbarous uncivilized people. He had been sent to a rest camp near some village behind the lines and he had been shocked by the privies. They were not like anything he had ever seen and they were much worse. "They ain't human, goddam it. They got these dam' little old houses and they ain't nothing in 'em but a couple of handles. . . ." He had been glad to leave France and get back to civilization.

Unlike many American soldiers, he had scorned the French women because you couldn't understand a damn word they said even when they were talking English. Yet he was a hot lover. He told me about affairs he had contrived in Mississippi with waitresses, farm girls, and married women. (He was married himself.) He was proud of the married women, but I couldn't imagine how this ugly, scrawny man could attract any woman because I believed you had to be handsome, vigorous, and rich for the job. I got one inkling, though. He was going on one day about some brakeman's wife in some river town. He said in a matter-of-fact tone that he had gone with her fifteen times in one night. Ordinarily I never questioned anything he said or made any comment on it, but this was the kind of statistic that had been hashed over pretty thoroughly my senior year in high school, and I said "The hell you did."

As if I had pressed a button, he began to shake all over and stride up and down the room, swearing in a high voice almost falsetto with rage. I just sat and shook my head.

At last he jerked off his fuzzy hat, threw it on the floor and kicked it.

"I *did*. I swear I did. I did it. *Yes*, sir," he shouted. It was the only time I ever saw him with his hat off. His forehead was a shiny greasy white, and he was bald with wild uncombed strands of hair fluffed up from the sides of his head. He was uglier than ever, yet his passion gave him a kind of dignity; at least you could take him seriously as a human being. He looked at me, waiting for me to acknowledge him. He was not exactly angry, not at me anyhow. My doubts seemed to have tainted his memory of the night with the brakeman's wife. He was waiting for me to make it right again, and the anger was the shock that his past could be tampered with.

At last I said, "Okay."

He picked up his hat without any embarrassment and went out and began to handle his game chickens.

Along about October the factory began to "run." I had very little to do with it. One morning I saw smoke coming out of one of the smaller chimneys. I went to the shop and found all the machines running, each operated by a colored woman. That afternoon, Cathey led them all into the office to sign the payroll sheet.

"They git fourteen dollars a week," he said. He turned to the first one. "What's your name?" he bawled.

"Willie Sue Mawson," she said and tittered.

"Kin you write it?"

"Naw, suh," she said.

"Write down Willie Sue Mawson," he said to me. I wrote it down.

"Make your mark," he said, and jerked her forward by the arm. She took the pencil and made a shaky cross after her name. There were about twenty women in all. Three or four could write their names, and one printed it out in block letters. When they had all signed, they began to file out of the office. Cathey stood beside the door jocosely patting the young ones on the behind, and they cooed and giggled.

My easy days were over. I came to work at eight o'clock in the morning because there was a much larger mail every day, more bookkeeping, a constantly shifting inventory, and I had to dicker with the railroad for empty freight cars. If I got to the offices a little early, I would see the colored women drifting past my windows toward the shop. Few of them wore stockings although the mornings then were getting sharp. Most of them had broken men's shoes on their feet, and one of them wore a man's staved-in-hat. They walked beautifully, languidly, cackling and giggling in high shrill voices. I never did anything but just barely notice them and I never could tell them apart.

One morning I had to go out into the factory to get Cathey to check a shipment of strawboard with me. He was in the machine room overseeing the work of the women. I told him what I wanted, and we went out to the siding and opened the freight car that had just been switched in. It was full of big yellow rolls of strawboard four feet high. It didn't take us more than five minutes to count them. We shut the car again, and Cathey returned to the machine room. I added up my figures and started for the office. I was always in a hurry those days, and it was shorter to go through the old factory past the huge gloomy power wheels and the bins of cottonseed hulls.

I came out of the building and was crossing the road to the office, when I noticed Cathey coming toward me. He was walking slowly, all humped over, looking at the ground as he usually did. He was too busy himself to come to the office unless he wanted something so I waited.

He took a match out of his mouth and spat. He looked up at me and gave his weak yellow grin. "One of them nigger wenches just killed another one out in the shop," he said.

"Killed her?" I suppose I said. "How?"

"Cut her." He sliced the air beside his throat with his forefinger.

I had already started walking very fast toward the machine shop, and Cathey had to hustle to keep up with me. He resented it and took it it out in the high complaining tone of his voice. "We wasn't gone five minutes. Goddam 'em."

I didn't say anything. I guess it was because I had to see the body first.

Cathey said, "Ain't no need to hurry thisaway. She'll keep."

She lay on the floor beside a machine. There was a long bloody gash in her neck, and a big pool of blood on the floor. Already the floating lint from the strawboard was speckling its surface. Her eyes were open and her hands lay open by her sides as if she expected to receive something. I don't think I had ever seen her before in my life.

There was no one near her. The other women stood in a group about ten feet away, staring at the body. Cathey had switched off the machines, and the place was still. I could hear a loud passionate whisper somewhere at the back of the group; "I tole her. Didn't I tell her, Loreen? I swear I tole her a hundid times." It was evidently the voice of the woman who had done the cutting.

Suddenly Cathey shouted, "Now, goddam it, all y'all git back to work. And git her out of here." He threw the power switch. The wheels began to turn and the belts started flapping. The women drifted back to their machines.

I said loudly to Cathey, "What were they fighting about?"

He nodded his head toward the door and started for it. I followed him. The day had turned out warm and bright with a haze in front of the red gum trees across the bottoms. We walked slowly up the bumpy cinder roadway toward the office.

"What were they fighting about?"

"Hahda I know? They're always fightin' about somethin'."

"We ought to send for the sheriff, don't you think?"

He stopped dead and looked at me. "Sheriff?"

"To pick up the woman with the razor. It's murder."

He began to quiver, walking back and forth across the road, cutting and slicing with his empty hands. "Goddam it, don't call no sheriff. They got enough to do. Come way out here?" he shouted. It was hard for him to say what he meant because he was so angry. "Goddam it to hell, they're just niggers. The law don't want iny part of a nigger killin'."

I said nothing. I was balked by the intensity of his anger, and by the stink of the cottonseed hulls, and the dull red of the gum trees. They had their own ways of doing things here and maybe I had better not monkey with them.

"I been to ever' nigger shanty in North Meffis to git these women. Now I gotta git one more. I don't wanta git two more. You call the sheriff and he taken her to jail and I got to start out again, askin', askin' . . ." He stopped, and putting a hand on a post, he jumped lightly over his chicken fence

and caught one of his cocks. He began kissing it. He took
its bill between his lips, cooing and clucking as he would to
a child, and stroking its long, black, shining neck.

He turned to me with the bird in his arms, smiling. "You
have to get 'em used to this. When they git hurt in a fight,
you spit in their mouths. It'll put 'em right back on their
feet sometimes. Why, I seen it when..." He went on telling
about cockfights and how game birds should be handled. I
stood there, and I must have been listening to him because I
didn't hear the car go by, or, if I did, I thought it was our
truck.

I saw the car when it came back, though. I don't know
how they sent word for someone to bring it. No one had
used the phone. Maybe some one of the women had run
down the tracks back of the factory. It was an old Model-T
touring car with the top down. One of the wilted fenders
flopped loosely up and down, and the colored boy driving
it kept slamming the front door that wouldn't shut, and
steering with one hand. Three women sat in the back seat.
The one on the far side was old. I could see gray hair sticking out under her red head-rag. The near one was about
sixteen. Her hair stuck out in stiff pigtails, and I could see
the neat pattern of parts on her skull like a map. The one
in the middle wore a man's dirty felt hat, and her throat was
bound up with a piece of calico. Just as they passed me, the
front wheels went over a small culvert, and the head jerked
to one side with a dreadful limpness. As the hind wheels
struck the tile, it jerked back to the other side. I saw the old
woman trying to straighten it up again, and at last, she put
her hand up on the back of the seat and held the head erect
so that it wouldn't show when they passed down the street.

I did not think Cathey had noticed the car. He was still
talking to his game cock, but when the car turned out our
front gate into Thomas Street, he looked up and said slyly
and cheerfully, "They'll be some sure-enough big doings
now. They always have a brass band at them funerals."

* IV *

"Dear Old Shrine,
Our Hearts Round Thee Twine"

*E*arly in September before I went to college I came back up North to stay a couple of weeks in my home town with a friend of mine. He had a brother who was home on vacation from a job in New Jersey. One afternoon my friend said, "Tonight Wynn's going to wear his Brooks Brothers suit. If we get downtown about seven-thirty, we can see it." Since Wynn was twenty-four years old, it didn't occur to his brother that we might watch him dress and see the suit without going downtown. No. At seven-thirty we were standing in front of Jack English's barber shop and Wynn passed us, the jacket buttoned up to his sternum, the trousers narrow. He nodded but did not speak. I didn't know at that time that Lincoln had been shot in a Brooks Brothers suit but I couldn't have been more impressed.

That was one of the things I expected college to give me, that kind of aplomb. I expected a great deal from college, and it was to come magically fast. While I didn't really believe I would walk away from registration an instantaneous amalgam of Casanova, the Admirable Crichton, and Johnny Weissmuller, I counted on it fairly soon. I was disappointed, of course. All I learned my first day was that the knot in my necktie was too big.

I had come up from Memphis where the Sewanee and

Washington and Lee boys wore knots in their ties as big as playing cards. Not only that, the shirt collar was worn modishly low and I had seen many a young man before a glass, pulling down the front of his collar with two fingers and plucking the flesh of his neck out of the collar with his other hand. The aim seemed to be to rest the collar on the clavicle if possible, and to let the neck itself jut upward like another limb, a naked arm or leg. No sign of the shirt collar should show above the jacket in back, and the bloods had developed a tic to prevent this, a spasmodic rolling of the shoulders forward as if they had the itch. All this was wrong in the North, I found. You wore a small knot in your tie and a quarter-inch of your shirt collar showed in back. This took some adjustment as I had the tic myself.

From a white-haired, motherly old lady with steely gray eyes I rented a narrow single room. I could touch both walls if I stretched. The first night I was settled in, I heard a repeated bony rattle which, as an adopted Southerner, I knew the meaning of. This rattle was followed by a metallic trickling noise that puzzled me. I rapped on the door next to mine, expecting to walk in on a crap game muted in fear of the landlady. A voice said "Come in," and I entered, ready for the action. A thin fellow much older than I, wearing a green celluloid eyeshade, was tossing a pair of dice against a little washboard that leaned against a pile of books on his desk. The dice would roll down, come to rest, and the thin fellow would make a notation in a ledger. "Oh," I said.

"Experiment in probability," he said and threw the dice again. I didn't know what he was talking about. It turned out that he was a graduate student in mathematics and he was working out empirically how many times the number seven would come up in a million throws. He threw those dice all winter.

I wanted to study English, French, Latin, and Greek but the catalogue forbade this. It said I would have to take a laboratory science or mathematics. However, I was an idealist then. I believed that what man can devise man can undo, so I put on a pair of overall pants, a sweater with a shawl collar and holes in the elbows and went to see my scholastic adviser. I was trying to give the effect of a learned farm boy and I think I was successful. I told him with perfect truth that I had worked a year and saved my money to come to college. Since there was no question of my taking a degree (an untruth), could I study what I wanted to for this one year? It was not an easy program and I think it was the Greek that won him over. Perhaps he had a picture of me back on the farm after my year of study, my head against the steaming flank of a cow, conning the *mi*-verbs as I milked, or plowing, stalwart, bareheaded, shouting verses from the *Anthology* over the about-to-be-fruitful land. He looked like that kind of guy, tweedy, pipy, booky. Anyhow he signed my program.

Greek grammar was a nightmare. I had a little grind-yourself phonograph and I had to play it all of every evening to shut out the monotonous clicking of the dice next door. Consequently, whenever I remember Xenophon's Greeks marching up that last long hill before the Black Sea to shout, "*Thalatta! Thalatta!*" they tramp along to the tune of Rube Bloom's *Soliloquy*, a piano study of the period which I can still whistle.

Every freshman rented a room somewhere. Every freshman had a program of study. These were essential, not important. It was fraternities that were important. Nearly every freshman emitted a kind of cloudy yearning to be pledged. Some were modestly willing to take any pledge pin they could get. Others went around smirking because they were legacies, merely waiting on a formality. Others, like myself, were fussy. During the first week I learned that the fraternities my friends belonged to in the South were not very highly regarded here. SAE, for instance, which at Sewanee was jammed with aristocrats, did not rank much higher than the YMCA. There were Yankee outfits new to me like the Dekes, Psi Us, Chi Psis, and Sigma Phis which seemed to have more class. And "class" was the right word. I wanted to be identified with the right people and I didn't think a couple of swimming medals would quite do it.

Had I known then that an ancestor of mine had sailed from Plymouth, England, in 1630 and settled in Connecticut, I could have rested secure in another kind of snobbery, but all I knew was that my grandfather had originated in Vermont and had taken up veterans' land in Michigan after the Civil War. Beyond him my family might have sprung from acorns, for all I knew. And I had very little money. I had to depend on my yearning and a few friends who didn't know me very well because I had been in the South for nearly ten years. One's sixth-grade pals change almost out of recognition in ten years.

I accepted invitations from inferior houses because the meals were free. It was understood that they looked you over for two meals, and if they asked you for a third, you could expect an offer to join. One night during my first visit to one of them, I was hustled upstairs and shut in a small room with the football captain, who had been sitting there all alone. He was wearing his sweater with the big *M* on his chest. He gave me a lot of prepared malarkey about "working for Michigan," insisting that the best place to do this was in his particular club. Statements like this embarrass me and did then. I didn't want to work for Michigan. I wanted Michigan to work for me, although I was polite enough not to say so. As he talked his face had a faraway look as if he did not keep his clichés handily in his head but down in his stomach and laboriously re-gurgitated them. It tired him and at last he reached a dead stop. I had begun to say, "I've got to be going," when he silently whipped a pledge pin out of his pocket and tried to stick it in my lapel. He was a good deal heavier than I and he nearly made it, but I got away safely.

If I cast my mind back over those years casually, I can say like everyone else that my college years were the happiest of my life. However, I kept a diary and when I look at the entries for the early days of my first semester, the truth comes back. I was numb with anxiety. The right people weren't rushing me. It was a rainy fall and in the diary I am always stalking around in a smelly green slicker with wet leaves stuck to my shoes, worrying, and when I was not walking I lay on my bed waiting for the phone to ring. I didn't know what was the matter with me. I looked hardly any different from other pledges, and my poverty, or what I thought was my poverty, didn't show. I considered, I thought quite seriously, running away to sea or going to Australia to raise sheep. Then with an oily celerity I was asked to lunch twice at one of the houses I had secretly chosen and pledged the third night. I relaxed. I felt worthwhile.

It didn't take me a week to find out that I didn't like the brothers very well. I couldn't admit this even privately and it made me criminally aloof. My adviser, an elegant senior, lectured me on my "attitude" whenever he could find the time, but he never had much to say since I never had much to say. (It reminded me of my grade-school days in Memphis, when, hating the place, I tried to get through every day without saying a single word. I made it only once.) I performed my freshman duties, waking the upper-classmen in the morning and answering the phone with as little talk as possible. And I didn't hang around the fraternity house trying to be a popular pledge because someone would find me an errand to run if I did.

Slowly I learned that the house was split down the middle into the Christers and the drunks. (I do not believe this schism still exists. I think they are all drunks. At least they were fined twenty-five hundred dollars a year ago for keeping a bar in the cellar.) The Christers were the more conscientious about everything, the drunks the more interesting. Although I was out for swimming, I resolved to line myself up with the drunks.

We had a long limber guy, a junior, a Christer who wore pince-nez glasses. (Not so many people seemed to wear glasses then.) He was the house intellectual and was confidently expected to make Phi Bete. He herded the freshmen into a room one night to give us the word about the pleasures of the mind.

There was once in Memphis a huge empty house on the corner of Third and Madison. It was right downtown even then, the old Napoleon Hill home. I had heard that the Grand Duke Alexis had stayed there once. In a corner of its cellar with an opening on the street, an old man with a corrupt, baggy face and delicate, crisp white hair had opened a bookshop. His name was Pickering. His feet had swelled and I performed repeatedly a single errand for him, to go around the corner and buy him a pint of gin. It was he who sold me a copy of Joyce's *Ulysses*, a second edition, rebound, for fifty dollars.

Behind his bookshelves were the long cool alleys of the cellars where, exploring, I stumbled over dozens of empty dust-covered champagne magnums. Once I had seen these, I couldn't resist the *Ulysses*. It was such a big investment that I read it all the way through, I daresay the first person south of the Mason-Dixon line to do so. I remembered Stephen's phrase "the ineluctable modality of the visible." I didn't know what it meant but I remembered it. When all of us freshmen were sitting there dutifully agog, I remembered it again. He was going on, this Christer, about Leibnitz and Kant, reviewing some course he had taken, and this to freshmen as if they cared. Suddenly I said, "What about the ineluctable modality of the visible?" It stopped him cold. I didn't go near the house for three days, and when I did, I learned that if I was not the house intellectual, I was certainly the intellectual pledge. This only confused people because I was also an athlete, and while they did not with today's jovial condescension call them "jocks," it was felt that you had to talk slowly and clearly to athletes. The Twenties, they say, appraised American life anew. One of the victims was The Athlete. Dink Stover was dead.

We had what is called in the South "a big old boy" from the hills of West Virginia whom the football coaches had their eye on. He was a twenty-three-year-old freshman. He weighed around two hundred and thirty and his fist looked like a peck of potatoes. Like most wrestlers and football players he had a sweet nature and with a docile somnolence he acquiesced in the brothers' attempts to teach him to play bridge all one winter. He did not quite learn the game properly as he always bid "two spades" no matter what cards he held, but he was always glad to play. He also took a mild interest in his textbooks, riffling the pages delicately with his great hands to see if there were any pictures, and if he found one, he would go, "Whooee! Looka hyuah now!" in a pleased falsetto.

He called all girls "poon tang" indiscriminately but he was gentle and smiling with those he met. He couldn't dance a step and didn't try, but parties were always crowded and he was very happy to hug some girl in a corner while the music played. If, however, misled by his open face and his gentleness, she went into a room alone with him, she came sprinting out thirty seconds later, disheveled and shrieking with disillusion.

While our house was not an athletic house, it was believed that athletes did no harm, and, in fact, it was wise to keep a couple in residence to back up our claim that we were a well-rounded group. Everyone knew that it was going to be hard to keep Maxcey around for very long. While it was not true that he was totally analphabetic, the printed word gave him a rough time. He could read, muttering every word and pointing to it with his toelike fingernail, but it was so hard for him and he was so relieved to finish any sentence with an approximate accuracy that it was like a ritual. We used to gather to watch him read, each of us forming the words silently with his own lips, mutely cheering him on, a mutual frown forming at every impediment, and an exhalation and wide general smile at the period. A successful paragraph would raise a ragged cheer, and Maxcey—proud as he could be—would clasp his hands over his head and cry "Heah now!"

I suppose everybody in the house had a crack at tutoring him one time or another. Maxcey was as patient as a turtle, obviously ashamed of his own deficiencies, and he meekly accepted correction from snotty youths he could have broken in two. His first two years we were aided by the Athletic Department, who steered him into courses in Physical Education where, to pass, he had little to do but ripple his muscles, but we feared his junior and senior years, when he would have to take academic subjects. We cooked up quite a few schemes to help him out. One we discarded might have worked. It was to register a moderately intelligent brother under Maxcey's name in two or three of his courses. Maxcey was delighted and offered to pay any *Doppelgänger* handsomely. (Maxcey had a lot of money some alumnus had sent him.) We didn't use this plan because we surmised that the authorities would throw everyone concerned out of school if they caught us. As it was, we put him into courses that at least two other brothers were taking. They moved him to class every day, lent him their notes, and explained what was going on as well as they could. At exam time they made cribs for him, either

writing in block letters on a small roll of toilet paper which
he could feed across his belly, from one pants pocket to
another, tear and stuff into the pockets if the professor came
snooping around, or packets of notes given to freshmen with
instructions to lurk in the men's toilet nearest the exam
until Maxcey came in when they were to read the notes
to him as quickly as possible. The freshmen got fairly tired
of this but it helped Maxcey. He staggered through his
program, dragging a tail of C-minuses after him.

In his junior year Maxcey signed up for a course in
Speech, charmed because he thought that all he would have
to do was talk, but the professor threw him a curve. Maxcey
had to learn the anatomy of voice production, and the differences between larynx and pharynx took relays of frantic
helpers because Maxcey had heard of the lynx, the furry
denizen of the forests, and that lynx kept creeping in.

It was a second-semester course and the grade depended
chiefly on a term paper. The subject was the endocrine
glands. In the month of April Maxcey was never seen without a book on the endocrines in his hands. The football
coach had told every member of the squad to keep a football on his desk during the year and to squeeze it and fondle
it while studying so as to get the feel of it. I think this was
what Maxcey was doing with the book; I didn't see him
read it. The paper didn't get written and Maxcey asked the
professor to give him an Incomplete and he was so genial
the professor did. Maxcey went off to work as a station-
master at some whistle stop in the West Virginia mountains
for the summer. When he returned in the fall, he still didn't
have the paper done although he said he had tried. He
called on the professor humbly, contritely, and the professor said, "I'll tell you what I'll do, Mr. Maxcey. I'll give
you an oral examination in lieu of the paper."

"Yassuh," Maxcey said, frightened. I don't think he
thought the professor was going to look at his teeth. I don't
think he knew what was coming next at all.

"Mr. Maxcey, name the endocrine glands."

"The endocrine glands?"

"Yes. Just name them."

"Well, suh, There's the thah-roid," Maxcey said dreamily.

"That's right."

"And there's the para-thahroid."

"That's good. Go on."

"And there's the tabloid ... and there's the hemorrhoid. ..." Maxcey sat there, the professor said, clutching his little finger and glaring at it. We had told him there were five endocrines.

The professor stared at him a second to see if Maxcey was kidding him, but Maxcey never kidded anybody. Then, as Maxcey said later, the professor "like to ruptured himself laughin' " and he said, "Mr. Maxcey, I'm going to give you an *A*."

Maxcey came loping into the house, cuffed the heads of all the bridge players, and shouted, "Where's mah jug? I got mahseff an *A!*" That evening he drank nearly a gallon of some white stuff we called "sheep-dip" that came off a farm near Jackson. He was the first man I ever saw drink from a jug with one hand, throwing it gracefully over his elbow. Someone had given him "asteroid" as the fifth endocrine and at midnight he was prowling up and down the corridors, the jug dangling from one finger, interrupting studiers, waking sleepers, shouting, "Son, you know the names of the endocrine glands?" and he would tick them all off. The House Committee fined him five dollars because A's weren't as rare as all that, but he didn't care. The Speech professor told the story and eventually it went all over the campus.

After I had gotten through first-year Greek, my own work went well enough. I moved into the fraternity house, a brand-new Elizabethan pile, and my roommate and I decided to study every day. But to keep from looking as if we did, we studied at that idle time, from five until seven.

While the rest of the brothers were playing bridge, taking showers, or listening to records, we had our door locked and we hit the books. Nobody caught us at it. Since we had to study only a couple of evenings a week in addition, we acquired the welcome reputation of intelligent bums because we were always ready to drop the books and go to a movie or a speakeasy.

I am not aware that I had, as some people do in college, a ripsnorting intellectual awakening, although several of my professors tried to jog me into one. My first class in the university was in English. On the first day, the instructor, a fresh-cheeked, lame young man, came in without a word to us, wrote "Great is Diana of the Ephesians" on the blackboard, and said, "Write for twenty minutes about that." None of us thought it silly. It cowed and appalled us all. The longer I thought about it, the madder I got. At last I wrote this on my paper and handed it in, "It's a hell of a note to expect freshmen to comment on the Pauline Epistles." I don't know what the instructor thought but he took me out of freshman English and put me into a sophomore class where I was immediately asked to describe a man doing physical work to the point of exhaustion but I can't recall the professor who assigned that one.

Only two or three of my teachers stand out in my mind. One is an old man, erect, with his open hands away from his sides, reciting Goethe's *Faust* from memory, as tears ran down his face. Some of the class giggled. Now that I am older, I know he didn't give a damn whether anyone giggled or not, but I was terribly afraid he was going to be hurt then and I poked the guy in front of me and told him to shut up. After that I got up my German before any other subject, and I have never believed that his tears were pedagogical.

Another was a tough little Scot from Aberdeen and Cambridge, all tweed and flying hair like the British. I say tough because I became his student assistant in my senior year and one night I saw him drink two bottles of horrible bootleg whisky and walk away. This was astonishing because he was no bigger than Jimmy Wilde, the flyweight champ, but he dominated his classes and he did it by contempt. He would ask wide-eyed students from Kalamazoo or Grand Rapids about Maillol, Braque, or Paul Klee, and when their tongues clave to the roofs of their mouths, he would sniff and go on about Rimbaud or Eliot—who was very new then and his special property. I asked him why he put these hard questions when it was so obvious that no one knew the answers. "They must hear the names sometime, mustn't they?" he said. My acquaintance with him was no protection. Once in a paper about Huxley's *Antic Hay*, I said that I didn't believe people like Gumbril, Lypiatt, or Coleman had ever existed. He wrote in the margin, "You just haven't been around enough." I knew that but it stung me to have it pointed out when I was trying as hard as I could.

Later he was fired. Only grave moral turpitude was grounds for firing a full professor, and the story was that he had been found in bed with the leading lady of an itinerant drama group. It didn't occur to me at the time but this is an inherently unlikely story. Who does the finding (a student, a dean, a uniformed policeman?) and how do they know when to time it? I am inclined to believe that he was as contemptuous of his colleagues as he was of us and they used the actress only as a lever. A few years afterward he died of yellow jaundice on Staten Island, oddly enough.

My roommate and I took a course in Fine Arts. The label didn't mean what it implied. It was, like all such courses, a history of painting, architecture, and sculpture. The professor was a thick bald man with a face like a mandrill. He wore a neat serge suit, and he moved and spoke with a briskness we all thought inartistic. When he threw slides of Sant' Ambrogio or Azay-le-Rideau on the screen, I had the impression that he was discussing valuable pieces of real estate which we could buy at a good price if we were sharp about it. He had reduced his course to a twenty-page outline, price a quarter at any of the bookstores. When it came to the final exam, my roommate and I decided to ignore the questions, learn his outline, and give it back to him.

Through two hot June days, lolling in our shorts, we conned that damned outline over like a poem until we knew it cold. (I have never been able to shuck some of the facts. They remain in my memory as cold and unfruitful as pebbles. The water for the aqueduct at Nîmes comes from the springs above Uzès. The "eye" in the Pantheon at Rome is 24' 9" across.) On the day of the final we wrote out the whole outline. We were the first ones to finish. As we turned in our blue books, he picked them up and thumbed through them. When he saw what we had done, he said, "If you have made one mistake, I'll flunk you." We hadn't, though, and he had to give us A's. Everyone said he had been a guard in the Metropolitan Museum.

As I read over this diary, on sheer inchage (is there such a word?) it seems that I spent my time not studying, not swimming, but either with women, pursuing women, or writing really frightful prose about them. Even in my memory, a notoriously unreliable repository for anyone, my college years are a frieze of pretty girls. As a freshman, I was told by my senior adviser at the fraternity that I was not to have any dates with co-eds. "You come to college to meet men, not women," he said. And we learned a song which we sang at least once a week after meals:

The co-ed leads a sloppy life, sloppy life.
She eats potatoes with her knife, with her knife.

And once a year she takes a scru-u-u-b
And leaves a ring around the tub, the dirty thing.
And once a year she takes a scru-u-u-b
And leaves a ring around the tub.

My adviser's command did not depress me at first because
I was too afraid of my studies to foresee any time for dates,
but the co-eds looked all right to me. At that time they
wore hats and gloves to class, their dresses up to their knees,
and high heels. I sat next to one in French and after I had
surreptitiously looked at her neck and found it perfectly
clean, I lent her a pencil and we talked. She was having
a tough time with the irregular verbs and this seemed only
normal. I made up my mind that when I found a good-
looking one I would date her, brothers or no.

The girls we were supposed to date were the Detroit
debutantes. The Detroit "season" was the winter months.
Engraved invitations were tacked to the fraternity bulletin
board on week ends which meant, I suppose, that every
member was welcome. This seems incredible, considering
the jerks we had, but it was true. Detroit was full of automobile money then, the older lumber money having somewhat sniffily retired into the background. Since I came to
these gatherings pure, hoping only for romance, it took
a while before I had any notion of what was really going
on. The fathers of these debutante girls were looking for
brisk young executive types as husbands for their daughters, and I discovered that several of our members were
eager to be found. It was one of my early lessons in the
radiations of power to watch one of my sworn brothers
hustling a big, fat, sweaty girl around a dance floor because
her father was vice-president of some auto company.

Two of our guys were thought to be shot with luck,
in spite of all the footwork and flattery they had exercised,
because they married the right Detroit girls and were thrust

into automobile companies at quite a high level—but all this was earlier than 1929, and both their fathers-in-law, as it happened, flung themselves out of the Penobscot Building, the highest in Detroit, after the Crash and my brothers had to find work just like the rest of us.

I didn't have enough money to pay any real attention to even pretty debutantes and the main attraction of these parties was the free liquor, some of it pretty good for the period. There was a distillery across the Detroit River at Walkerville, Ontario, and while I doubt if any of their whisky was over six months old, it was a good deal older than a lot of the stuff we bought, and sometimes a hospitable official would set out some genuine prewar Scotch, but this was hardly appreciated because it seemed so weak.

We were compelled to drink—it was thought genuinely rude to turn down a drink if offered one—and I have often discussed this old compulsion with my contemporaries, some of whose faces have that spanked reddish look, with others who are steady and clear-eyed from a long vacation with the AA's. I have gathered that we were participating in a moral upheaval. Each drink we took was a ritual defiance of ancient Puritan strictures unworthy of a free people and all like that. Hindsight makes it sound pretty good but not good enough.

I can remember making a two-inch puddle of a purported Old Crow on the edge of a bathroom washbowl, touching a match to it, and watching the flame to see whether it burned blue or yellow. It was never true blue. There were always yellow halos even with the seven-dollar stuff, but if there was any blue at all, we drank it. Drinking it straight, out of a bottle, was a heroic act. You took a deep but unobtrusive breath, filled your mouth, braced yourself for the swallow, forced it back, hoping your stomach wouldn't buck when it landed, and, tears flooding your eyes, you gasped "Gimme a cigarette" if you hadn't had the foresight to light one beforehand. According to the code, you couldn't ask for a chaser or have one ready. This brings me to what I believe to have been the actual compulsion: We were performing one of the *rites de passage*. The trouble was that where the Sioux could fast a few days, go off into the piney woods and have a dream of some totem animal, and Malinowski's Trobrianders, lying flat on their faces, could have the hell temporarily scared out of them by a bull-roarer, our rites went drearily on and on, year after year, because it was not within human capabilities to drink bootleg whisky neat with grace and dispatch. You couldn't *learn* how to drink. You drank and took the consequences. This is why so many of my generation have remained sogged in a state of chronic adolescence. They feel sheepish.

But the girls. Nothing makes me see what a Prig I was more vividly than the lists I kept in the back pages of this diary: the titles of the books I read, the slowly descending swimming times, and the names of the girls I kissed. Is there any American who does not believe that there is a technique for everything? As a people we believe in the foolproof recipe. And that was what we—not I, all of us —were looking for. Necking girls, getting them into bed, were matters of the right passes, the effectual incantation.

With the spring, characters used to appear at fraternities— a man with cavalry mustaches who sounded like Harry Lauder, peddling genuine Harris tweed in bolts, smuggled into the country, he said (it fell apart in the first rain); a surly youth who wanted someone to tie him up so he could get loose against a five-dollar bet (you furnish the rope); and a Levantine in a derby with a suitcase. Out of the suitcase came copies of the *Kama-Sutra*, Frank Harris' *My Life and Loves*, Cleaveland's *Fanny Hill*. They were expensive and we formed little book clubs on the spot to split the costs. Then we studied them, looking for the charm.

We had serious discussions of aphrodisiacs like dropping cigarette ashes or an aspirin in a girl's beer, either of which was supposed to render them complaisant but never did, or wrestling holds that would immobilize the girl and leave you one hand free, but these conversations never resulted in anything sure-fire. Each of us had to peg away all alone. Not once did we consider the girl's point of view, that she might simply be looking for a husband because we were not looking for wives. There was no Bomb then, no hurry.

While I cannot find faces for some of the names on my list, and while there are strange lovely faces from that old time that something pricks into my head, surrounded by clouds like a girl on an old valentine, a few I remember utterly. They are the ones I would have taken to Paris. The aim then, not mine alone, nearly everyone's and impossible for nearly everyone, was to live with a girl in Paris, not in the Faubourg St. Germain, not in a villa in the suburbs with a vitreous sign saying *Chien Méchant* on the front gate; no, but in a garret on the Left Bank. Nobody would have lived with a girl in Detroit, or Elkhart, or Akron. Greenwich Village might have served, but the ideal was Paris. It took a certain amount of financial conniving to get me to Detroit for a debutante party. How could I have taken a girl to Paris? Yet I had a list of three or four in my mind all ready in case of fortune. I don't know whether they were ready to go, but I was certainly ready to ask them.

When I was a sophomore, a freshman came scuttling into the house one afternoon, excited, with tidings which, if he had not been a freshman, he would have kept to himself. His name was Johnny McGinty, and, to use an archaic word, he looked like a sport. He wore checked suits and you rather expected him to give you a sure thing for Tuesday at Laurel or Pimlico. The impression was false—he was a dumb freshman drunk but I was only a sophomore; I

didn't consider for one second that his taste might be unreliable. I believed him instantly and I'm glad I did. He
said that the most beautiful babe on the campus had just
been elected vice-president of the freshman class. He was
too stupid to be coherent and his assessment ran "She ain't
so pretty for nice but she's hell for stuff. With a shape,
man. With blonde hair. With a leopardskin coat, too."

Now leopardskin is not like sable and I knew it wasn't
then but it is identifiable and I started keeping my eye
out for babes in leopardskin coats on the campus. I saw
a couple, one fat, one thin; too fat, too thin. They reminded
me that Johnny McGinty was dumb and I quit looking.

Puffed up as we were from being asked to the brawls and
levees of Detroit, we paid little attenton to dances spon-
sored by the university but one Saturday night I was loung-
ing down the corridors of the second floor at the house,
looking for something to do. I was convinced as I believe
the young are today that something fascinating, something
important was happening elsewhere if I could only find it,
especially on a Saturday night. Many of the rooms were
dark, the occupants already having gone to look, but I
found one door open with the light on. Sam Claflin, an
architecture student, was bending over a drawing board at
his desk, apparently working.

"You must be damn hard up for something to do," I said.

"Uh-huh," he said. He was busy.

I walked in and looked over his shoulder. Tacked to the
board was an engraved invitation to the Freshman Frolic
which was being thrown that night with George Olsen's
band, as I remember. He was holding below it a white card
of the same size and doing a very creditable job of imitating
the engraving with a pen, freehand.

"You're going to that?" I said. Claflin was a soph like
myself.

"No. I'm just learning fancy lettering."

"I suppose you can afford the fine," I said. We were fined five dollars if we associated with co-eds. "You didn't actually buy that real ticket."

"McGinty's. He loaned it to me. He can afford the fine."

"What do you want to go to a frosh hop for?"

"Becky Black," he said. She was the girl in the leopard-skin coat.

"Make me one," I said.

Claflin looked up for the first time. "Oh, Christ," he said. "Why don't you go read Greek or something? I'm already making one for Honeycutt."

"Make another."

"Got any whisky?"

I had cached away about six inches in a forty-ounce quart of Spey Royal, the preferred "Scotch" of the period. "A few snorts."

"How many?"

"Three for you, three for me, say."

"It isn't really worth it. Those tickets cost five bucks apiece."

"But you'll do it, Sam, because you're a drunkard through and through." He wasn't. He was just beginning. He had been an Eagle Scout. I was flattering him.

"Well . . . go get dressed. We haven't got all night."

I went and got myself duded up in a hard shirt and a dinner jacket. When I returned to Claflin's room there was a pint of Old Crow on the table. Honeycutt was standing behind Claflin at the mirror, tying his black tie from behind, a difficult operation usually performed by women, and McGinty, resplendent in tails, was mewing on the bed for a drink of the Old Crow.

"I wouldn't think of it. You're just a little boy," Honeycutt said.

"Aw, come on, Ted. Just one. You wouldn't have any tickets at all if I hadn't loaned . . ."

"You goddamned little bastard," Honeycutt said mildly.

"If you don't shut up, I'll break the bottle over your head. I mean it. Broken glass causes dandruff."

At last we were ready to leave for the party, eager, alert, reeking of Ed Pinaud's Lilac Vegetale and Sta-Comb. We had all had a snort out of Honeycutt's Old Crow, except McGinty. Since the forty-ounce bottle of Spey Royal was too big to go on anyone's hip, we poured the "Scotch" into the pint of "Bourbon" without hesitation. "What the hell, it all tastes lousy," Honeycutt said.

McGinty, sore at being deprived of a drink, tried to scuttle away ahead of us as we left the house but Claflin grabbed him by the collar. "No, you don't, McGinty. You've got the real ticket."

"We swarm in after you, laughing and talking. Laugh and talk, McGinty," I said.

"Aw..." McGinty rumbled.

"Practice laughing and talking or I'll fine you ten dollars," Honeycutt said.

"Sophs can't fine," McGinty said.

"No, but sophs can kick your ass so it will hang right up between your shoulder blades. Get hot, McGinty," Honeycutt said.

McGinty babbled conscientiously until we got to the Union, where they were holding the dance. We drew off into some coniferous shrubbery and each took a drink. McGinty hovered bleakly nearby. "Let's give him one," Honeycutt said. We called him and he took a great big slug with more ease than any of us. "Watch it, McGinty. You'll never graduate," I said. (He never did.)

We went in. When we got to the door of the ballroom, we laughed and talked so persuasively that Claflin's three false tickets got us all in. Again McGinty tried to slip away.

Honeycutt seized his arm. "Look, McGinty, you're unattractive as hell. Nobody's waiting to meet you. Now which one is Becky Black?"

McGinty hung his head, playing stupid.

"Learn, McGinty. Don't try to get even with sophs. They'll cut your heart out and fry it. Now which?"

As if he had had his eye on her all the time, McGinty said, "She's that one," and pointed out toward the dance floor.

"You can go home now," Honeycutt said.

The great population shifts had not yet occurred and Michigan co-eds were, in the main, what three generations fixed in one place and the hard water had left them. Beauty was apt to be big, highly colored, opulently curved, the attraction of the perfect Northern Spy apple. There is not one thing wrong with this and, after the build-up, I expected to see a big blonde beautiful dame who would go a hundred and thirty and have a loud voice.

Instead, I saw something suave, delicate, raffinée, blonde sure enough but not a girl who reminded me of stone fireplaces and tobogganing, rather a clutch of names I knew but had never experienced, such as Biedermeyer, Chateau La-Tour Blanche, and Proust. She was dancing. I watched her. She was not talking to her partner. She was not wearing an evening dress, which suggests a garment with ruffles run up over a Bertha at home, but an evening gown bought for the occasion. Her shape was not striking but insidious. I kept watching it. McGinty was right, she wasn't so pretty for nice but she was hell for stuff.

I had come to the dance bursting with condescension but, watching her, it leaked away. She had a longish lock of blonde hair hanging beside her cheek and occasionally she threw her head back a little to move it. (Later I touched a match to that lock as she bent forward to light a cigarette. Later that year.) However, I was paralyzed.

Honeycutt poked me in the back. "Come on, come on. Let's get the show on the road. I'll introduce you."

I didn't ask how he came to know her. I walked out with him among the dancers. He tapped her partner on the shoulder and he fell away.

"Miss Pumphandle, Mr. Pumphandle," Honeycutt said. He had gone to school in Switzerland.

She smiled vaguely. We danced. She danced well but I was a slick dancer myself. I gave it thirty seconds, watching fiercely over her shoulder to keep off any cut-ins. "I'd like to talk to you," I said.

"Well . . ." she murmured.

I broke off dancing and took her into a kind of sun-room that ran parallel to the dance floor. "Who are you?" I said.

The dialogue began. It is the great dialogue when you come to think of it. What else has ever engaged anyone with like intensity? It lasted three years and it ended in the porter's lodge at Oriel College, Oxford, where the only public telephone was. She had written me she was getting married. At stunning expense I put in a transatlantic call and said "Marry me."

"Oh, we'd never get along," she said.

We never had but I said, "You're sure?"

"Yes."

"Good luck," I said, three pounds fourteen shillings sunk in the ocean sea. On mature consideration I believe she was right, but I didn't think so then. I went all alone to the George Restaurant and started drinking down the cocktail list, A for Absinthe, Alexander, Avocaat; Bacardi, Bronx. . . .

V

The Nicest Girl in Cook County

*I*t may seem an odd way to do it, but I once became acquainted with a Chicago gangster and his family through the distaff side and the novels of André Gide. It happened the summer before my senior year in college. I was working as a lifeguard at a swimming pool on the west coast of Michigan with a fraternity brother of mine, a big quarter-miler named Arno Bevins. In the early summer, the water of the pool still grew cold at night, and no one came in. Arno and I would get into his Model T and drive down to the Big Pavilion to dance. The Big Pavilion looked out over the little harbor of the town nearby. It was bigger than any three barns I ever saw, and at night it was full of girls, all kinds of girls—from the town, the yachts anchored in the harbor, and the summer cottages up and down the beaches of Lake Michigan. The roof was the introduction. You bought a string of tickets and asked any girl you fancied for a dance.

Nearly every girl had her hair bobbed then. One night we saw a tall, I thought handsome, girl with her hair done into a bun at the nape of her neck. This made us want to dance with her. I asked her politely, employing the relic of a bow I had learned in dancing school. She said "No, thank you" coolly, with a certain hauteur. Arno followed me and she refused him, too, unsmilingly.

At the beginning of the season, we had noticed this halfwit

boy looking in through the fence at the edge of the pool. He was there every morning at nine, and he stood there all day, patiently hanging by his fingers until we started letting him in free. In return, he used to wait for us at the edge of town every night. We would pick him up, and he would hang around with us for the rest of the evening, enthralled. He was twelve years old and his name was Everett Cartwright. We gave Everett a quarter to ask the long-haired girl to dance. He teetered up to her with his high, whinnying giggle and asked. She smiled, patted his arm and looked over at us. She knew we had put him up to it, and I guess she thought better us than Everett, because she accepted when I asked her again. Arno asked her for three dances and she accepted. Going home in the car, Arno said he thought she was a darb. At that time there was no higher praise.

The next morning, our boss, the proprietor of the pool, called us in. "I hear you two were dancing with Sara Egan last night," he said. (Her name was neither Sara nor Egan, but that is what I am going to call her.)

I was looking for beautiful girls, knockouts. I had thought her merely handsome, and, satisfied at having broken down her resistance, I had not asked her name. Arno had, though. He said, "Yes."

"You want to watch it with her," the boss said.

"Why?" Arno asked.

"She's Bone Egan's sister."

"Who's Bone Egan?" Arno asked. He was six-three and he knew how to box.

The boss sensed Arno's covert belligerence and extinguished it. "He's in Chicago. He's got the beer for an alderman's district."

I didn't know exactly what this meant, but the boss's ominous tone gave it importance. "You mean he's a gangster?" I said.

"You tell 'em he's a gangster. And that sister of his is the nicest girl in Cook County, so don't go getting any funny ideas. You wouldn't want a doctor peeking into your bullet holes, now, would you?"

This was incredible to me. We were college men. Occasionally a bootlegger's car would roll up under our hushed and sacred elms. The bootlegger would get out and come up the front walk of the fraternity, carrying a suitcase, and we would buy the frightful cut "whisky" at seven or eight dollars a bottle. Bootleggers always appeared on Thursdays, just as that wonderful tension was beginning to mount before a football game or a houseparty, and they were as much a part of it as the pretty girls or the dance bands. One, a Mr. Fox, portly, white-haired, circumspect, used to work both sides of the corridor I lived on, and, when he came into my room, if there were friends of mine who didn't know him, they stood up, thinking him a professor. We had heard that these staid, friendly men were in the pay of gangsters but we only read about gangsters in the Chicago *Tribune*, where they shared the dubious journalistic reality of Lindbergh or Dr. Coué. They were famous. They probably existed but they were shadowy, distant, vague. Yet here was a man telling us that one of them might shoot us full of holes.

"Why *Bone* Egan?" I asked.

"You'll catch on the first time you see him," the boss said.

I didn't see Sara Egan for a couple of weeks. It was not caution; it was the warm weather. People began to swim nights at the pool and one of us had to watch them. The nights I was on, Arno took the Ford and lit out somewhere. The nights I was off, I walked downtown to the Big Pavilion. (I didn't know how to drive.) I didn't see Arno there, or Sara either. I asked him if he were dating her. He said "Yes," and that was all. Usually he gave me his speculations about any girl he took out until he produced a tedium almost sublime. I asked him if he didn't think it was pretty risky. He said "Maybe." He acted scared to me.

When we were hired, we were supposed to sleep in a room at the pool building and eat there at the hamburger stand. One night after the boss had gone home, Arno and I tried an experiment. We set out to prove that it was possible to make a malted milk thick enough that you could stand not a straw but a spoon in it. We packed the can nearly full of chocolate ice cream, added the powder and about a gill of coffee cream, and stuck it on the machine. The machine spun and caught, spun and caught, went "oo-ah, oo-ah, oo-ah," and flew all apart. We gathered the parts into a neat little pile, but the next morning we were asked to take our meals elsewhere, and the boss' wife devised an elaborate system of mapping the ice cream every night before she went home. We were both on duty during the day but we alternated nights and mealtimes. That is how I came to be eating alone at a summer boardinghouse in the town a mile away.

One hot day in July, trying to find a shorter route, I went up a different street from my usual one. It was in the older part of town, away from the summer cottages, an alley of gigantic maple trees. As I was passing a big white frame house, I heard my name called. I heard the squeak and clash of chains on a porch swing, but I couldn't see the swing because the porch was enclosed by a honeysuckle vine. Then I saw Sara at the top of the steps. I walked up. She looked very cool in a white cotton dress and she had no tan. She said, "How would you like a bottle of beer?"

Like a cup of tea. In those days, no one asked you to have a "bottle" of beer. You bought a case of the filthy stuff, drank it up, and called it a party. I said, "It would be wonderful."

I went up on the porch and we sat on the long wicker swing. Almost at once a colored maid came out with the

beer and a glass on a tray. The maid was in uniform, and
the beer had drops of moisture running down the bottle.
Sara must have seen me coming and counted on my acceptance.

She was marking the place with her finger in a yellow-
back French novel. I said, "What are you reading?"
She held up the book. "*Les Faux Monnayeurs*," she said.
"André Gide."

I had never heard of him but I felt I ought to have. Without a dictionary at hand, my own French was still desperately and precariously concerned with the hat of my aunt
on the table. I hurried into my beer while she told me about
the book with the flattering assumption that I would want
to know. As she talked, I noticed she used none of the current college slang. She seemed older, and she was. She told
me she was taking her Master's in mathematics at Northwestern.

"Calculus, eh?" I said, immediately exhausting my knowledge of that field. I was beginning to be uneasy. The beer
was so good it was sinister. She might, if she liked, hide behind this fragrant honeysuckle, these screens of French and
mathematical sophistication, but she was still Bone Egan's
sister. I think I was waiting for a gun to go off.

When I finished my beer, I stood up and said, "I've got to
get back and relieve Arno. Thanks a lot."

She said "Stop in any time," but I never did.

I had deliberately not brought Arno into the conversation
because I didn't know what tone to take. He hardly ever
mentioned her name but, a few days later, as I was sitting
on a bench beside the pool watching the customers, Arno
came back from lunch and sat down beside me. I could
smell beer three feet away, and it was the middle of the
afternoon. He said as offhandedly as he could, "I've just
been talking to Bone Egan."

"How'd you meet him?"

"Sara."

Bone Egan had come into the harbor with a bunch of guys on a fifty-foot cruiser from Chicago. They were already *guys* to Arno, not Bone Egan's gang. They had a ginny hunchback to play the accordion.

"Ginny?" I asked.

"Italian," Arno said.

They were all sitting around, having a few drinks on deck, and somebody knocked a can of alcohol over the side. Arno had stripped down to his shorts, dived in, and come up with it.

"How deep is it there?"

"About thirty feet."

This was modesty, waiting until I had asked him about the depth. It is quite something to go down thirty feet without equipment, and there were no aqualungs then. It must have impressed Bone Egan and the guys.

"He offered me a job," Arno said, watching me.

"What doing?"

"Driving a truck. A hundred and fifty bucks a week and no shooting. 'We'll have a guy on the truck to do the shooting,' he said."

A hundred and fifty bucks a week was a lot of money then. We were roomies and members of the swimming team and all that, but I realized that I didn't know Arno very well.

"Good-by, Arno," I said.

"Oh, hell, I'm not going to Chicago."

"What kind of a guy is he?"

He was not big, Arno said, a black Irishman who had gone East to Holy Cross for some reason, and then to the War as a lieutenant in the Rainbow Division. He had won a Croix de Guerre. He had come back to Chicago, seen the opportunity, and gone into the liquor business.

"That's what he calls it, huh?"

"Yes. They don't look any different. They're just a bunch

of guys getting drunk on a cruiser. They were singing 'The Camptown Races' when I left, close harmony."

The sky was a deep, clear blue, and the sun was so bright all the shadows seemed black. Before us in the water the children of the summer people screamed and splashed, watched by their mothers or drowsy nursemaids. Bone and his boys singing in the harbor seemed a platoon of soldiers in a rest camp, and Arno's job took on the aspect of a brisk little military operation. I had been in Chicago only once, to visit an aunt in Oak Park. If Arno had taken the job, would someone have shot at him from Marshall Field's windows or the steps of the Art Museum? I didn't believe it.

The summer ran down in a string of beautiful moonlit evenings I spent with a girl of my own. During the calm, slack days, I actually taught Everett Cartwright to swim a crawl. He was badly coordinated and it took a long time, but when his face was in the water, I couldn't hear that giggle. I didn't see much of Arno and Sara. I said to him, one morning as we were dressing, "Look, if somebody tosses a pineapple from a speeding car some night and blows us out of our beds, if there's anything left of me, I'm going to take a hammer to what's left of you," but I said it only to use the word *pineapple*, which I had read in the papers. Arno looked at me quite seriously but he didn't say anything.

We went back to college in September. On a Saturday morning before one of the early football games, Arno took me down into the cellar of his fraternity. "We are now going to make some blowtorch. It's a drink," he said. Two clean quart Mason jars and an oblong can of shiny tin sat on an old workbench in front of us. Arno took an orange out of his pocket and peeled it. He dropped the skin into the bottom of one Mason jar and bruised it with the handle of a ball-peen hammer. Then he poured the jar full from the can. He took another orange out of his pocket, shoved it whole through the mouth of the other Mason jar, and pounded it to a pulp with the hammer handle. "Now you let that stand for two hours," he said. "Then you strain it into the second jar and let it stand two more hours. Then you strain it again and drink. It's the oils in the peel that does it."

I nodded solemnly. I still believed, earnestly and idiotically, that the juniper oils "did it" to gin, and that, of course, the orange oils would do it to this stuff. "Where'd you get the alcohol?" I asked.

"Sara."

"When'd you see Sara?"

"About one o'clock this morning." Arno had quit being gabby months ago. I had to pry it out of him.

After his last afternoon class the day before, he had climbed into his old Model T and taken off for Chicago, two hundred and fifty miles away. Anyone who has taken that long a trip in a Model T will remember that you could make about thirty-five miles an hour on the average, and Arno had pulled into Chicago about midnight. He had sent a post card saying he was coming, and his intention had been to bring Sara back for the game. She wouldn't come. Instead, she had made him a present.

Somehow I had gotten the notion that gangsters, in spite of their money, lived in the back rooms of mean little flats. They ate in flashy restaurants but their homes were squalor. "She just keep this stuff around the apartment?" I asked.

"She don't live in an apartment. She lives in a great big house on South Halsted Street."

I moved her into the big house. "In the cellar there?"

"No, you dummy. She gave me an address and called somebody. It was up a flight of stairs. Big door with one of those slots in it. I rang the bell. The slot opened. A guy said, 'What's your name?' and I told him. He said, 'Stand back away from the door.' I did. He let me in."

"Why stand back away from. . . ."

"He said Miss Egan told him a big guy named Arno was coming for a can of white. He wanted to see how big."

"*Miss* Egan, huh?"

"They all call her that."

Until the swimming meets started in January and we went into training, Arno went to Chicago every Friday and came back with a can of white. By the end of October he was wearing his fur coat; in November a heavy sweater with a shawl collar under it, and fur-lined gloves. When it started to snow in December, he cut his Friday-afternoon classes, and he would spend half an hour getting into a sweatsuit, corduroy pants, a flannel shirt, the sweater, and over and around it all, the coonskin coat. Then he would stuff the front of the sweater with newspapers, tie a long woolen scarf under his chin, cram a hat over it, pull on mittens over the gloves, and go creeping off over the icy roads with the top down.

Sara had put him into the liquor business. Alcohol cost fifteen dollars a quart, retail. Arno kept one quart for our own use and sold the other four. He was the only student bootlegger I ever knew, and he did a nice trade on football and houseparty week ends. Our private blowtorch was awful. To this day, I can gag on a glass of orange juice. It's the oils that do it.

At the end of February, the swimming team took a long week-end trip to meet both the University of Chicago and Northwestern. Sara met us at the I.C. depot, but not with a Cadillac and chauffeur as I had expected. True, she was wearing a mink coat but she had a Buick sedan and she drove it herself.

The house on South Halsted was enormous. It was red, brick, and Victorian, and it had a louring mansard roof like an old woman with her hat jammed down over her eyes. Inside, the ceilings seemed about fifteen feet high, and the rooms were cluttered with furniture. The living room contained four huge chintz-covered sofas set in a square. In the middle of the chief one, propped by archaic satin-covered circular cushions, sat an asthmatic old woman with white hair and thick hands clutching a rosary, Sara's mother. As we talked, Mrs. Egan breathed heavily and didn't say much, and I counted four different servants, one a man in a white coat, passing through the hall and the other rooms on mysterious errands. There was obviously more money around than Mrs. Egan had ever expected to see. From the conversation I gathered that she had four children, "all living at home," she said proudly. Bone and his three brothers, and Sara, her baby, but when Howard (Bone) was mentioned, her pride became timorous. I don't think she had the slightest notion of what Bone was up to, but she had divined that it was dangerous, perhaps illegal, and she probably never inquired too closely.

After a few minutes, she got up to go to the kitchen. Sara and Arno went into another room to talk privately (for all I knew, they were engaged), and I was left alone. I discovered a curious thing. Feeling something hard under the cushion behind my back, I lifted it up, and I found a bottle of beer. I lifted up the next cushion, and there was another. I picked another sofa at random, lifted up a cushion, still another. It was not conspicuous and it was not waste because there were no bottle-openers, and the beer was warm from being leaned against. I didn't know the protocol of the house. Were you supposed to knock the top off the bottle against the marble fireplace? Or was this a little joke the servants had cooked up? Now I am inclined to think it was somebody's sign that the Egans were now rich, but whose sign I never learned.

Mrs. Egan came back from the kitchen, and Arno and Sara from the other room. We were making that lame conversation people make when they don't know each other very well when Bone came in with one of his brothers. I saw him take off and hang on the hall-tree a snap-brim hat and a double-breasted blue overcoat, which I knew to be the proper uniform, but when he came into the parlor, "natty" was my first impression. There were sharp creases in his trousers and no bulges at his chest or hip. His hair was black and slicked down. He was about five-nine and he looked like a harassed young executive. I could see his nickname in his face at once. He was not a bad-looking guy but he had high, very prominent cheekbones, and a ridge that jutted sharply out over his eyes. He didn't look odd but he sure looked bony. Thin hands, too.

By this time, I was so confused that I didn't really expect him to snarl "Hahzit, Jack?" but I was still surprised when he shook hands exactly as we did at the fraternity and said, "Sara tells me you're swimming Chicago and Northwestern both this week end. How do you think you'll make out?"

For a man whose mind was stuffed with liquor, tommy guns, and gorillas, it seemed pretty tame for him to remember anything a sister told him, but a few minutes later, he turned his head and shouted "Emily!" One of the maids stuck her head in the door.

"I want a drink."

"Oh, now, Howard, the minute you come in the house . . ." his mother protested.

"I said I want a drink, Ma." At last I saw the expected power. It was the true, flat, ominous gangster tone I had constructed from the news stories, and I wouldn't have been too shocked if he had jumped up and clipped her one.

The brother had not joined us. He had that awful shell-shock from the War, his mother said. Arno told me he also had all the nickel slot-machines in Chicago. He spent his time going around with a truck, making collections. The collections came to eight thousand dollars a week in nickels. I never saw any of the other brothers but this one and, when

I did see him, he looked like a rummy to me. I think the shell-shock was something he told his mother.

When Bone finished his drink, he said to Arno, "I've got to go see a man. You fellows want to come along?"

Arno said, "Sure."

We stood up, if *morituri*, OK.

"I'll be home for dinner, Ma," he said as he went out.

We drove several blocks down Halsted, off on a side street and into another, a dirty little street full of warehouses and a few stores. When we stopped, Bone said, "You go on ahead. It's that Acme Floral Company there. I'm going to lock my car." He took out one of those steel rings with a heavy spike on it that you locked around a front wheel, and, if anyone drove the car, it rang on the pavement.

In the window of the Acme Floral Company stood a large bouquet of dusty red paper roses. We went in. There were no flowers inside. It was just a bar. Two nondescript men were sitting behind a baseburner stove at the back. As we came in, their right hands went up simultaneously and mechanically to their chests inside their lapels. I saw them. Arno and I turned to the bar that ran the long way of the store.

"A beer." Arno said.

The bartender shifted a toothpick, spat, and said "Yeah?" He looked me square in the eye and did not even unfold his arms. I have never been so scared in my life. I could hear the frightful squeak of a piece of paper blowing against the sidewalk outside. It seemed to go on forever.

At last Bone came in. I turned to look at the men behind the stove. The hands went down as automatically as they had gone up. The bartender was busy drawing our beer, which neither of us tasted. Bone was kidding with the gunmen. With an insane punctilio, he even introduced us. The dizzy slide from terror into palship convinced me. It was all true, not something I had read in the papers. One of the gunmen said, not without admiration, "So you're one of dese swimmin' guys, eh?" At least he talked like a gangster. On the way back to the Egans', I cased every car that drew near us just as Bone did. He talked only when it had a woman driving. The rest of the time he looked and so did I.

As we were swimming Northwestern that evening, Sara took us out for an early dinner at a place called the Menander Grill Room. It looked like a respectable Greek restaurant. There were white cloths on the tables. The waiters wore the uniform black, and there was an orchestra, not a band. We ignored all this and walked straight through into a little back room. About thirty people were sitting at small tables, eating and drinking. As Sara came in, everyone stood up. There were bows and murmurs of "Good evening, Miss Egan."

I was well into a big steak when a young woman at the next table tapped me on the arm and said, "How about a little congenial drink, dearie?" I was jumpy. If she had suggested that I eat the steak bone, I would have done it. My hand was closing around my glass when her approach turned out to be a *faux pas*. Her companion, another young woman, pulled her upright with a jerk, and said in a loud whisper, "Nix. Lay off him. That's Bone Egan's sister."

The young woman turned back to me and said, "Oh, excuse *me*," and then, louder, with a big wet smile, "Excuse me, Miss Egan." Sara didn't look at her.

As we ate, I asked Sara to tell me something about the ups and downs of the liquor business. She knew the Aiello girls whose menfolk were established further north in the city and were having a rough time. She told me about Dion O'Banion, who had often visited the Egan home, his flower store, and his murder, and how the box office at the Unione Siciliano hall was really a concrete pillbox. I asked her if anyone she knew was "hot" at the moment.

"Yes. Diamond Joe Esposito," she said.

Far away in Paris Gide was working on his *Journals*. In them, his remarks on his contemporaries are sometimes genial, oftener tinged with his peculiar spite, but when he went out of an evening to a soirée, say, at the Comtesse de Noailles', I am sure he displayed the same acid tolerance that Sara allowed Diamond Joe Esposito.

"What's he done?" I asked.

"Why, it's an intramural difficulty," she said. "He had a group called the Forty Thieves. They were quite successful. They made a considerable fortune, in fact, and it was enough for Joe. He bought a big farm up in Wisconsin and announced his retirement. The other members thought this grossly unfair. Joe was the brains. So they called on him and tried to persuade him to stay in business until they all were wealthy. Joe said no."

"So they're going to get him?"

"Yes, any day now. The interview was two or three days ago."

Sara was certainly an interesting girl to talk to, but Arno and I had to swim. She drove us as far as the Loop, where we caught a train for Evanston. Two hours later, mere college boys again, we had beaten Northwestern. When the coach asked us where we had been, we said "Visiting friends."

The next week we were in Philadelphia for the National Collegiates. At the hotel newsstand was a rack of out-of-town papers. I picked up a Chicago *Tribune*. A banner headline said DIAMOND JOE ESPOSITO SLAIN!

I never saw Sara again and I don't think Arno did, either. I don't know whether he had any real affection for her or not. Hers was the first social group Arno had moved in where his height and his two hundred and fifteen pounds of muscle did not count. They were impressive, but these people had their own ways of leveling men out, and maybe Arno didn't like to miss the slight deference usually given a big man. And, in the end, he may have been scared out as I was without hardly being in.

Three years later, I was in Paris, standing in a long line of people waiting for mail at the American Express. To pass the time, I was looking at some Paris editions of the home papers. Among these was the rotogravure section of the Paris *Chicago Daily News*. In it was a photograph of a room that had been bombed, centrifugal splinters and broken glass all over everything. The caption said "Room where body of Howard (Bone) Egan was found, victim of rival gangsters."

That was the last time I ever heard of the Egans. For Bone, the liquor business had been a calculated risk that he must have foreseen might be thwarted any time. To his mother, wandering perplexedly through her big house, it must have been the bitterest of mysteries, what had happened to the family she had tended so carefully, but the one I wonder about is Sara in the calm center of this vortex, reading Gide, conducting her Riemannian equations thoughtfully, knowing exactly where the money came from, yet, with an almost aristocratic confidence, never seeming to be afraid.

VI

Actress with Red Garters

One evening in the fall of my senior year in college, a group of us went to the play. It was a student production of *Hedda Gabler*, I think, although my memory is hazy. Two or three of us were taking a literature course with the play as part of the syllabus and we figured it would save reading.

The theater was built like a shallow barn. From the middle on back, any play was a pantomime because of the bum acoustics, so we all sat in the front row. The girl who played the lead (was it Hedda?) was tall and beautiful with black hair done into a chignon. None of us had ever seen her before and, the moment she appeared, all our heads went together, asking each other who she was. She was a challenge, almost an affront. My fraternity was full of a turbulent pride and, while its longing for beauty resembled less the connoisseur's than a beagle's after a rabbit, yet there she was, unknown.

We forgot our scholarly purposes and took to applauding every speech she made, and I think she responded, for once, to make some dramatic point (or maybe not), she crossed her legs and we all saw a garter, as red as a stoplight, gleaming above one knee.

The man next to me, Sherman McIntyre, said hoarsely, "Five bucks I get that before you do."

The wager astounded me. Sherm's father, his grandfather, all his ancestors back to the founding of the Miami Triad had been members of the fraternity. He was a legacy. You have to pledge legacies and, like most of them, Sherm was repellent: (A) He studied all the time. He was not very bright but he kept grinding away and later in the year, there was a rumor he had just missed Phi Bete. (B) He never drank anything but beer. (C) He was tighter than the bark on a tree.

I remember one evening we were sitting around a bridge table, grumping because we had nothing to do. Sherm came in. He lived in town and he could get his family's car. (Cars were banned to nonresident students.) We made Sherm a proposition. If he would drive us to Detroit, we would buy him all the beer he could drink.

He didn't jump at it. He took a bridge pad and a pencil and for ten minutes he puttered around with figures on mileage, the cost of gas, and how far his family's old Jordan would go on a gallon.

A guy in law school said, "I could draw you up a regular contract, Sherm."

Sherm didn't hear him. He looked up smiling, as if he were our friend. "If I have a flat, we pro-rate it, huh?"

"The hell with that, Shermy-wormy. All we buy is beer. You provide transportation. If you have a flat, you pay," we said.

He thought a minute, checked his figures, and said "Okay."

"You've got it straight, now? We buy all the beer you can drink. Any expenses connected with that big auto are yours."

"Okay."

We were going to a speakeasy at First and Fort streets in Detroit, about thirty-five miles away. The reason we patronized it was the free lunch. (I was too young to remember the noble free lunches of my father's youth like the hams at the Holland House, the cold barons of beef, and the oyster stew in the winter time.) This great and genial institution had dwindled to bologna sausage, rat cheese, crackers, and pickled Italian peppers, but it was still free and we liked the delusion that we were getting something for nothing.

You approached the building from the rear, passed a little tree, and went down four steps into the cellar. Archie, the bartender, had locomotor ataxia. He was all right behind the bar where he could step sideways, but on straightaways he sometimes went further than he was going before he could get himself stopped. I saw him coming to work one day, stepping off vigorously—too vigorously to take the steps down to the cellar. He grabbed the little tree, walked busily for twenty seconds in place, then slowed down and stopped. "They cut down that tree and I'm going to walk off the top step and break my goddamned neck," he said.

The beer was ordinary alley beer, moderately bad, but it didn't make your lips numb and every fourth round was on the house. Sherm was too green a drinker to pace himself. I had glanced at the bridge pad and I knew he had to do two dollars' worth before he was making any money on us. He larruped four beers into him in less than half an hour, then he slowed down. The next two took him another hour and his face changed. He didn't sing when we sang. He didn't talk. I could tell he was gunning his will to make the break-even point, and then he would have to drink one more to get ahead. The schooners must have looked as big as washtubs. It took him until one o'clock to make it. Then he began to smile a secret drunken smile and ate a few peppers.

On the way home we had hardly gone a block when his car began to clank. He stopped and lifted the hood. I don't know what he expected to find, rabbits with hammers or what. We crept around the dark city until we found an all-night garage. I forget what was wrong but it cost old Sherm

nineteen dollars and it took until dawn. We left one guy
with Sherm to keep him from running out on us and went
back to the speak. When he came to pick us up, he tried
his smile again and asked us if we didn't feel sort of honor-
bound to help him out with the bill. We told him we sort
of didn't. He didn't say another word. He drove home in a
sulk as thick and rigid as a little brick house.

This was the man who was wildly betting five dollars on
his ability to snake a garter off that girl's leg before I could.
I knew I could trust his avarice but I didn't know about his
looks.

All through Philosophy 69, Psych 31, and Anthropology
159 next day, I tried to gauge my chances. I still thought
you had to be handsome to get anywhere with a woman, and
realistically I couldn't conclude that I was handsomer than
Sherm. He had a heart-shaped face, I mean a real heart, a
beef-heart, say, and his cheekbones stuck out but he had a
swell complexion, red and white. He dressed all right, too. I
couldn't possibly imagine what he would say to a girl but,
with five dollars on it, I knew he would say something. I had
the uneasy feeling that he had known her all along and was
betting on a sure thing which is illegal.

Michigan had twelve thousand students even then. It
was useless to hunt around for her, and the only place I
knew she would be was the theater that night. By dinner-
time I was too nervous to eat. I went for a walk and about
seven, I went to the theater. It wasn't the five dollars that
bothered me. It was the girl. I believed with a bone-shaking
solemnity that if a man could take a garter off a girl's leg,
she had to be his. All the way.

I knocked at the stage door. A courteous old man opened
it and pointed out her dressing room. She had just come
in, he said. I walked slowly toward it, composing myself,
for meeting a new girl was always exciting. I rapped on her
door. She opened it. She was in a black satin peignoir, her

long hair over her shoulders, her face shining, ready for the make-up.

"Good evening," she said. Meeting a new man obviously did not excite her.

"Miss van der Puyl?" I said. I had gotten her name from the playbill.

"Yes."

I didn't want it to come out in a blurt but I'm afraid it did. "I've got a bet with a guy that I can get one of those red garters before he can," I said, honest as the day is long. She didn't for one second pretend that she didn't know what I was talking about. She lifted one knee. The peignoir fell away. "One of these?" she said. She still hadn't smiled.

I nodded. "You haven't seen this guy today, have you? Tall, long face, sort of blond hair, name of McIntyre?"

"No."

"Well, can I have the garter? I'll take you to dinner on the money I win."

"All right."

Naturally I had run this scene over in my mind a dozen times that day, but my somewhat steamy hopes and my sober expectations were so confused that I almost expected that she would acrobatically thrust out her leg with a provocative rakehell air and say "Take it." She didn't. She took it off herself, standing on one foot, and dropped it into my hand. Her stocking fell down over her knee at once.

"Now how am I going to keep my stocking up?" she said.

"Can't you—I don't know—kind of pull it up and tie a knot in it?"

"Maybe." She pulled up her stocking, put her foot on a chair, and went to work on the knot.

Since I was fourteen, I had assumed that some day I would hang around green rooms with actresses lightly clad. I justified this by calling it part of my education, but these scenes, these lovely actresses had always kept a safe couple of years ahead. Now one of them had snapped back on me in a spasm of truth. I was breathing pretty hard but I felt I ought to look good, that is, sophisticated, now that the moment had surprised me. I said, "That's some leg."

She looked up at me coolly. "The other one's just like it."

"I didn't mean they weren't mates. I mean they look good."

The knot was finished. She put her foot down. "I know it," she said.

My confidence was butting itself to pieces against this marmoreal poise.

I said. "Thanks for the garter. I'll call for you tomorrow evening?"

"All right."

"Where?"

"Martha Cook."

As soon as I was no longer looking at her, I felt apprehension as a chill. Martha Cook was the dormitory for female honor students.

Dinner was just over when I got back to the fraternity. Sherm had settled into a red leather chair in the smoking room with the evening paper as I'm sure he does yet. I went up behind him and tossed the garter over his shoulder so it struck the paper and dropped in his lap. He picked it up and looked around.

"You bastard," he said.

"Pay me," I said.

Again he tried smiling, saying, "How do I know it's the same one?" but too many people had gathered around to bullyrag him if he didn't, so he paid.

At Martha Cook the next evening, I was let into a long sun-room with paneled walls and a floor set with black and white tiles. It surprised me somewhat, for while I didn't really believe intellectuals preferred attics, I didn't expect luxury. I could hear the receptionist sound the buzzer and a few minutes later she entered at the other end of the sunroom. She was wearing a wide-brimmed floppy felt hat, not a cloche like everyone else, and what looked like a man's double-breasted blue overcoat. Her hands were in her coat pockets and she stared at the floor as she approached. She looked somber.

I suppose the chief reason a very young man likes a woman is that she is willing to let him do the talking. Talk, then, is plumage. He can tell her all about himself and hardly anything is more fun than that. This evening, however, I was leery. I wanted her to do the talking.

I took her to the best steak place in town. (PORTERHOUSE STEAKS, $1.00) I ordered setups and gave her a drink out of a hip flask I had borrowed from my roommate. Then I went to work. Her name was Marta van der Puyl. She was from Grand Rapids. Her family were of Dutch descent. She was twenty years old and a senior. She had no brothers or sisters. She answered all my questions as briefly and soberly as if I had been a police examiner. She would speak but she wasn't talking. I wanted to give a fillip to the monotony of the questions, so, in the same tone as "How old are you?" I said, "Do you like me?"

She ran her tongue over her lower lip and looked at me as if I had been a dress on a rack and said at last "Yes."

I wanted to say, "Well, act like it, then," but instead I asked, "What does your father do?"

With her answer she threw me the key to her character, maybe her whole life, but she didn't know it and I didn't pick it up. She did not tell me how her father made his living. She said he was head of some big national organization, something like the National Association of Manufacturers or the Mystic Shrine. She drawled out his title slowly, with the fiercest contempt, watching me as if she expected me to burst out laughing.

I didn't care what her father did. I wasn't going to marry her. (I wasn't going to marry anybody for a long, long time. I had to get to Paris first.) There were certain technical moves I had to make and I began them with "You know you are very beautiful, don't you?" One move followed another with almost syllogistic perfection, and, if I had been dealing with logical matters, I would have had more women than I could count. I always thought I could talk my way in. I must have been thick in the head.

Tediously brilliant, I carried on through the steak and two more drinks. She could stay out Sunday nights until eleven-thirty but at nine she said she had to go home and study. She said it calmly as if someone were paying her.

"Study?" I jeered. "What're you trying to do—make Phi Bete?"

If I had not responded to her contempt, neither did she to mine. "No. I made it last year," she said.

A *junior* Phi Bete. I was stunned. I don't know what I expected in the way of intellectual fireworks, something like naming the kings of England all in one breath probably, yet she was so laconic her intelligence had no play. I paid the bill and found a taxi.

Possibly convinced that this would be the last time I would see her because she wouldn't want to waste time with a dummy like me, and, since there was nothing to lose, willing to chuck my sly technique and act boldly, I reached for her the minute the taximan shut the door. She put her arms around my neck and kissed me warmly but somewhat absent-mindedly all the way back to Martha Cook. My clichés were taking a beating. Intellectuals, I knew, had nothing but scorn for the pleasures of the flesh. I wonder where I got that idea.

"May I call you again?" I asked.

She smiled for the first time. "Will you?" she said. "Ihada-verynicetime," she said as if it were something her mother had taught her. She walked slowly away down the sun-room with her hands in her pockets and her head down as she had come, and I didn't know what to think.

That was the fall I was making blowtorch with my swimming buddy Arno Bevins, and, since I had a lot of liquor, I thought I would have a lot of dates, but none of my lady friends would touch the stuff. They said it tore the throat out and why couldn't I supply Old Crow as decent people did? Except Marta. She drank it like water.

I used to call her on weeknights, stick a flask of blowtorch in my coat, pick her up at Martha Cook and walk her to the center of the campus. It was dark there and we sat under a big elm tree on a stone bench given by the Class of '92, alternately drinking and clutching at each other. If anyone passing on the sidewalk forty feet away saw us, he probably didn't believe it. Why should two people sit on a cold stone bench in the chill of late October? That was not the way it was done.

We didn't talk much. About ten-thirty she would disengage, stand up, put her hand in her pockets, and we would walk slowly back to the dormitory. Nothing diluted the alcohol in blowtorch except orange juice. She drank with me drink for drink yet, walking home, she never staggered. When she spoke, she spoke clearly, and I surmised that she was a girl of vast experience with the bottle.

After a few of these dates I was just getting so her intellect didn't bother me when we had a young philosophy instructor at the house for dinner one night. We had such guests frequently. It was a way of ingratiating ourselves with the faculty, and we needed all the ingratiation we could get. I have seen brothers yawning through nine-o'clock classes in dinner jackets. The impression we were trying to convey was that, even if we didn't study, we were personally faithful. We had to drink, of course; social pressure saw to that. And whenever anyone could get a car (hidden in a garage at

the edge of town away from the university police), we who
had to walk everywhere couldn't resist taking off in it. Often
we would wind up in Cleveland or Chicago or deep in In-
diana at some little pineboard dance pavilion listening to
Bix Beiderbecke. (Oh, we all knew who he was and groaned
when he went with Whiteman.) And there were these girls
all around us. It must be clear that study had to be carefully fitted in. Sometimes it didn't make it, hence our lavish
hospitality to the faculty.

After dinner a few of us took the philosophy instructor
up to my room where I was able to offer him the choice of
a fine, cut Golden Wedding or my humble blowtorch. He
took the blowtorch and ginger ale. Within a quarter of an
hour and his second drink, little beads of sweat lay above his
eyebrows and he was talking about ideas. He prophesied
what an impact Freud would have in the next few years. He
was clear, voluble, and he knew his stuff. And we were interested. (It occurred to none of us that this might be an
intellectual discussion. We were just getting the faculty
stewed.)

Someone said, "Why can't we get courses in Freud?"

"Too new," he said. "Too hard to understand now, too
many iron preconceptions. I doubt if there's a single student
who really understands him. Yes, there's one, a girl. She has
the best student mind I ever met. Understands Marx, too."

This was 1929. How many people understood Freud and
Marx then? I said, "What's her name?" with a suspicion
stirring in my head.

"Marta van der Puyl."

One of us said, "Some babe, I'll bet. Glasses, hump in her
back, creeping around."

The instructor was answering another question and I made
no denial but I couldn't see her again for two weeks.

The library of the fraternity was an oak-paneled room
with two blue leather sofas and a Jacobean worktable and

chairs, installed at great expense through the generosity of some alumnus. Except for the freshmen who had to study there, we used it only as a place where we could sleep off hangovers unmolested. However, I sneaked in and looked up Marx in the *Encyclopaedia Britannica*. There was no article on Freud. It seemed incredible that a girl with a shape like hers could be interested in such stuff.

Paul Whiteman's band came to play on the stage of a local theater. He had the tuba all shined up but we thought his arrangements were solemn, pompous—in a word, *wet*— but we all knew that Beiderbecke was playing second trumpet and that Harry Barris, Al Rinker, and Bing Crosby would take a chorus or two. We went in a body. Then, during the performance, the word circulated that one of the fraternities had hired the whole band to play for a dance afterward.

It looked like a riot around that fraternity. Everybody in town was trying to get in and they had a cop at the front door. My roommate, a shrewd fellow, took me around to the back. He had found the opening to the coal chute and down it we went. It took us a few minutes to clean up so we wouldn't rub off on any girls we danced with, but it was a wonderful party. As I stood against a wall, watching, I wanted a girl too, but I didn't dare call a girl at ten-thirty for a date that same evening. It would insult her. Then I thought of Marta. I didn't think she had any dates but mine. She had been willing to sit on a stone bench and drink blowtorch in the cold. She might be willing to come to the dance.

I called her from a phone booth on the second floor and asked her if she could be ready in ten minutes. She said she could. I met her and walked her to the party. I gallantly slid down the coal chute again and opened one of the back doors for her. We stepped into the privacy of a pantry for a drink of blowtorch and joined the dancing The floor was so crowded that all you could do was tap your foot. My room-mate saw her, recognized her from the play, and cut in on me, eyeing her with little blue lickerous eyes.

The big Whiteman band was playing "Song of India." There was nothing in that for the Rhythm Boys, and I asked Bing Crosby, then a slender young man with a wilted bow tie, if he wanted a drink. He leaped up and we went out behind the fraternity and sat on the coal pile. He drank and said huskily, "My God, man, you drink that stuff all the time? Liked to turned my voice bass."

When we went in, I cut in on Marta. She stood in my embrace and occasionally we inched a little forward or a little back. At last, near one of the corners, I saw an opening and went to swing her in a fancy turn. She nearly fell down. She wasn't drunk. I had an illumination. "You can't dance, can you?"

"I never did before," she said. She was not perturbed.

"And you never had a drink before this fall, did you?"

"No. I like it, though."

I felt I had the edge on her for the first time. The moment had come to put the capstone on the intricate logical structure I had been working on. I took her out to the coal pile. We had another drink. I kissed her. Then I said, "Marta, I want you to become my mistress." (Think of saying a thing like that out loud! Who was I imitating, Edgar Allan Poe? As if she had no other way of telling, I wanted the girl to know what she was signing on for.)

"I wouldn't mind," she said, "only I'm engaged to be married."

"Married? Who to?"

"A man named Raynor Wilkie."

I was astonished again. I knew Raynor Wilkie. He was a friend of mine, a tall, shambling, tweedy fellow who, somewhat unusually, wore a mustache and looked, I believed then, like a British lieutenant cashiered for cooking the mess accounts. He drank like a fish; he had spent a couple of years at the University of Virginia, where they were methodical people. They trained their freshmen on Mason jars full of water until they could hold the muscles of their throats rigid and pour a pint straight down without swallowing. When they could do this, they were ready for the Mason jars full of applejack that came out of the templed hills around Charlottesville. Raynor had been a Beta at Virginia but he was an Alpha Delt at Michigan, the only man I knew who was a member of two brotherhoods, and he used to compare their rituals sardonically. Late in any evening, he could not be prevented from reciting, in a sepulchral voice, "The great gray-green, greasy, Limpopo River, all ringed round with fever trees."

While I could applaud his choice, I didn't think his looks, his drinking, or his taste in verse were capable of arousing her love. It must have been his money, I thought. He didn't fling it around or keep a secret Stutz like some, but he did live in an apartment. This was expensive and it was obviously the way he had gotten to her. It was hard for students in love to find shelter, and Raynor most have used his advantage for many a long mumbling hour of his mating song.

"May I give you my felicitations?" I said with gloomy propriety.

"No. Not really. I don't like him very well."

"Then why in hell are you marrying him?"

"Three things. One, it will get me away from my family. Two, I can lose my virginity in all honor. Three, it will get me to New York."

I muttered that I didn't see where the honor lay in as devious a scheme as this. The truth was, I didn't believe a word of it. People our ages did not dispose of their lives as coolly as this. I should have realized that her pat little list of reasons could have come only after long consideration.

"You're going to live in New York?" I asked.

"With *his* parents," she said disdainfully. "Do you ever get to New York?"

"Not since I was a kid. With my aunt," I said. An aunt of mine had married late in life a widower of fifty. For some obscure reason I was taken on the honeymoon. This included a few days in Manhattan. All I really remembered was a deep-dish apple pie à la mode.

"If you come to New York any time after the first of February, look me up."

"For a homey evening with you and Raynor? No, thanks."

"Oh, I'm only going to stay with him a month. We're being married at Christmastime."

I have never thought I had a limber face. Joy or sadness do not ripple its muscles very deeply but I was glad it was dark then for I felt that my face was wrenched into a cramp of disbelief.

"Naturally, Raynor doesn't suspect any of this."

"Naturally."

"You're not afraid of ..." I hesitated a little here "... breaking his heart?"

"Oh, now, really. All I'm asking is a month of his time and a one-way ticket to New York."

I didn't believe it would break Raynor's heart either. I thought he was befooled by lust as I was. If it were true, it seemed a fair enough exchange.

"You're really going through with this?"

I could feel her looking at me in the dark. "Yes. I've wasted enough time around here."

"All seniors get that way," I said. A faculty man had told me. I felt that way myself but I had no projects that had crystallized until they clinked.

"That hasn't anything to do with it. Give me another drink." She drank glug, glug, glug, better than Crosby. "I'd have gone last year if I'd had the chance."

I could see she had already broken through or perhaps

she had never acknowledged the boundaries that enclosed the campus. What impressed me was that she was the first contemporary I had met who knew exactly what she wanted to do. Oh, we all talked about getting rich, certainly. There was a guy in the fraternity who had run up a month's allowance to ten thousand dollars in the stock market. People said quite casually, "As soon as I make my first million . . ." but what followed was vague, a haze of women, yachts, liquor, and big new cars. Nobody had any real plans.

"What are you going to do after you leave him?"

"Read. Write."

"You can do that here."

"At my family's expense? No. From now on almost anyone else can keep me but not they."

"I wish I had enough money."

"It would have to be New York."

"It would be New York if I had the money. Or Paris."

"I told you. If you come, look me up."

"Fat chance. I haven't even got train fare, but send me an address anyway, will you?"

After this there seemed to be no point in going back to the dance. We climbed down off the coal pile and I walked her back home. I think what I was feeling was awe.

When I returned to college after Christmas vacation, I found a note from Marta. It was postmarked December 21, New York. All it said was, "Today I become Mrs. Raynor Wilkie. Wish me luck." I wished her luck, all right, but I was sure I had seen the last of her. New York was a long way away.

During the first week in February, I got another note, "I am living at 13 Cornelia Street, Greenwich Village. Let me know if you come." There was no one to laugh hollowly for but I did tear up the note as useless information. (Naturally, the address became part of the mental lumber I carry around in my attic. I forget my own addresses but not this one.) She seemed to have exploded her marriage but it was an explosion in another country, a catastrophe like the floods in China that did not concern me.

Suddenly in March a rumor began to circulate that Michigan was going to swim Yale after the Nationals in Philadelphia. I asked the coach, Matt Mann, point-blank. He said it was true and I began saving my money.

I came down to New York from New Haven with my hand in a paper bag. After the meet the night before, we had been celebrating in somebody's rooms in Harkness. Later we had gone out to get something to eat. I went downstairs in the restaurant to wash my hands and I saw approaching me a big ugly guy, lurching menacingly, who was obviously going to slug me. I cagily struck first and broke a full-length mirror. I was aware of what I had done, enough so that I got out of there at once, but I felt no pain, and, after the first pick-me-ups the next morning, it hardly seemed worth the trouble to clean up my cuts so I put the bag over my hand. It was a bag some gin had come in.

I had assured a place to stay by writing a friend of mine from Memphis, Frank Adams, who had a job in the advertising department of *The New York Times*. He was living with three other men at 56th and Broadway in what was then, the upper stories at least, a theatrical rooming house. There were two beds. They slept two in a bed, and I made a third in one of them. There was a kitchen but nobody cooked. The only other room beside the bath contained a long sagging sofa. To sit down on it or in it was like diving into water whose depth was unknown—your knees just about hit your chin before you touched bottom. Against one wall stood one of those semicylindrical china cabinets with a curved glass door. In it were six Havilland teacups, no saucers, and a good deal of dust. There was a circular table, bare, two old rocking chairs, and that was all. No curtains

at the windows, no rugs on the floor. It had the look of
having been stripped for action.

It was hardly nightfall before the action began. Frank had
taken the afternoon off to welcome me. We had spent it in
a speakeasy near Broadway and he had come home with his
arms full of bottles. He set the bottles on the table, and, as
if summoned by the clink, two sweet little old ladies in bath-
robes and those lace caps women used to wear, breakfast
caps, they called them, came marching in the door. Frank
gave them each a teacupful of gin and they sank nearly out
of sight on the sofa. I don't suppose they were much older
than fifty, actually. They had sung with the D'Oyly Carte
Company in London and the provinces, and now they had
a sister act singing patter songs. They were followed almost
at once by a family of delicate Japanese, all clad in pajamas,
hissing and smiling and bowing. They had had the foresight
to bring their own glasses. "Jugglers," Frank said, hissing
and smiling and bowing as he poured. Frank's roommates
came in with three girls who lived somewhere upstairs. They
were pretty good-looking but I saw little of them because
the roommates took them into the bedroom and shut the
door. "Showgirls," Frank said. "Their show just went into
the tank."

The word spread through the building like a fire alarm.
The apartment filled up with everything but a dog act, and
it acquired a low roar so steady and seemingly so solid you
could almost touch it. I remember submitting to the gaze of
a hypnotist who looked as if he had two glass eyes, an impression that probably kept me from going under. I had a
short chat, conducted in shouts in a corner, with a robust
fellow who had an enormous chest. He had just finished
thirty weeks on the Pan time, playing Jack London's *The
Sea Wolf*. I asked him if he could crush a raw potato in his
hand. "Get me a potato!" he bellowed. I looked in the re-

frigerator but there was nothing in it but a half-empty bottle of something and a moldy lemon.

At the height of the evening, a heavy-set brunette was rendering "O Sole Mio." On the other side of the room, the Savoyards rattled off "the very model of a modern major-general," and in a corner almost unwatched the papa Japanese lay on his back spinning his youngest child with his bare feet. This bedlam did not surprise me in any way. I merely thought it was life in New York.

Next morning after my hosts had gone to work, I was waked gently by a gaunt blond young man in a pea-jacket. This was Cheney and I had been warned about him the night before. He was a merchant sailor looking for a ship and he was wanted by the authorities of the State of Maine for shooting deer with a tommy gun. Apparently he looked for the ship only at night for he came every morning to sleep in one of the beds as soon as it was vacated.

I took a subway down to 14th Street and started looking for Marta. After four inquiries and an hour's walk, I found 13 Cornelia Street. It was a small apartment house; on the cards in the lobby, I found the name *Marta van der Puyl* coupled with the name of some other girl. I pushed their button. There was no answer. I pushed it vainly several times more and went out and walked up and down Cornelia Street for half an hour, followed by a group of Italian children singing. I tried the button once more. No one was answering. In desperation I sent her a telegram, giving my 56th Street address, and asked her to get in touch with me.

I waited in the apartment all the next day, talking to Cheney as soon as he waked up. He had hired a rowboat on some lake in Maine and fixed a gigantic gasoline flare to the bow. In the dead of night, he laid his tommy gun beside him and rowed silently to a cove where he had been told the deer came down to water. A few yards offshore, he lit his flare, dazzled a buck and two does, and mowed them down. I mumbled something about "unsportsmanlike" but Cheney seemed affronted. "I was hungry," he said. "I was shooting for the pot." The racket had raised every game warden for miles and Cheney had scampered, leaving the gun.

It was five o'clock before I got an answer to my telegram. Marta gave me an address on East 4th Street, and said she would be glad to see me.

East 4th Street looked like pictures of slums in my high-school civics book. Marta lived over a dry-cleaning shop. The stairs were dark and smelled bad. I thought, however, that she knew what she was doing. She must have had a reason for picking the place. I knocked at a door. I heard her say "Come in."

A lighted candle stood in the top of a tin can on a wooden packing case. Three army blankets lay spread out on the floor and on them Marta had been reading with her overcoat thrown over her. That was all there was in the room. I assumed that she was living like this to enjoy the monastic asceticism of the intellectual. I said, "Nice layout you've got here."

"Yes. I'm terribly grateful to these people for taking me in."

"What people?"

"Oh, there's a man and his wife live here, too."

"And you all roll up together in these blankets?"

"Yes. He's an architect but he lost his job after the Crash."

"What happened with that girl on Cornelia Street?"

"She wanted a little more intimacy than I was willing to provide." I had kissed her when I came in, but now, looking at her in the candlelight, I saw that she was dirty, not a smudge here and there but the sheen of the unbathed. Suddenly I knew she was scared, for all her talk, and I no longer felt any awe of her.

"How long has it been since you had a hot meal?"

"Well, I haven't had anything today . . ."

"Haven't you any money at all?"

"A nickel. I was going out later and get some day-old bread."

"You haven't got a job?"

"No. Jobs aren't easy now." She was working on a play, she said.

"But how do you eat?"

"I have made as much as fifty cents a day in subway stations. I try to find prosperous-looking old gents and I say, 'I'm terribly sorry. I seem to have left my purse at home. Would you . . . ?' One of them gave me a dollar and tried to date me up."

"Come on. We'll eat," I said. The room was not ascetic now; it was only poverty-stricken and I wanted to get out of there. As she was getting her hat off a hook in an alcove, I noticed the title of the book she had been reading. It was *The Decline of the West.*

In those days in that part of town, you could get nearly all the Italian food you could eat for thirty-five cents but I splurged. I bought the sixty-five-cent dinner. She put away the antipasto, the minestrone, the spaghetti, the chicken cacciatore, and the spumoni almost without speech. When we had finished, I was ready to sit and talk but she said, "Would you mind if I did it again?"

"Did what again?"

"The dinner."

This delighted me and I ordered her another dinner. Her aplomb made it seem funny and I didn't once think how hungry she must have been. She was performing a trick, that was all.

The second time around she ate more slowly and we talked. Even with her hair dull and her face shiny, she was a beautiful girl and I believed that such a girl had only to wait, and some man would come along and make her

happy—or if not he, the next one. At my time of life, girls
were hardly human. They were lovely trophies to be acquired and whether they were happy except with me was
not a matter I was curious about, but Marta's long, grimy,
exquisite fingers, so busy with the spaghetti, were helping
me to cast that old skin, and again I asked her question after
question.

No, she did not really want a job. A job was like marriage.
It took too much time. She wanted to work on her play.
She had talked to Philip Moeller at the Theater Guild and
he had told her to send it to him when she finished it. ("I
primped in the Ladies Room in the 14th Street subway station before I went to see him.") She would not mind living
with someone who would keep her, provided she could
go on writing.

"In return for the pleasures of your fair white body?"
I said. My Sunday School teachers would have been proud
of me.

She had a big mouthful of chicken. She merely nodded.

I didn't ask her what her play was about. I said, "Come
up and see me tomorrow and I'll give you a bath."

"All right. I'd like a bath."

I walked her back to 4th Street, a little irked that her
attitude toward sex was as casual as I thought my own was.
How did she get that way? Damn it, I knew what kind of
people she came from. I could guess exactly how her father
and mother looked, how they talked, what they wore. I
asked her, "Did you live in a big white house with a screened
porch halfway around it and maple trees in the front yard?"

"No. Stucco. The porch was there all right. It was their
summer arena."

"Their?"

She looked sideways at me. "My parents'," she said with
the old contempt.

"There was a winter arena?"

"The living room where they made me entertain the Campfire Girls. My name was Wa-wau-tosa."

I didn't smile. It wasn't funny to her.

At the foot of the stairs, she said, "I can't ask you up. They'll be home now. It's gotten so it makes Charles nervous to see anyone with money."

"I haven't got *money*."

"Any money. A dollar bill. I'll see you tomorrow."

The next afternoon I had tossed Cheney, yawning and bellyaching, out of the apartment by two o'clock. I had bought a bottle of gin, an expensive oval cake of bath soap, and a new towel. I was ready.

She came in about three. I drew her the bath and scrubbed her back for her. Afterward we enjoyed ourselves very much. She was cheerful, warm-hearted but, as she went to go, abstracted again as if she were already thinking of something else. I had twelve dollars and my ticket back to Michigan. I offered the money to her. I was intending, quite unconsciously, to imitate her without any of her reasons for doing so by starving a little. She took the money and thanked me. I kissed her and she walked away toward the head of the stairs, her hands in the pockets of that big coat. It was the last time I saw her.

Toward the end of the following summer I went fishing in northern Michigan with Raynor Wilkie. I had known him long enough before he met Marta so that we didn't have to talk about her and I didn't bring up her name. We had one of those no-fish-no-pay guides, and, after trolling for an hour, we had our limit for the day. We went back to his cottage, cleaned our pike and perch, laid them on ice, and went out on the porch with drinks in our hands.

We had hardly sat down when he took out his wallet, drew from it a folded newspaper clipping, and handed it to me. It was a photograph from the Chicago Tribune. It showed a picket line in front of a strikebound factory. In the foreground was Marta with an *Unfair* sign around her neck. Beside her was a big colored man. The caption read, "Mr. and Mrs. Robert Blake on a picket line. Mrs. Blake is the daughter of Samson van der Puyl, national head of" whatever it was he was head of. The date was less than a week before.

Raynor had a smirk on his face. "What do you think of that?" he asked. It was plain that he thought it was a fate worse than death for Marta and serve her damned well right.

"If that's what she wants to do . . ." I said.

He was eager to talk. He told me all about his marriage, every detail. I couldn't stop him. He had to justify himself, of course; there are too many reverberations when your wife walks out on you, so she had to be a devil. She had insulted him. She had insulted his father and mother, deliberate, shrewdly given insults, unforgivable. I couldn't tell him he had been only a temporary convenience to Marta. You can't tell people things like that.

I said, "Still, she was beautiful." I noticed that we talked about her as if she were dead.

"She was that," Raynor said. "Man, you don't know. But she was a devil all the same."

A year or two later, I ran into Raynor in New York. He hustled me off to the edge of the sidewalk, holding onto my arm. "You know what Marta's done now?"

"No. What?"

"She's gone to Russia with that nigger. She's had a kid by him. Communists, see?"

There was nothing much I could say.

"Remember that picture I showed you?" he asked.

"The one in the *Tribune?* Yes."

"It killed her parents," he said almost gleefully. "It wasn't a week after it appeared, her old man had a heart attack and her mother died a month later."

I never heard of her again.

The instincts that drew her toward the stage were her deepest ones, I think. She was an actress with a good deal more sincerity than she could command. She told me once that she was sick of hypocrisy. She wanted some honesty in her life and she didn't care how many rocks lay in the path toward it. But they were prop rocks, really, hard but papier-mâché, and the truth was already behind her as she spoke. If she is still alive, she is living and working in Moscow, Kharkhov, some such place, compulsively performing a role that so shocked its only possible audience that they would not stay on the front porch to watch it.

*VII *

Miss Anglin's Bad Martini

*I*t sounds like a riddle, but does anyone recall both Margaret Anglin and Pastor Russell? Those who remember the one are not likely to remember the other. Yoked or tandem they spring, I daresay, to no one's mind but my own. Hardly any connection exists between them except that you sat in seats to watch them. When I was at the age to regret I was too young to lead a pair of the enormous Great Danes who played the bloodhounds for Eliza in the parade before the annual Tom show, Margaret Anglin brought a road company of *The Iron Woman* to our opera house and played the leading role. It was the first time I had watched a dramatic performance from the dark side of the footlights, although earlier I had created the leading role in a fifth-grade operetta, *The Smuggleman*, cheeping away in little brown jacket and little green pants of shiny paper cambric. The only sediment I retain from this appalling cruelty is the brooding fear that my pants would split in front of all those people.

A few years later I led the Great Danes and I "carried" the *Saturday Evening Post* and after I had made my collections on Thursday afternoons, I usually took the sixty cents and went to the Garden Motion Picture Theater to watch a serial which seemed to run through my entire grade-school days. In it a man named Ravengar was constantly in trouble but he had three pills that would make him invisible. Query: would he use one this Thursday? I sat in the darkness wolfing down two packages of raw Jello—I liked the sweet piercing flavor—watching Ravengar hang from cliffs by his fingers; Ravengar, tied to a log, approach a buzz-saw, fling himself about in the coils of a loathsome python, or skedaddle as the target of a dozen guns, aghast in the boundless credulity of childhood and my tongue puckered like a rosebud. But the Garden cost fifteen cents. When I saw that Pastor Russell had an earth-shaking message to deliver at the opera house, and, moreover, that the message was free, I went one Thursday afternoon.

I had my Jello in my pockets, chocolate and strawberry, and I saw the first talking picture. What you read in these twelve-pound histories of the movies is all poppycock. *The Jazz Singer* is surely a late and somewhat better synchronized theft from the Pastor's grand design. Pastor Russell was founding the Jehovah's Witnesses. He could not be in ten places at once, not in the flesh. He used the movies.

There was a good turn-out to receive his message and, since the contraption was still new enough to inspire awe, we all sat silently in the dark for quite a while, listening to the operator and his assistant knocking and banging around in the gallery, making ready. The film started abruptly with a ratchety noise we soon ignored. It showed a speaker's platform. On it stood a plain wooden table. On that was a glass jug of water and a tumbler. The scene continued for about thirty seconds until it was well impressed on our minds.

Pastor Russell strode onto the platform in a driving rain. (Ravengar also struggled in this rain, as did John Bunny, Bronco Billy, and Flora Finch, and I remember beautiful Kathlyn Williams fleeing from an African grass hut. The

rain poured down as usual but the hut was afire, burning
briskly, and I wondered why the rain seemed to have no
effect.) The Pastor was a tall gaunt man with a full beard
and a Prince Albert coat. Immediately he began an im-
passioned harangue with wide, full pulpit gestures. Ten seconds later the sound came on. (It was a guy with a big-
horned phonograph in a front box. We could see him
dimly.) The Pastor had enough of a start so that the rest
of the film was like the capering of dream. Where Russell
(heard) would be softly pleading for us to give up tobacco,
Russell (seen) had his fists raised to high heaven, his beard
tilted, the cords standing out in his neck, and his mouth
wide open. Where Russell (seen) would be drinking from
a glass of water, Russell (heard) bellowed of the wrath
to come. Since I innocently thought they were playing
it for laughs, I enjoyed myself. Now, when one of the
patient Witnesses comes to my door carrying a record-
player and tries to play a sermon for me, I tell him I have
seen and heard Pastor Russell. This baffles him and he sometimes goes away.

I did better with Miss Anglin. I entertained her in the
flesh; in fact, I had her over for cocktails my senior year
in college but, I am sorry to say, she was rather like the
eggs, a mere panache.

In Ma Brown's rooming-house my freshman year, three
guys from Fort Wayne lived across the hall from me. Since
then I have considered the Fort Wayniots to be the most
contentious wrangling lot since the Athenians. They were
always arguing and putting feisty little bets on things, a
dime here, two bits there. To shut them up one night, I
went in and said, "I'll bet you each five dollars I can eat
a dozen and a half eggs in thirty minutes." They did not
believe I could but there was a twenty-minute set-to to get
the bet straight. Finally I wrote it down—I stood to win
fifteen dollars if I ate the eggs in half an hour, the loser

to pay for the eggs. We went down State Street to an all-night restaurant with an original name, The College Inn. We sat down in a row on stools and I said to the waiter, "A dozen and a half soft-boiled eggs." With commendable *sang-froid*, he turned and called, "Eighteen soft-boiled." The cook jerked his head out of his cubby like Punch and howled, "What did you say?" It is hard to surprise anybody in a college town.

They brought them in cereal bowls and I ate them in a little over twelve minutes with an order of toast and two cups of coffee. It wasn't hard. I still like a soft-boiled egg, but it was not that I had a passion for eggs or a passion for money, although the fifteen dollars came in very handy; I was only showing off, tinkering away at the persona I wished to display. A psychiatrist would argue that these are the rickety poses of the insecure and I would not argue back for anything in the world. Pychiatrists are like priests. They both present impenetrable surfaces, the one opaque, the other clear.

So Miss Anglin was rather like the eggs but the mask I was working on was not the Gargantuan nor was it, in the old phrase, the stage-door Johnny's, for while Miss Anglin was not then so far advanced in years as to be called an old lady, she was a good deal older than my father and not, although green she might have been, a dish. She was in town for a drama festival. I forget the name of her play but I wanted to entertain her as the only celebrity in view. A cosmopolitan suavity was, I think, my aim.

The problem of serving a woman a cocktail openly in a fraternity house was not insurmountable but it was steep. I could hardly bundle a famous actress upstairs to my room, still less could I plunge her into the cellar. We had a faithful Danish porter named Chris who sold a little whisky to a rigidly selected clientele in the house. He lived in a cellar room and next to his was another just like it, furnished

with bed, bureau, a rocking chair and a washbowl. For a
dollar he would give you the key and put clean sheets on
the bed. I have had many's the drink in that room with a
girl who thought it funny to sneak in when it got dark.
I didn't believe Miss Anglin would think it funny to sneak
into a room which looked like a cell in a high-class jail just
to get a cocktail for I knew that her career parallelled, give
or take a few years, Ethel Barrymore's. She would have
drunk champagne at Delmonico's before the war.

How not to sneak, then? How to give her a drink as
if casually, a quick turn through the ground floor to allow
her to admire the oaken paneling, then an offhand retirement to chambers sufficiently private so we could break
out the liquor. But whose chambers? There was only one
possible answer—Cara Lemay's. She was a maiden lady in
middle life who consoled herself with eating. Famished, I
doubt if I could have eaten head-to-head with Cara. Her
pace was slow, ruminative but devastating. She must have
gone three hundred pounds at five feet five. She had delicate little ankles like Babe Ruth's but her feet were breaking down, forcing her to wear ponderous health shoes except at parties, when she would put on Cuban heels. Crossing a simple floor was like walking a tightrope then. One
slight uncorrected list and she was done for. (Once I tipped
over on a load of hay. Watching Cara fall was like that:
soft, slow, grand.) She was the house manager, although
for obvious reasons she liked to be called the housemother.
We supplied her with a small apartment, two rooms and
a bath at one end of the second floor.

Luck rarely assists arrangements of this kind but on the
day of Miss Anglin's projected visit, it was reported that
Cara was going to tea at a real housemother's up the street.
(Sororities had real housemothers.) To juice up the luck,
I bribed a freshman to lurk at a window and when he saw
Cara trundling back down the street from the tea, he was

to run out and ask her to dinner downtown. He was to
have a taxi waiting at the curb and his invitation was to be
urgent. The bribe was a dollar down and four dollars more
if he returned no earlier than eight o'clock. (My God, you
would think I was trying to seduce Mistinguett.)

Young as he was, the freshman's face was seamed with
despair. Cara loved freshmen. She gave them little cakes and
pitchers of milk in her apartment, adopting the pose of
an old auntie. Only very frightened little Christers responded to her invitations—the kind of boys who *needed*
an old auntie—because of the fug in her room. Her bathtub was too narrow. I have never seen a bathtub that wasn't
too narrow except one in Rio de Janeiro, a magnificent
sunken pool. The only safe way she could have gotten in
and out of her tub was with a hoist and we didn't have one.
It would be, I think, impossible for someone as pneumatic
as she to take a nasty fall but I suppose she feared it.

Nonfreshmen saw her only in brief interviews pertaining
to the business of running the house, and she had a whole
armory of sly lures. Occasionally they worked. Once Ed
Hayden, our other football player, came down with pneu-
monia. Ed was a very handsome fellow with muscles bulging all over him, and Cara said that while we were waiting
to see whether his case was grave enough for a hospital,
she would bring him into her rooms and nurse him. Ed,
weakened by fever, consented.

The first night Cara selflessly gave him her bed and prepared to bunk on the sofa, which she was finally able to
do. About midnight Ed had a chill. The shivering of his
two hundred and twenty pounds in a metal bed woke Cara.
The poor tormented woman shuffled into his room in her
nightie, mercilessly offered to warm him and rolled into
bed with him. Ed said he felt his hair turning snow white
with horror, but his reason stayed put nevertheless. He pretended to be delirious and claimed that a big brown bear

was trying to hug him to death. Bellowing with simulated fear, he fought and kicked and lashed out until she left him. Most beds wouldn't have stood it.

The next day Ed sent for friends and said, "You gotta get me out of here." Everyone agreed. Although he was ready to run on his own legs, six of us carried him out in a blanket to make his story look good. He was taken to the hospital. I have never asked Ed, naturally, any intimate details about his sexual fantasies, but I'll bet that big brown bear ramping around doesn't do them any good.

My freshman asked me dully, "Why am I asking Cara to dinner? I run when I see her."

"Oh, that's all right," I said jovially. "You want to discuss your problems."

He merely looked at me.

"Since you left home, you are worried about your father and sister. An incestuous relationship, see?"

He sighed. "I haven't got a sister."

"I know you haven't," I said menacingly. "You've got three brothers younger than yourself who will be coming here one, two, three. And you live in Tucson, Arizona, so your family won't be coming to the games."

He began to see the beauty of it. "My old man is a dope fiend, huh?"

I nodded. "After a severe gall-bladder operation, the doctor put him on morphine...."

"Okay, but ..."

"You don't sit next to her. You sit across from her. All you got to watch is in the taxi. You're worried. You cry a little. But you're not worried enough to sit on her lap."

"She hasn't got a lap."

"She tries, so watch it."

I was determined to serve Miss Anglin a Martini cocktail. I had never drunk one. We had quicker uses for gin than that. But I had read about them. To prepare, I bought a gin kit. It was a little bottle of glycerine, a packet of juni-

per berries mingled with coriander seeds, and a gallon of
distilled water. You set the alcoholic content yourself. I
wanted things genteel so I made it half and half—which
I now know is 100 proof gin, but I didn't know it then.
Vermouth was a mystery and I had Mr. Fox, our staid little
bootlegger, bring me a bottle a week ahead of time. It cost
seven dollars and, even more than it does now, it tasted like
sucking lead pencils in the fourth grade.

My date with Miss Anglin was for a Thursday afternoon
after her matinee. Tuesday morning I made my gin with
finical care. I let it age during the late morning and early
afternoon hours. About five o'clock in my bedroom I made
a Martini, a trial run. I had borrowed a cocktail shaker.
(The deadening protocol of stirring Martinis to avoid bruis-
ing the gin came much later. You couldn't have bruised
this gin with a ball bat.) I made the proportions three to
one, shook it briskly and poured it out into my toothbrush
glass. Then I tasted it. My throat constricted and my tongue
shrank in my head. It was as nearly undrinkable as anything
I had ever tasted except some honey highballs, so-called,
in Memphis two years before.

A man named Cleary had phoned me and asked me to
come over to his house. His family had gone out for the
evening. He said he had some gin. Alone in the house we
did not need to hide or hurry. We could drink openly and
Cleary said we would make some honey highballs. It was
a drink new to me and, I suspect, to him. He got out a
lemon squeezer, gave me a dozen lemons, and told me to
get the juice out of eleven of them. He took a large crystal
water pitcher of his mother's, emptied a jar of honey into
it, and poured a quart of gin on top of the honey. He mixed
this with a long spoon. As soon as the lemon juice was ready,
that went in also. He sliced the twelfth lemon for show and
added that. He filled the pitcher with ice, let soda water
into the interstices, and stirred it again.

It was a hot night. Imagine heat that begins in May and

lasts until October with rarely a day under ninety and many over a hundred, a damp heat. It makes for crime. When I lived there, Memphis edged out Port Said after a close race as the leading murder city in the world.

As Cleary stirred the pitcher, beads of moisture broke and ran down the sides. We were thirsty. It looked good. When he had played the stirring for all it was worth, he poured out two glasses.

We both took big swallows. Both of us were taken with violent spasms. I do not like to spit on the floor in houses where I am a guest so I spat mine out in the sink but Cleary was at home. He spat from where he stood. "Wow!" he cried, and we stared at each other mystified, with impulses toward nausea still twinkling around our palates. It was gin he had bought from an Italian he patronized regularly, but it tasted like poison. Maybe there had been a dead rat in the batch.

The pitcher sat there, demurely perspiring, hideously attractive.

"One more try?" Cleary said.

I shook my head.

"I don't think so, either," he said. With the elan of defeat he lifted the pitcher high and poured it splashing down the drain, all wasted.

After all this trouble we felt we owed ourselves something. We went down to Mother Bianchi's. You sat in her kitchen, ate her spaghetti, and drank her homemade beer. The spaghetti was wonderful but the beer was very strong and it threw a beach of yeast in the bottom of the bottle. We were joined there by Frank Adams. I have seen him many times, switching his profile back and forth in front of a glass, always asking, "Seriously, did you ever see anyone as handsome as I am?" To avoid argument, I always said no. Later at Washington and Lee, he used to sleep with a raw beefsteak over his face the week before the dances to enhance his complexion. He pitched for the Memphis University School ball team. After our spaghetti we sat drinking beer and listening to Frank pitch. After a while he tired and said, "Let's go to the Peabody."

To stay us if we grew thirsty we bought a half-dozen quarts of beer and put it into two big brown paper sacks. At that time everybody went to the Roof Garden on the Peabody Hotel. The garden was paper flowers over wooden lattices but it was certainly on the roof, the roof of the thirteenth floor as I recall. Cleary was rich but Adams was poor and he objected to paying admission prices anywhere. We were willing to go along with him on this. Instead of buying tickets for the garden at a table in front of an express elevator in the lobby, we went up to the mezzanine floor and each sat in a telephone booth to drink a quart of beer.

Refreshed, we took the elevator to the twelfth floor and scuttled down corridors until we found an outside fire escape. It was a narrow iron ladder twelve stories above the street and we went up it like cats, still carrying the paper sacks. Once over the parapet we were in the Garden. We found a table by the dance floor and we had barely got our last quarts of beer open when—I don't know how—policemen seemed to spring up from under the table like djinns and before we could say knife, we were in custody. They took us down in the elevator and led us across the lobby where troops of our friends were standing in line to buy tickets.

All they were going to do was throw us out, I think, but Cleary, a man whose hair fell into his eyes after the third drink, had a spleen against one of our ushers, a house dick named Bob Crosby. Just as we reached the door, Cleary swung on him. I don't see how he missed because Crosby had a face the size of a snare drum, but miss him he did and Crosby said "Ride 'em."

We waited on the sidewalk with artificial nonchalance while some more of our friends passed by. In the distance we heard the clanging of the Black Maria coming for us. It sounded like a fire truck and we hoped it was but it pulled up in front of the Peabody and we trooped in the back door. At the jail we gave false names and they booked us on D & D charges. We had spent all our money but they took away our watches, matches, neckties, a penkife, and Cleary's pocket nailfile. "He's a great dandy," Adams said to the cop. "He imitates Beau Brummel."

"Bo who?" the cop said.

We were let into the drunk tank, the white drunk tank. I believe for once the nigras had separate but equal facilities. I don't see how theirs could have been any equaler than ours. The walls were of iron. The seat along the wall was iron. There was a zebra of strap iron in front of us and beyond it, a turnkey walked back and forth once in a while deafly.

Abruptly there was nothing to do, nothing to look at, nothing to read, nothing to smoke, nowhere to go. We felt it. We were sober by then. It was not in the least remorse. It was shock, the shock of being unfree.

Quite unconsciously we each explored our little den, *touts conforts*. One at a time we walked the length of it and back, took a drink of warm water from the tap, and pissed in the can. Then we sat down and stared out into the corridor. For half an hour we didn't talk. Shocked, we sat there.

Then in a marvelous but shameful way we began to live there. We noticed the stifling heat. We noticed the two other guys in with us and like them we took off our shirts.

One of our buddies was a middle-aged man with a dreadful carbuncle oozing on the back of his neck. "What are you in for?" we asked.

"I'm in for beating my wife and I'll beat the son-of-abitch again when I get out," he said, so enraged his genders had loosened. He didn't speak again that night.

A boy younger than any of us was lying comfortably on the iron bench along the wall with his hands behind his head. "What are you in for, bud?" I asked.

In one of the deepest bass voices I ever heard, he said "Highway robbery." He told us with immense satisfaction how he had stuck up the Anderson-Tully payroll car with a Daisy automatic squirt gun and taken forty-four hundred dollars from the terrified driver. His getaway car was an old Model T which had cast an essential part somewhere in the Wolf River bottoms, and the law had caught up with him. "I only had mah hands on that money about fo' hours," he said. "But I had it."

"What do you think they'll stick you?" we asked.

"Five-to-ten on account of mah youth, 'reckon. Maybe ten-to-twenty. I dunno."

Like most misdemeanants, the three of us thought it only bad luck that we had been picked up at all. A little more finesse and we might have been dancing on the Peabody Roof at that moment, yet here was a felon whose luck had really gone sour nonchalantly facing five or ten years in a place like this. To us jail was a ludicrous interruption. It dawned on us that there were people who took jail as an inevitable part of their lives.

"What were you going to do with the money?" I asked.

"Flahda. Miama," he said, explaining everything. He told us he was seventeen.

We wore away the rest of the night canvassing the possibilities. Cleary was working that summer as a reporter on the *Commercial Appeal* and he was in and out of the courthouse all the time. The judge we would come before tended, he said, to be lenient with first offenders.

"Lenient?" we asked.

"Ten dollars."

That was bad enough, but our worst problem was how to get out of jail. Frank's father was sick, he said. My father was out of town. This left Cleary's father, unfortunately. Only the week end before Cleary had been drinking with some new friends. He was overtaken by a ten-year-old corn whisky, red as blood. The friends, barely knowing his name and nothing of his address, had lifted him into the Chisca Hotel and lain him in a room there. Next morning, a Sunday, Cleary reached his father just before church and his father came down and paid him out of the Chisca. To have to call him from the jail this Sunday morning seemed excessive.

"He's an old man. He can't go banging around Sunday mornings like a milk route," Cleary complained.

"How long until we go before the judge?" we asked.

"About three days usually," Cleary said. "I know. We can't stay here."

Cleary was wearing a new gray worsted suit. Already the trouser legs clung damply to him and were gathering smudges of dirt.

About dawn they gave us breakfast, hot grits covered with melted pork grease and coffee that tasted like the cell, of iron. We needed something on our stomachs but those grits seemed to fly spherically together and I felt as if I had swallowed a warm bowling ball.

About nine o'clock the turnkey said we could make a phone call. Both of us looked at Cleary. He got up as though his legs ached and walked out with the turnkey. In ten minutes he was back.

"What did he say?" we asked.

"He said, 'In jail, eh?' " Cleary said.

"Is he going to get us out?"

Cleary sat there, spat between his feet, and shrugged.

"But didn't you ask him?"

Cleary looked at me. "He hung up."

The heat had returned with breakfast and we sat there, quietly sweating. After an hour or so the turnkey let us out, saying mockingly, "Yes, *suh*. Step this way, please." Mr. Cleary was waiting at the desk, overwhelmed with fatherhood. A pile of money was on the counter in front of him. He didn't look at us. He didn't speak. He turned and walked away, Cleary following, hangdog. I caught up and said, "Thank you very much, Mr. Cleary. I'll return the bail money as soon as I can." He didn't say a word. At nineteen you think that most adults like you rather than not. It was strange to get a full blast of adult disapproval. We asked the cop behind the desk; it had taken twenty-five dollars a head to get us out.

We went out into the hot Sunday street full of papas and mamas and their broods going to the big Methodist church a couple of blocks away. We watched the churchgoers a minute and Frank said, "They're the ones that keep their noses clean." As I went down the jail steps it occurred to me that I could turn right if I wanted to or left if I wanted to. I have never forgotten that feeling.

Tasting my trial martini, I remembered all this. And, as if floating in the nasty mixture, jammed down small like homunculi, was a passel of cops pulling a minuscule jail after them, I determined that Miss Anglin's visit would be conducted with rigid propriety, a drink or two (if I could stand it), a nibble at some crackers spread with whitefish eggs working as caviar, and then conversation—the drama, art, the great world.

I enlisted two of my friends as hosts. I didn't want to receive her alone. To seem to have a date with a woman as old as she would give rise to lewd remarks. My friends hung back at first. They couldn't see any sense in squiring an old dame around gratuitously, famous actress or not. They did not have, as I had, the occasion confused with a fictive situation in the Second Empire. (I must have been reading *Nana*.) I knew little of Miss Anglin but I saw her then as a queen of the Parisian theater like Réjane or Bernhardt. At the blue hour I would call for her in a four-wheeler (Sherlock Holmes) and we would trot softly through the darkening Bois to my flat where a cold bird and a bottle would await us, and, after a couple of whacks at the bottle, she would regret that I was too young to have been her lover like Gautier. It was something like this my imagination was burrowing toward. I could almost feel a top hat sprouting from my temples and patent-leather shoes creeping over my feet. My friends didn't have these advantages and it was only after I promised them free liquor that they promised to come with me.

When she came out of the stage door after the matinee, Miss Anglin was not swathed in satin or ermine. She wore a tweed suit. The three of us were freshly bathed and pomaded, wearing the hard linen collars of the day. She stopped short, looked us up and down, pursed her lips, and winked. It is only as I write this that it occurs to me she liked our looks. I thought she was doing me a tremendous favor, but maybe she liked going somewhere with three painfully clean young guys.

In the taxi, I kicked off with a suave little paragraph, precooked and jawbreakingly casual, "I know, Miss Anglin, that you rarely leave Broadway. I thought you might like to see something of the student life here. Just as a curiosity."

One of my friends on the jump seat whispered "Jee-sus" in the direction of the driver and Miss Anglin said, "Why, yes. It would be very interesting."

We had not tried to prepare the other members for Miss Anglin's visit for fear they would try to horn in on the cocktails. We took her in cold. She hadn't said much in the taxi and now I think she was watching us, very likely with amusement. We entered a small lobby that opened into a long room we had been instructed to call the solarium.

To the right, one end of the solarium gave into the smoking room. No one was in the solarium and what could be seen of the smoking room looked safe enough, four guys playing bridge as usual. I ground down the silence with banal identifications: "This is the solarium. And here"— interval of three or four steps—"is the smoking room."

We walked through the archway and it took only a glance to show me what was going on. Lying on a big red leather sofa called the Senior Bench was a tired senior. He was sound asleep and one hand dangled over the edge of the sofa. Crouched beside him on the floor, giggling noiselessly, were two sophomores. They had a basin full of warm water and they were raising it to inundate the dangling hand. Properly done, with the water at the right temperature, this will cause a dreadful accident.

There was a snort from one of Miss Anglin's escorts and I turned her around by the elbow firmly enough to leave a bruise. "But what are they doing?" she protested.

Foundered utterly, I babbled, "It's a rite. It's a fraternal rite."

"Secret, I suppose," she sniffed.

"It's one of the most secret things we got," said one of the escorts with decent human feeling.

"And here is our garden," I said weakly, pointing out of the solarium windows at the no flowers, the barely any grass, and the big brick wall.

Phase One was over and I was ready for Phase Two. "Perhaps you would like a cocktail, Miss Anglin?" I said.

"That would be very nice," she said demurely.

We had to go up a flight of stairs and down a long corridor to get to Cara Lemay's apartment. It was the time of day when people took showers.

"Would you run ahead, Jack, and see that the coast is clear?" I asked. I know I sound like Dick, the fun-loving Rover, but that was the way I talked.

He leaped up the stairs ahead of us and we could all hear him bawling, "Into your rooms, you bastards. Za dame coming up here."

"Why, it's like a monastery," she said. "Aren't you allowed even to look at women?"

"It's the other way around, Miss Anglin," I said, I thought neatly. "You aren't allowed to look at us. We're taking showers. You wouldn't want to run into a nude young man."

"Why not?" she said crisply.

I didn't know why not but at least I didn't say, "Well, gosh..." I only laughed nervously.

Our little procession walked alone down the corridor and into Cara's apartment. On a table beside a bisque lamp were the cocktail things and the plate of crackers with the whitefish eggs. I made the cocktails as I had done the day before and offered her the first one.

I had concocted a couple of pushbutton questions and I hoped she would do the rest, that is, regale me with her memoirs. I said, "The theater is your great love, Miss Anglin?"

She was looking at me with a sort of smile and raising her drink at the same time. Perhaps a touch hurried to answer a question like that, she may have taken a bigger swallow than she intended. She coughed, and then, full projection, aimed at the cheap seats, she cried, "*OH MY GOD!*" She set the cocktail down and clapped a handkerchief to her mouth as if she had been shot in the throat.

Well, it made me sore. Maybe it wasn't a very good martini, but she must have tasted bootleg liquor. She didn't have to rattle the windows about it. I got her a glass of water and after a few feebly solicitous questions I took her back to her hotel. She seemed glad to arrive there. I think she feared for her vocal cords.

At the time I thought I was angry with her because I

had made all those arrangements and spent all that money for nothing. (I had to give the vermouth away.) I am no longer of that opinion. I can see that I was the one who had done all the acting and at the one moment when she might have obliged with a little, she refused. An actor spurned is a mad actor. So I learned something about the theater after all.

VIII

The Old Man,
a Nineteenth-Century
Steel Engraving

I was idle, something he would have hated, watching a fraternity bridge game when I was called to the phone to hear of my grandfather's death. I picked up the receiver and the message came in a long shout: "Hey, Allan, your grandpa died last night." With the first blast of the "Hey!," I knew it was my Uncle Brad, the one who had stayed with the farm. He was a grown man with children of his own before his father would allow a telephone in the house, and I don't think Brad ever got it straight about the electricity. He acted as if the telephone wire were a hollow tube. Even making a local call he would take two or three deep breaths and, as soon as the party came on the line, he would bellow his first sentence in a voice seemingly full of rage and anxiety. Then he would listen to see if he had made it. An intelligible answer and he would relax, winking a sharp blue eye at any bystander. After I had reached him and said it was too bad, he shouted that my Uncle Charlie would pick me up Tuesday for the funeral.

I had seen my grandfather no more than a dozen times. I felt nothing but a vague dutiful regret but I knew I would go out in the country for the funeral. A sense of family decorum, a decorum I see now that he established, left me no alternative. I put on a dark suit and a black knit tie and was ready when Charlie came.

He came in a new Buick. After thirty years of keeping a village store, he was getting rich off silver foxes. The fact that money could be made by giving the natural instincts of these exotic, pungent little beasts free play instead of the staid hogs and sheep of his childhood excited him.

Charlie was the husband of my grandfather's only daughter, Maude. In the store he always wore a cap and swore every breath he drew. Today he was wearing a fedora and a blue serge suit and his manner was quiet and solemn. I don't think I had ever been alone with him before and I didn't know what to expect. I had grown up in town, effete, and my country kinfolk had a vigor—even a wildness—that made me feel soft and awkward with them. I sought for some innocuous question that Charlie could answer without exploding into profanity. "How's Aunt Maude taking it?"

He looked away from the wheel at me for three seconds before he decided not to curse some mistake I had made by asking. "She's fine."

He said nothing more for five minutes. The road was icy. It was reasonable to suppose that the driving was taking his attention, but suddenly he burst out, "They don't teach you much back there at college."

"How do you mean?" I asked.

"Asking how Maude was taking it. How would she take it?"

"He was her father. I suppose she's sorry he's gone." *Sorry* was too weak but I couldn't say *grieved* in front of Charlie, not if I wanted to be stalwart. The old man had been living with them for the past seven or eight years. "She'll miss him."

"Hah!" Charlie said scornfully, almost loudly enough to rattle the side curtains.

"Well, won't she?"

Charlie's face had begun to sag and in profile he looked gloomier than he sounded:

> Old Bowm' is dead and there he lies
> And nobody laughs and nobody cries
> And where he's gone or how he fares
> Nobody knows and nobody cares.

The members of my family were still tricked out with the emotions I had been taught in childhood—Mother loves you, Daddy loves you, Daddy loves Mother, we are all happy. I had not had to do any thinking about filial pieties and I was shocked. I couldn't quickly believe that the little poem expressed a real indifference. I was certain Charlie hadn't made it up himself. Composition of this kind was somehow barred to a man who cut meat and raised foxes but he had remembered it and applied it to my grandfather and the rhyme and repetition gave the indifference a dignity, even a truth that made me uneasy. Something was beginning to crumble.

"If you think you're going to find your Aunt Maude grieving you got another think coming. Or Brad. Or your Dad. And if you could holler through Mac's gravestone, or Mac." He had named the old man's four children and his voice took on the rhythm of an incantation. I was sure he was releasing things he had never said before. "He lived in my house eight years. He paid his board on the nail but never once did he say a bed was soft or a beefsteak was tender. He gave Maude her orders as if she was a servant. She was his. He got her. He figured he had the right. Why, once when Maude was fifteen years old, he had her pushing hay back in the barn. It was ninety-five in the shade, probably a hundred and ten up in that mow. Maude fainted dead away. He told the boys to lay her out under a tree and throw some water in her face. 'She'll be all right in a minute,' he said. So they laid her under the tree and threw the water over her. When she came to, he said, 'It'll take us fifteen, twenty minutes to get the next load up. You can rest up till then.' These are the fruits of the goddam earth, and they're important, to be sure. And your grandmother stood on the back porch with her hands under her apron and watched the whole thing, just watched it. She'd learned by that time. You didn't protest nothing to him." He looked around at me. "Didn't your Dad ever tell you about him?"

"Not much," I said. And he hadn't, but I didn't feel then that I had to believe Charlie. Although he had been mild enough that morning, I saw him as a violent man, given to willful excesses, and his opinion of the old man merely personal. Now I know he was kind-hearted and the profanity a habit that accompanied his breathing.

"Your Dad'll talk now. You ask him. He come in on the Lake Shore this morning. Brad went in to the station to get him."

To me my grandfather had been a withered little nearly silent old man with crisp snow-white hair and two blades of a white mustache hanging slanting over his mouth. Although my father had said once that he had been six feet tall with black hair and a sandy mustache, I had never imagined him young or tall or speaking in any but the high husky voice of extreme old age. Now, illumined by another light than my own, I began to remember him again.

I had seen him oftenest on Thanksgivings. We would drive out the nine miles from town in a buggy hired from a livery stable, nine miles of icy hub-deep mud where we would let the lines lie loose over the dash and give the horse his head, heaving and throwing himself against the collar and making the plate covering the crock of oysters rattle. We always brought two quarts of oysters.

It was a big family dinner, a concession allowed my

grandmother, who liked to see all the cousins and grand-children once a year anyway. The table was made of saw-horses with boards laid over them. It was shaped like an L with chairs for thirty people, beginning in the living room and turning into the parlor, the folding doors of which had been opened on that day for that purpose. The kitchen was a congregation of women all the morning, and, after the men had gone out to the barns to look at the stock and view the state of Grandpa's corncribs, they would settle into the parlor, smelling faintly of the barns, and pour them-selves nips of rye whisky from a cut-glass decanter that sat on a marble-top table. The old man never took any himself. The smallest man, he sat in the biggest chair, initiating none of the conversation, settling arguments when appealed to, occasionally volunteering a caustic remark that exposed the foolishness of something his sons had said. The nephews and the grandchildren got no closer than the door.

Customarily the dinner began with oyster soup, possibly an obeisance to the memory of the seacoast our forefathers had struggled away from. It was followed by two gigantic coop-fattened turkeys filled with a bread stuffing flavored with sage. They were flanked by dishes of potatoes, creamed onions, and mashed squash. It was the yearly festal display for the women of the family and each one brought a jar of pickles, jam, or jelly she had put up.

Grace was never said. I remember him when he stood up to carve. He made the knife ring against the steel with negligent efficiency as if it were contemptible to make work of as simple a job as this. He carved elegantly, giving every-one big platefuls and eating little himself, as if to imply that we were all gluttons. The women—except my grand-mother—all pressed their jams and jellies on him. Some-times he took a little but he never said it was good. After the procession of pies and the coffee, the women cleared away. The men—all but my grandfather—lit cigars and retired into the parlor, where they talked crops and land prices, seldom politics, as my father once pointed out, because they were all Democrats and agreed. The old man had been a Vermont Democrat before the Civil War when it was the party of wealth and power. After the war, he had taken up veterans' land in Michigan only twenty miles from Jackson, one of the two birthplaces of the Republican Party, and all his neighbors had voted for Lincoln but he dismissed them all as a lot of higgledy-piggledy farmers. After all, he had introduced the Merino sheep into southern Michigan. (I was about nine when Brad told me that and, for a hilarious moment, I could see my grandfather leading a big Merino ram around the neighboring farmsteads, saying, "Sheep, this is Mr. Greenleaf" or "Sheep, this is Mr. Stoddard," the ram gravely sticking out a trotter to be shaken.) He always kept sheep with big curling horns, Merinos or Rambouillets. His sons meekly became Democrats and he even named the eldest in defiance of his neighbors George Brinton McLellan Seager after a well-known Democrat who had been his commander, the only commander he ever had, I guess.

As I looked back at these holidays, my grandfather did not seem to change. He remained the little white-haired old man. What came forward now was rather the anxious deference everyone paid him. If they had failed in it, what could he have done, a little old guy like that? I couldn't understand it then, in the car with Charlie, although I understand it now well enough. It puzzled me because I couldn't feel it.

When I was fifteen I had been marooned one summer afternoon at Charlie's house alone with the old man. He was eighty-seven then and he sat rocking in a big wicker chair with all his decades straight in his head and he didn't seem at all lonely, so that any attention I paid him was not a kindness to the aged but a gratuitous intrusion on an established privacy. He wasn't talking, but after thirty squeaks of the rocker the quiet became unbearable. I can see how much his presence influenced me, for I didn't start with a banality. It was obviously a nice day—sun, maple leaves quivering in the light airs—but if I had said so, I am sure he would have looked me up and down as a fool, a fool's son, therefore another fool. I began with something that interested me. I said, "You were at Gettysburg, weren't you, Grandpa?"

He looked at me and nodded. "Fourteenth Vermont. Stannard's Brigade. We won it."

I knew we had won it and I thought he had slipped a cog by giving me this schoolboy fact. I ignored this courteously and went on, "You must have seen Pickett's charge."

"We broke Pickett's charge," he said.

Was he too old to get anything out of? He seemed to recover only the grossest history. "It must have been something to see," I said as suggestively as I could.

"Oh, we knew they couldn't make it. It was a hot day, hotter than the hubs of hell, and we lay there in a clover field and watched 'em. They had three-quarters of a mile to come and, first we see of 'em, they come marching out of a little swale, the whole bunch, like a parade, ranks was straight, flags a-flyin'. I counted over thirty flags myself. We lay off to the left. . ."

"Behind a stone wall."

He stopped rocking and looked at me. "Wasn't any stone wall where we was. We laid in little holes we dug out with our hands, our bayonets, anything we could dig with. We just laid there and watched 'em come. Fifteen thousand men, I guess, and when the artillery opened up, a ball'd slam into 'em and take out one or two, and they'd close up. Another ball'd go through and they'd close up as if it was a drill. Captain says to us, 'When they git close, aim at their knees' . . ."

"Can't go far with busted kneecaps," I said knowledgeably.

"Wasn' much of a grade in front of us, but enough. Shooting downhill, you aim at a man's chest and your bullet'll go over his head. So we loaded and waited. The sweat was just a-runnin' off us. Then three, four hundred yards away, our boys started feeding canister to the guns and seven or eight men'd git knocked out at a time and they couldn't close up. They lost that fine parade-ground look and come a-runnin', yellin' the way they always did." ·

"The Rebel yell," I said.

"Sounded like a bunch of women to me. It was right then they made their mistake."

"How? What mistake?"

"We overlapped 'em. Our left stuck 'way out beyond their right. They should have come an oblique and fought us all, but no, they passed to the right of us, whooping and yelling up the hill. Fool thing to do. I saw it. Old Stannard saw it. He picked us up and we struck the Rebs in the flank. They couldn't endure that so they broke. Run off the way they'd come in dribs and drabs or stood still waving dirty handkerchiefs, hollering, 'Don't shoot! Don't shoot!' " His face didn't change but he made a series of soft little puffs and I took it that he was laughing. He sniffed and stopped. "And that was the end of it. It ended it for Pickett. It ended it for Lee but he had to go traipsing off for nearly two years till Appomattox."

Only then did I realize what he had been telling me all along, that his brigade, Stannard's brigade, had won the Civil War at Gettysburg. I have looked it up since. It is a tenable point of view. I didn't talk to him alone again.

My Uncle Charlie's house was one of the biggest in the village, built in this century of white clapboard with stained-glass borders on the windows and a wide porch across the front. Three or four cars were parked in the road, a great

many in those days. Inside, the house was full of my kinfolk, the women in the kitchen as usual preparing a meal.
I saw my father, who had just come from New Orleans.
Usually he was a genial man and would have embraced me
and clapped me on the back. He shook hands almost coldly
and said, "How are you, son?" Then I noticed that the
parlor was full of men, the two living sons, the older nephews and grandsons. They were sitting, most of them, with
folded arms, none smoking, barely speaking. Was this the
family's observance of formal grief? Was it perhaps real
grief? Was I supposed to sit down and fold my arms, too?
Charlie noticed it also, as soon as he had hung up his overcoat. "Oh, you fellows don't have to set there like cobs
stuck in tar. You can talk. He ain't going to hear you." No
one responded to this or smiled.

I sat examining from a distance my cousin Harold's trom-
bone which lay beautifully polished on top of the piano, a
relic of his high-school-band days and I wondered if he
ever regaled his family with a solo. The thought seemed
out of place, however, for no one was speaking at all now.
We could hear Charlie, who carried none of the old man's
blood in him, kidding the women in the kitchen and them
trying to shush him, but here there was silence. It struck me
that there was no sadness in this quiet at all but a tension,
perhaps the tension of waiting for the old man's death to
take hold of them and become real, and since unfamiliar
emotions are usually recognized as anger, these men seemed
grim and surly to look at. Maybe I did myself.

Charlie sauntered in. "Come on to lunch," he said.

We all filed into the dining room and, after a flurry of talk
to get us seated, the women were infected and they said no
more except to offer dishes to pass in whispers. No one ate
much except Charlie, who was always a good doer at table.
When he finished he lit a cigar and sat back in his chair.

"Who's settin' with him?" he asked.

"Cora," Brad said. Cora was Brad's wife. "She said she didn't mind."

Abruptly it occurred to me that my grandfather was going to be buried from his own house, the one he had built on the farm four miles away. It was only natural but I was surprised. I had thought that somehow, with all the solemnity in the parlor, the funeral was going to be here at Charlie's.

All the men got up from the table, put on their coats and hats, and went out to the cars. I heard Charlie driving the women out of the kitchen, "Come on, let's get it over with. Let the damn dishes go." They let them go and they, too, went out and got into the cars, some of them sitting on the men's laps. Ordinarily there would have been country jokes and pinchings, but that day we rode the four miles like mutes.

The preacher was already there, a moon-faced young man with pince-nez glasses, fussing around the coffin. A single bouquet of chrysanthemums sat at the head and by that time I wondered who had sent them; Brad probably. Everyone sat down at once in the undertaker's chairs as if bidding the preacher to begin. Before I did, I sidled up to the coffin and looked in. He lay there with his big hands folded, his cheeks ruddy, his hair and mustache as white as ever. He might have been the teller of Pickett's charge who had just shut his eyes.

I sat next to my father. "He wouldn't have liked this," he muttered, nodding toward the preacher who was just opening his book. "He never said aye, yes, or no to a preacher in his life." But I think the family didn't know how to get a man buried without one.

The preacher began, "Gracious God, it hath pleased Thee to call Thy servant, Bowman Seager, to his eternal rest," and he went on a long time, sinking down to "Gracious God" whenever his breath or invention ran out. He could have known my grandfather only by reputation, yet he was impelled to give him a eulogy. It seemed to be a standard piece full of vague phrases, sentimental and imprecise, interchangeable for any recipient. It was so false and long-drawn-out that I could feel a tension mounting in the room and my father said loudly enough to raise smiles, "He'll need more of a boost than that." I looked out the window at the big bare maples. The old man had planted them all. What had he expected?

I was brought back into the room by Brad saying sharply, "The grandsons." It was over. The preacher was discreetly wiping his brow. The grandsons stood up, Mac's two, Brad's two, Maude's one, and myself. "Carry him out," Brad said. I had not seen him stern before. He was the gentle one of the old man's sons. We sorted ourselves out around the handles and lifted. We were none too many. It was heavy, copper I realized. It must have cost a thousand dollars even then.

The hearse went to a little graveyard down the road. There was no marquee then, no carpet of imitation grass, just the big hole under a pine tree. They always have pine trees in graveyards here and this one whirred and sighed in the wind and dropped clots of snow on our necks. Maude was the only woman who came. The undertaker had little equipment and we had to let the coffin down, the undertakers and gravediggers giving us a hand. When it was in the grave, the preacher gave a long prayer. The men did not stand back in a clump; they stood in a ring around the grave looking in, every one of them. At last the preacher began to finish, scattering a little loose dirt. He stopped and stepped back, thinking he had ended it. The men did not move. My father motioned to one of the gravediggers and he started shoveling. When there was a foot of dirt over the whole coffin, my father said, "There, by God." He looked around at Brad and Brad nodded.

"Let's go back to the house and get a drink," Charlie said.

His kitchen was full of whisky. The women had set it out. The men got drinks and went into the parlor. I hung back. I drank but I didn't know how well my father knew this and I thought he would be less likely to forbid it if I appeared with a glass in my hand than if I asked him first. Aunt Mary, Uncle Mac's widow, gave me the ice. She was a tall, handsome woman with gray eyes. "Why didn't you go to the grave? Too cold?" I asked.

"I know you owe the dead something but I didn't owe him that, not after the way he treated Mac," she said. Mac had died three or four years before, the head of a hospital in Detroit. She didn't tell me how he had treated Mac. She was busy making ham sandwiches as if we had to eat, and I didn't ask her.

I took my drink and went into the parlor. Most of the people had dispersed. Only my father, Brad, Charlie, and Aunt Maude were there and Maude had a drink. I don't think she had ever had one before, but she was of the blood and whatever rites were being performed she was determined to take part in. As I entered she was saying, "... but I don't think you ought to talk that way about him."

My father said, "Maude, how do you forget? Is your memory getting weak? Does soft living here with Charlie blot it out of your mind? You go to the phone and call him and he brings home a porterhouse, but it was meat once a week and flour-and-water gravy the other days. Have you forgotten that? And you and Mother lugging fleeces of wool to the creek to wash when the snow was barely off the ground because he had to shear early to catch the Boston market and the sheep blatting their heads off up against the straw stack because they were cold. And when he put that tin roof over the side porch, that was a good place to dry apples but he didn't get up there to spread 'em and get his knees scalded and Mother putting mutton tallow on 'em, the only medicine we had in the house but horse liniment. This is all true."

"I know it is but why do you wait until he's underground? Why didn't you tell him to his face?" The drink was making Maude, a retiring woman, brave.

"I did tell him once. I was scared of him every time I saw him but I told him once," my father said.

"I never heard you. I never heard anybody."

"The time I bought my first car, I told him good," my father said. I had heard of that. My father's first car had been a Mitchell and he had bought it at the factory in Racine, Wisconsin, and driven it back to Michigan. It was a big black touring car with white wheels and it cost $1528. I can't remember what I paid for my own cars but I can remember the price of that one. Full of pride, Dad had taken it out to the farm to show his father. The old man gave it one careless glance and said, "What do you want one of those damn things for? Throwing your money away." For once my father didn't knuckle under. He fought back and at the end he said what he had meant all his life, "You're not my father. You're just my sire."

"That's true. Arch told him," Brad said.

"But only once in all that time. Mother might have been alive today if you boys had stood up to him," Maude said.

(And the night I wrote the last word of my first novel, I came out of my room with the six-hundred-page manuscript in my hand, full of pride to show it to my wife and my father, and he said, "What do you make it so thick for? Nobody'll read it." But I said nothing because I could hear the echoes and by that time I knew what kind of people we were, I guess.)

I could barely remember my grandmother, a frail, sweet old lady. They began to talk about her marriage but inevitably, it seemed, the old man became the subject. He had run away with my grandmother when she was fifteen, the daughter of a prominent farmer in the neighborhood, David

Jerrells. It was a come-down for her because Grandpa was still clearing his land and he had only a log house to put her in. My Uncle Mac had been born in the log house, the other children in the "new" house, but the clearing of the land went on well into my father's lifetime. He could recall columns of blue smoke rising from the piles of walnut logs his father burned to get rid of them. After the elopement David Jerrells and my grandfather never spoke to each other again. When it was Jerrells' turn to head the gang repairing the road, my grandfather would pay his road tax rather than work under him, and when my grandfather was head, Jerrells would pay his, apparently an almost unheard-of extravagance in those days. He had built one of the largest houses in that end of the county, white clapboard, green shutters, like a New England farmhouse. Sometimes he would spend the evening in the grocery in the village and come back a little bit tiddly. He walked with a cane and he would stop in the road before his house in the moonlight and lean on it and holler, "Who owns that big fine white house?" Then he would slide the cane up over his shoulder and say, "David Jerrells, by A'mighty," and go marching unsteadily in. As she has in this account, my grandmother seemed to get lost in other people's lives.

The men got fresh drinks, Aunt Maude refusing, but she remained in the parlor, and the talk went stubbornly on. It did not sound like reminiscence. It was accusation with a bill of particulars, belated, useless, and their tone was a bitter pride as if he had been a catastrophe they had survived. Years later, when they spoke of him, the tone had not changed, it was full of hatred. Time softened nothing.

"Show Allan your hand, Arch," Brad said. I had seen the scar that ran white across my father's hand below the knuckles but he had not told me what made it.

"I got that plowing," he said. "I was ten years old, first crop I made, and I had a pair of oxen, Buck and Joe . . ."

"Buck and Jack," Brad said.

"All right, Jack. And the old man came up behind me with a big long ox whip. He whirled it round and let fly and it caught me here." He held out his hand to show. "Then he said, 'You draw them furrows straight.' "

"What did he do to Uncle Mac?" I asked. "Aunt Mary wouldn't come to the grave."

"Oh, that was terrible," Brad said. "It come on Mac's twenty-first birthday along in the fall there. Dad took him to the front door. We never used the front door much so Mac knew something was up. Dad opened the door and he pressed a hundred dollars into Mac's hand and says, 'My son, there's the world.' And he made Mac pack right up and get out that night. Now he knew Mac wanted to be a doctor. . . .

"So he loaned him the money to get through medical school and charged him six per cent, same as the bank, and he had the gall to tell Mac he was lucky to get it; 'The bank wouldn't give it to you. You don't own nothing to put up as collateral.'

"That was to teach us to git to owning something as quick as we could, I expect," Brad said.

"You don't believe that. You know he never cared whether we learned anything except to work. We were just free labor until we came of age and he couldn't hold us," my father said.

"You got out," Brad said, looking down at the floor between his hands. "And I stayed."

"You bet I got out. I took my hundred dollars and lit out for town. If I'd stayed I might have killed him," my father said.

"I hated him, too. It's a bad thing to say about your own father. But I never got so mad as you and Mac. And then there was Mother," Brad said.

"Yes. There was Mother." My father stood up. "I've got to go. Charlie'll drive me. You think three months for that will to get through probate?"

"About. I'll let you know," Brad said.

My father got his overcoat and I got mine. "I didn't think I was going to see this day. I'd begun to believe he was immortal," my father said. He shook hands with Brad and patted Maude on the shoulder. We are not a demonstrative family.

"Remember the time Aunt Pam and Aunt Corneel come to see him?" Brad asked. "You were too little, Maude. Took the train all the way from Brandon, Vermont, to Adrian and hired a surrey and drove it out here themselves. They were wearing black dresses and half-mitts and they carried one of those carpetbags with a deer's head on the side embroidered in yellow wool. I sure admired that deer's head. Dad showed 'em the barns and the sheep and the cows and they come and set in the front room and asked him for a glass of his cold well water, and says, 'Well, Bowman, you've got a nice place here,' and they sipped the water, got up, got into the surrey and went right back to Brandon. They didn't stay but two hours."

"They probably didn't like him, either," my father said. "They were just nosey." My father put on his overcoat. "Well, good-by. Come on, Son."

Going into town to the railroad station we had to pass the farm. It was getting dark. The woodlot stood out black. The fenceposts were capped with snow and in the corners the skeletons of milkweed clicked in the wind. My father told me that the old man had left fifty thousand dollars and a hundred and sixty acres free and clear. Part of the money would see me through college. "Not that I didn't earn every penny I get," my father said.

At that time I was shocked and confused by what I had seen and heard; now I think I can see what my grandfather was up to. He had started with a chaos of walnut trees. He had cut them down, used them or burned them as he pleased, and made a farm out of the land they stood on, and I don't suppose there was a foot of any ground I could see that he hadn't walked over a hundred times behind his oxen, sowing broadcast, or swinging a scythe. He had peopled it, too, and made it prosper. The stiff papers of his title and his bonds were only signs of all that labor. The hatred and any random joys were irrelevant. They had glanced off him.

* IX *

The Scholarship

I was asked to tea at my professors' houses quite often when I was in college. In the front halls of those who had married well, a maid in a starched cap took your coat. Card trays sat on the hall tables with cards in them. Your host greeted you in a manly voice, throwing out tentatively bits of slang to put you at your ease, and led you to the teatable to present you to his wife. The professors seemed to dress alike, in dark suits, starched collars, string ties, and waistcoats laced by heavy golden chains from which depended Phi Bete keys as broad as matchbooks. I remember them by their beards. A few had just let the hair grow anyhow like Rutherford B. Hayes. One or two had fussed, training it into points. Some preferred a rough General Grant effect. Their wives, however, have receded into limbo. They all had gray hair, flowered dresses, demeanors so gentle as to seem cowed unlike today's Democratic committeewomen, and absolutely indistinguishable faces as if time and the weight of their husbands' learning (which I now know was not really leaden for some) had pressed out all the differences. After I had shaken hands, the tea was poured. Little sandwiches and homemade cookies were passed and there was a dish of peanuts, limp and stale.

When anyone asked me why I went, I said it was for the

food—I was always hungry and I inferred that it was smart to keep in good with the faculty, but these were only public excuses and I often wondered myself why I went. I never got enough of the sandwiches to hold me until dinner. The talk was dull. Their manner had the reticences and indirections of an earlier generation. Nothing ever seemed to get itself wholly said but dwindled away in smiles and the settling of cushions. Then one day it came to me.

Photographs of chateaus and cathedrals hung on the walls of their studies and I was handed a little dish of Provençal ware to put my cigarette ashes in. They made allusion to Seville, the Sorbonne, or the Alte Pinakothek. One, a bachelor professor of English history, had no buildings on his walls, instead a photograph of Julia Marlowe and another of Minnie Maddern Fiske, each inscribed, as I noticed when he went to fill the teapot, to "My darling Arthur." He was rumored to keep quart perfume bottles with big glass stoppers full of the finest Bourbon in his bedroom and people said he was never quite sober during the last years of his incumbency. Amazed, I used to see him padding across the campus at a kind of formal stumble, for I had not seen anyone who used liquor as mere fuel. All the same, he was as sharp as a tack, and, challenged, I heard him tick off the catskin earls of England glibly at a tea party. These men, I believed, had lived. They had been to Europe and met the great. Wasn't that living? I ignored completely what kind of men they were, dazzled by where they had been and the hands they had shaken, and, since I had shaken their hands, a kind of bond was formed and it was easy to borrow the decors of their sabbaticals and insert myself into them. Once there, I didn't horse around with elderly actresses. The hands I shook were those of Josephine Baker and Raquel Meller.

I couldn't go to Europe because I had too little money and so did my father. He was an anti-investor and the boom of the period was only something he read about in the papers. He had been approached about 1903 by a lank, seedy-looking bicycle repairman and begged to put a thousand dollars into a horseless carriage Ford was tinkering with, but my father was too shrewd for that. He knew they would never replace the horse. Later in life on windy nights, he would get out a bridge table and set it up, grimly snapping the legs into place. He would take a pencil and paper and start figuring. The last figure I remember was eleven million. When it arrived, the Crash was naturally a great consolation to him.

Nevertheless there came a day when I slid away from Pier 56, New York, hanging over the rail of the *Aquitania*, whistling "Great Day" between my teeth, waving good-by to Frank Adams and a girl named Peggy who had come to see me off, and I am inclined to think that these kindly professors had more to do with putting me there than anyone else.

It was they who turned me into a Scholar (not a scholar, which is sometimes a serious occupation). I merely liked to read. The real imperatives of college life were learning to be smooth with women and to hold your liquor like a gentleman. Since these studies took place chiefly at night, I read during the days. I didn't get to class much my junior and senior years. By that time I had learned that the lectures of many professors were the redacted essences of textbooks they had written and I didn't want to be routed out of bed on a frosty morning to listen to what I could read warm in a bathrobe over a cup of coffee, and, during a semester, not only that professor's book but half a dozen others in the field. It was not a method of study. It was self-indulgence but it seemed to work.

At the beginning of my senior year, two or three professors told me I should apply for the Scholarship so I did, somewhat diffidently, for I couldn't believe anyone was going to give me three years in Europe free.

The benefactor who had founded the Scholarships, his brains tingling with dreams of an Anglo-Saxon supremacy, was too acute flatly to demand supermen. For his Scholars he wanted brainy athletes or muscular intellectuals (are the two interchangeable?) who were Leaders of Men. Emphases like that scare me and I doubted if I had any of the qualifications. My roommate used to say that he could always tell when I went into training for swimming because I stopped buying cigarettes and smoked his. Did real athletes behave like this? It was true that I had more *A*s than *B*s on my scholastic record, but I had gotten them loafing around reading. Intellectuals seemed fiercer than I. And I didn't think I was a Leader of Men. I had been a leader of boys once when I was in knee pants. I had led them into a strawberry patch where we lay gorging ourselves. The man who owned the patch had thrown a charge of rock salt at us from a ten-gauge shotgun. The crystals whizzing above me carried any dream of leadership with them, and I had avoided campus politics mostly out of apathy but partly because I didn't own a blue serge suit.

I got up a dossier to submit to the Committee, a transcript of my grades, a birth certificate, letters of recommendation, a photograph with my hair slicked back in the manner of the period, and a letter telling why I wished to study at Oxford. I wonder what I said in it. Whatever it was, it couldn't have been the truth. The truth was clear but amorphous like an oil stain on water and I couldn't have written it down. I had to get to Europe, that was all.

I had assembled all this bumf listlessly, my hopes corked, but the moment I turned it in to the Committee, I suddenly wanted very much to win the Scholarship. Promptly and somehow properly a difficulty arose, the Phi Beta Kappa elections. All the Phi Betes I had ever seen were dopes and I had often stated to my friends that if I were ever favored with an invitation to join, I would turn it down, but when I was, I didn't. By that time my desire was so great that I was sure the Committee was exerting a force against me to match it by posting spies all over the campus like the MVD. If one of their agents heard that I had turned down Phi Bete, they might think me too shirty to consider, so I became a member but I have never bought a key. Beyond this slightly shameful compromise I did nothing but get my clothes pressed and wait for the oral examination. Everything hung on this, I was told.

I got very nervous waiting. I knew without asking anyone that I should act naturally before the Committee, but which naturally? The athlete? a sinewy handshake and a seemly aw-shucks modesty? The intellectual? a red flannel shirt, my head full of Platonism and prickly disagreements to cast at my questioners? The Leader of Men? Impossible. I didn't have the flow. Squire of dames? Malapropos. Had I known which persona to assume, it still is hard to act naturally when so much hangs on it. As the examination date drew near, I began to feel more and more like the nineteenth-century parson who had a compulsion, just after he had announced the Collect, to break into a minstrel song from the pulpit. I was afraid that if I let the clutch down for one second, my gears would shift.

On the day of the examination I dressed as if for church. I wore a hard collar, an Arrow Dart, I believe, and combed my qualms down with my hair. The public ordeal began with a luncheon given by the Committee for the applicants. "Just mingle around and introduce yourselves," we were told. I hate to mingle around and introduce myself. I froze against the wall paneling and let the Leaders of Men do the work. I knew the Committee were watching us like hawks but I stood erect as if I had just refused to have my eyes bandaged, muttering my name when anyone approached, my face cramped into a dreadful rictus of affability.

Luncheon, I surmised, would not be so much a feed as a proving ground for table manners. It was December. They served a sinister fresh asparagus but I was too cute to let them catch me with that. I lifted each stalk between my fingers and watched the others covertly to see if they did, too. To a man they cut it up with a knife and fork and I felt I had gained a little ground. The only thing was, I kept sighing.

After lunch we were led across the campus to a room outside the office of the Dean of the College. We stood in this room patiently like donkeys looking over a gate while the Committee conferred at one end of it. At last the Dean said, "We will talk to you one at a time in alphabetical order. Come along, Mr. Atkinson," and he took Atkinson by the arm, thrust him, it seemed to me, into his office with the Committee, and shut the door. "Talk to you" was, I thought, a specially fatuous euphemism. I knew they weren't heating plowshares on a brazier in the Dean's office but I didn't know what else they were preparing.

We all sat down, about twenty of us, around a long table to wait, and one of the silliest conversations followed that I ever heard in my life, spouts of clichés, *non sequiturs*, verbal twitches, and bursts of high, almost demoniac laughter. We were trying to display *sang-froid*. Almost simultaneously we saw it wasn't worth it. Talk stopped and we sat there staring at one another inimically, waiting for Atkinson to come out.

Someone said, "Are we allowed to smoke?" We didn't see any ashtrays. We didn't smoke.

It seemed two hours, but at last Atkinson came out. He didn't look much different from when he had gone in.

"What did they ask you?" we all said.

"Oh, a lot of stuff," Atkinson said.

"What kind of stuff?"

"Oh, just—you know," he said.

Already we had gone through enough together to en-
gender a slight but definite *esprit de corps.* When we saw
Atkinson nursing his own chances by refusing to give us
any clues, we stared at him with loathing. Then I think we
saw what a good idea it was tactically and we didn't ask
any more questions of anyone.

It was a situation for boredom but we weren't bored. The
office was very plainly furnished, only the long table around
which we sat, a few green file cabinets, and portraits of earlier bearded deans around the walls. All it needed was a drain
in the floor to look like a place where you were taken for
political interrogation, but that knowledge was a few years
ahead of us. We sat there silent, most of us, each man finding
something to do with his hands, not daring to leave the room
for an instant because the Committee were allotting a different length of time for each man.

A janitor came in and began to stroke the leaves of a rub-
ber plant with a cloth. Each leaf shone when he finished.
We watched him, hypnotized, as if he had been cutting
diamonds.

"What's that stuff?" someone asked him.

"Castor oil," the janitor said.

"—learn something every day," one of us said.

We roared with laughter. It seemed just funny then but I
think we laughed because we were all sitting there being
good boys as if we were being punished, and very likely
none of us had escaped being punished or the threat of
being punished with castor oil in our boyhoods and this got
tangled up with the incongruity of helplessly learning something on the one occasion when we were not going to take
in but give out learning, all we knew if asked.

We sat there fiddling with our hands and possibly what
kept us from yawning or screaming was that we sensed
the jostling of all these hopes. On the back of an envelope
one man drew a recognizable Stutz Bearcat being leaned

against by a gaunt man in a flat cap, all in the aloof classy manner of Laurence Fellows.

The man next to me was a cadet from the Naval Academy. He was in uniform, neat, confident, cool, and I feared him. He mumbled to me, "Say, how are you on this literature stuff?"

"Oh, fair, maybe," I said.

"Well, naval gunnery's my specialty, but all I been doing for the last three weeks is read literature, literature, literature—Galsworthy and everything."

As far as it was possible, this cheered me up.

I wanted a cigarette and I thought I needed a drink. Only three hundred yards from where I sat, a block away from the campus, I could have bought one. Mickey Phelan, a bootlegger I knew, had rented a room in a student rooming house and, with a lighthearted disregard for the authorities, had been selling whisky across the desk to anyone who entered for the past month, two bits a shot. He kept the bottle in a drawer. He, too, was one of my professors, I guess, for I learned a lot from him that seemed valuable at the time. He was beardless but his hair was white and it had the sculptured perfection usually seen in toupees. He had a professional Irish manner, verbose and twinkly.

I bought his whisky and he told me how it was made. This was as fascinating to a contemporary then as the procedures of the Marquis de Lur-Saluces at Château Yquem today. Deep in a cellar on Grand River Avenue in Detroit stood two vats holding about a thousand gallons apiece. Each batch was 20 per cent real whisky, bonded stuff, Mickey claimed. The rest was alcohol, water, and caramel flavoring. Two men, absolute teetotalers, mixed batch after batch all night long.

"Why teetotalers?" I asked.

"Because they're blind drunk at dawn from the fumes," Mickey said.

This was the stuff I thought I needed a drink of. Maybe I did, at that; after three hours in that room, the strain of our anticipations and the bad air were making me light-headed and I wondered dreamily what kind of act I would put on when my turn came.

At last the Dean stuck his head out of the door and said, "Mr. Seager?" I stood up. All I was thinking was, "Oh, God, keep me from being clean-limbed," and I floated in, knock-ing at things gently like a bubble.

The Committee seemed to stare at me with the forced geniality of a row of Toby jugs. One chair was empty. They told me to sit in it. I sat. I think I smiled but if I did, it was an idiot reflex from nervous tension. They began their ques-tioning under the somewhat labored pretense that I had hap-pened to drop in on a conversation about the ideal Scholar and, just for the hell of it, would I tell them casually and candidly how I thought I would measure up?

I could not have sat there mum-chance; I must have an-swered, but it is all a blur. I remember only two questions clearly. The first was "What have you been reading lately?" I answered, among other things, *The Case of Sergeant Grischa*. They asked me how I thought it compared with *All Quiet on the Western Front*. I said that the first gave an individual's experience of the war, the second, a military unit's, but the conclusions of both were the same, war was bad. They pursed their lips, nodding. Was I right? Was I even plausible? I didn't know and I was beginning not to care. Their second memorable question was "Do you drink?" I knew the answer should be a ringing "No, sir, not a drop!" but I was too tired. I just said "Yup."

It was a little after six when they let me go and told me to wait. I went back into the outer office. The aspirants had been in that room four hours and I sensed a change in tone. Now they were like a gang of prisoners waiting for the brass to decide on a decimation. People were getting sore. Nobody talked any more at all and I felt that it wouldn't take much to get them to kick the door in. The stimulus did not appear, however. We merely sat there. Perhaps some were fitting the Scholarship into their careers and jerking it out again like a piece from a jigsaw puzzle. Maybe they were nearly comatose from hunger and fatigue as I was. Whatever our conditions, they lasted until nearly eight o'clock, when the Dean flung the door open and said very quickly, "We've decided Mr. Seager has won the Scholarship," and, almost as if dodging something, ducked back into his office again.

I didn't feel anything. I was numb. We all stood up. A few were genuinely polite. They shook my hand clammily and congratulated me. What we all wanted most was to get to the men's room.

I emerged from the building into a splendid silent snowstorm. It had been a clear day when we went in but I seemed to have been in there long enough for not only the weather but the season to have changed. The snow was at least three inches deep, the heavy wet kind, and I had worn no galoshes. I wanted two or three quick ones at Mickey's the worst way. I had even unthinkingly started for the place but my feet plopping in the slushy snow decided me against it. I could send a freshman for a bottle when I got back to the fraternity.

As I went in the door I caught a freshman named Bill Clark. I told him, "Flip over to Mickey's and get me a bottle." I gave him the money. "And step on it."

"Yes, Sir," he said. All our freshmen said "Sir."

I avoided the smoking room where they were playing bridge and went out to the kitchen. The staff was just washing up. I wheedled a bottle of milk and a couple of ham sandwiches out of them. I ate slowly, trying to feel the Scholarship, trying to see myself on shipboard, but it was too soon. I had seen myself coming out of the Opéra in Paris in a tailcoat often enough, Lord knows, but that was just moonshine. Now that they really might happen, I couldn't summon up my visions.

When I had finished eating and thought I could stand the congratulations of my brothers, I started for the smoking room but someone called me to the phone.

"Your name Seager? This is the Ann Arbor Police Station. You got a guy named William F. Clark there?"

"Yes."

"No, you ain't. We got him here."

"What's the charge?"

"We picked him up in that room of Mickey Phelan's on Maynard Street."

"Is there anything I can do?" I asked.

"Nope. He just said to call you. We're going to hold him overnight, turn him loose in the morning. Put the fear of God into him."

I have always felt bad about Bill Clark but not half as bad, to be honest, as I would have felt if I had picked up the paper the next morning and seen a small headline something like POLICE RAID YIELDS NEW RHODES SCHOLAR. I never would have gotten to Europe then.

* X *

The Drinking Contest

*R*ecently an aunt of mine sent me a letter about my grandfather. Here it is:

Blue Coat Hospital
Liverpool, 27th March, 1852

I have much pleasure in stating that John Allan while in
this institution has been a very good, honest, truthful, active,
and intelligent boy, and in his conduct I have very great
satisfaction.

Had he been able to have remained here to complete the
full period, I do not doubt that he would have made a very
good scholar. As it is he has made good use of his time and
for his age is very well advanced in his instruction.

Thos. Wood.
Master

There were two Blue Coat schools, I believe, one in London where Charles Lamb had gone earlier, and the one in
Liverpool. Like the Deserving Poor and the Afric Slave,
my grandfather was one of the great butts of nineteenth-
century pity, an Orphan Boy. He knew nothing of his parents and later when I looked him up in the birth registry at
Somerset House in London, all I could find was that he had
been born in Cumberland somewhere.

He died very old when I was very young but what little I knew of him I liked. He was a stern, bent little man with white hair and a white mustache that covered his mouth like Nietzsche's. He wore a zinc insole in one shoe and a copper one in the other to seize terrene electricity and conduct it to his rheumatics. I asked him once about the Blue Coat School and he said, "Lob scouse every day and plum duff on Christmas."

After his death my aunt sent me his Civil War diaries and his *Book of Common Prayer*. The diaries were faithfully kept but dull. "Rode twelve miles. Went into camp" was the usual sort of entry. The most interesting was one from Georgia, "Saw the Old Man today. They say all he has up behind him is a slicker, a bottle of whisky, and a box of cigars." The Old Man was Sherman, of course. There was nothing remarkable about the prayer book except the end papers. On them he had written in a very fine hand a scheme for a system of natural philosophy he had devised. Stuck in the middle of the book was a thin sheet of gold leaf. Why, I have no idea. It fascinated me. It seemed the proper bequest from an old man to a boy. I couldn't spend it. I wouldn't swap it. I could only admire.

I was thinking about my grandfather when I came to England to take up my Rhodes Scholarship. Since he had been English, as had my father's people once, three hundred years before, I felt I might be coming home. I had never been in England but as I leaned over the rail waiting for the gangplank to go down, watching the chimney pots of Southampton in the rain, I was listening for some sort of echo.

The Rhodes Scholars moved in a clump, ungraceful, shy as mountain goats but sturdily determined to smother it under loud talk. On the way to Oxford we stopped at Winchester to see the school and the cathedral. I had heard of Eton and Harrow but nothing of Winchester. I had, in fact, worn an Eton collar to church when I was a choirboy.

My mother never quite learned how to tie the tie. I can remember standing in front of her, my chin lifted, while she struggled, unspoken curses hovering around us like flies. I have always wondered what my mother would have said if she had let 'er rip, but she never did, and I showed up for the Processional sad, harassed, my neck sawed red from the edge of the collar. Aside from some dim cloister where we were stared at by whey-faced little boys, the only thing I really recall from Winchester is a high vaulted room where a guide pointed to a huge thick circle of oak and assured me that it was the veritable Table Round of King Arthur, a claim my later studies taught me must have been a misstatement.

I had been warned at home to be self-contained in dealing with the English, not to speak first, never to say, "Hi, pal," to any of them. (I didn't say, "Hi, pal" to anyone in America.) Nevertheless I was not prepared for Bough, the porter of my college. A taxi trundled me down a narrow, winding street and stopped in front of a Gothic archway like a church door. I passed under it. To my left, set into the wall, it seemed, was a dingy office. I went in. A bald little man, built like a seal, with the same mustache and the same eager lift of the chin, lunged courteously at me. "Yezzir?" he said. (I couldn't spot the accent then. It was Somersetshire, in which all *ss* are *zs*.)

I didn't know he was the porter and I didn't know what a college porter was. Beneath his deference, however, I caught an inkling of his encyclopedic knowledgeability. (He kept all the members of the college in his head, dons and undergraduates, and he could tell you where any of them was any hour of the day.)

"This is Oriel College?" I asked.

"Yezzir."

"I am Allan Seager."

I had been startled to find that the college buildings were

not gray as in the photographs but black, probably from soot. The fine English rain was falling outside. Bough had a fireplace bellying out into the office but no fire in it. I would not have been surprised if he had said, "Never heard of you," but he found my name at once on a list on a slate. "Yezzir. Number Zix is your zuite, zecond doorway, zecond quad. Hainez will be your zervant, zir."

"Thank you," I said humbly. I was expected. I hadn't come all that way for nothing. I bent to pick up my bag.

"Hainez will bring that along, zir."

I went out into the rain. The front quad was covered with hard gravel like a county road. The second quad had the lawn I had been taught to expect, green as if it had just been painted, lush and shining in the rain. Around the border under the windows red and white flowers grew. They bloomed all winter, they or their successors, for as soon as the frost killed any, the college servants planted new ones. The second doorway led into a dank corridor that grew darker as I went. I walked in ankle-deep ruts in enormous flagstones where people had walked the past three centuries. Two of these ruts led up to my door. A cat could have slipped into the room through either and in the winter they provided ventilation that only an anemometer could have measured properly.

I had heard of dark oak paneling gleaming in the firelight. My room was papered and when I drew a finger down the wall, it left a moist track like a snail's. The bank of windows gave out not over gardens but over the college coal pile, great bituminous lumps shining in the rain like the grass. A fire was laid in the fireplace. I lit it and after a quarter of an hour I learned one of the chief characteristics of the small English fireplace. It gives light, not heat. Later I burned the soles out of two pairs of shoes with my feet on the fender but back where my head was resting, reading, I could always see my breath going up in plumes.

The door opened and a man surprised me by coming straight in.

"You've lit your fire, sir," he said reproachfully. It was only the middle of October. I didn't know who he was. He was a rosy, plump-faced man of about forty-five, the kind of face you expected smiles to furrow, but they never did. He was Haines, not the Dean or my tutor, but my servant. (I had not yet picked up the salient fact of English social life—your inferiors "sir" you.) It made me uneasy to have a man old enough to be my father tell me he was going to serve me. Actually he didn't seem to do much. At six in the morning the skivvy, an old crone in a blue dress, crept in, softly cleaned out the ashes and laid the fire. About eight Haines would bring my breakfast on a tray with the morning mail, lay it on a table before the fire, and wake me: "Good morning, sir. Raining today." He brought my lunch, the customary half a round loaf of bread, a slice of gorgonzola cheese that tasted like soap, and a half-pint of beer. Later he brought my tea; that is, he brought the anchovy toast and cake, if any. I made the tea myself, tossing a blackened kettle on the fire until it boiled. Dinners we ate in the college hall; the servants were the waiters.

Dinners were bad but they were served with great éclat. At each place lay a menu printed in French, but no matter what it said the dinner was always the same—soup, a cut off the joint, and two veg (cabbage and brussels sprouts), and either a sweet (raspberry fool or a trifle) or a savoury, a lorn little dead fish on a slice of toast. The kitchens were in underground caverns and it was my fixed belief and still is that since the time of the Protectorate, two gigantic cauldrons of soup bubbled there eternally, one thick, the bill-poster type, the other thin, like the drainings from an umbrella stand. These two soups alternated night after night, jazzed up with croutons or barley and, by the time they reached the table, stone-cold and horrible. The silver, how-

ever, was something to see. I have drunk beer out of a silver
pint pot dated 1662 and the forks and spoons were worn
thin by the butlers' thumbs. None of the Oriel silver bore
a date earlier than 1640; we had been a Royalist college and
had melted down all the silver and given it to King Charles
when he held his court at Oxford. If we complained about
the food to the servants, they only laughed.

It took a while to find out what Haines' real work was or
what, in fact, was the real work of most English servants,
schoolmasters, tailors, and haberdashers. It is to instil and
preserve the traditions of the English Establishment. It did
not seem to be the job of parents, for in my day, before the
advent of so many government scholarships, your English
undergraduate was a young gentleman and had seen little of
his family. He was shipped off to prep school at the age of
seven or eight, to his public school at twelve or thirteen,
and then to the varsity. The molding of his character was
done by underlings and they were conscientious as the very
devil.

Haines soon let me know that he had been butler to Lord
'ill and regarded his present situation as something of a
comedown. His incessant question, "Will you be want-
ing . . ." a hot luncheon for guests or an almond cake with
my tea not only instructed me in the things I was supposed
to want but subtly conveyed by his tone that he was doing
the Lord's work in polishing a shaggy barbarian like myself,
an American in fact. After the bootleg booze at home, I
was delighted by the Oxford wineshops where you could
buy anything openly and I spent a good deal more than I
should have the first week or so. Every day Haines had to
lug bottles from the porter's lodge to my rooms. One afternoon I was sitting reading. Haines came in, banged a bottle
of Cointreau down on the table and said, "You won't be as
lissom as I am when you're forty-five and you go on drinking that rotgut stuff, sir."

You know how you can always remember the right crack five minutes too late? For once in my life I caught the proper timing and said straight out of some novel, "That will do, Haines."

"Yessir," he said, shocked as if I had bitten him. From then on the molding process took less of his time and slowly I learned that Oxford scouts liked to feel they were serving proper gents.

It was lissom Haines who told me I should call on my tutor and gave me the hours he would be in. He was the famous Ben Jonson scholar, Mr. Percy Simpson. Aldous Huxley and Robert Graves had been his pupils. I towered over him. His hair and mustache were white but he had a good red-beef-and-old-tawny-port complexion. Not perceptibly appalled, he received me standing before a bright fire in his college sitting room. (He lived miles away on Boar's Hill and walked back and forth each day. He still does, I understand, at ninety-five.) I was ready to shake hands but he fended that off by waving me to a chair. He sat down and began to talk in a tone of fatigued stateliness. He had, I thought, the true Oxford manner.

There is undoubtedly a manner. Some say it consists in the ability to talk intelligently for five minutes on any subject whatever, but those who say this are Englishmen who do not know they have the manner. Personally I think it is the peculiar confidence instilled at Eton, Harrow, Winchester, or wherever but kept impounded there and released afterward, the confidence that "we are the people who will run the nation and the Empire," a confidence that, considering the state of the Empire, must be diminished, fairly free-floating, even aimless by now. (When Churchill said, "I did not become the King's first minister to preside at the dissolution of the empire," his was the diapason of tradition. Not so, although more intelligent and realistic, Sir Hugh Foot's, who said not long ago, "We regard each colony released into independence as a victory." But, to be sure, the British have never demanded intelligence in their principal function-aries, only the right emotions.) I am aware that my defini-tion of the Oxford manner is not clear, that it would leave you utterly unprepared to deal with an Oxford man, so I had better tell a couple of stories that illustrate the manner perfectly.

The first is an old one from the days when Jowett was Master of Balliol. Every undergraduate had to appear in chapel so many times a term, so many mornings, so many evenings. They would let you in mornings in a dressing gown but come you had to. One day a youth appeared in Jowett's rooms and said, "I'm sorry but I shan't be able to keep my chapels. I'm a sun-worshiper."

"You are a sun-worshiper?" Jowett said out of a mar-moreal imperturbability, as if sun-worshipers were as com-mon in England as Druids.

"Yes."

"Very well. I excuse you from chapel."

The youth went away chuckling. Put one over.

At six next morning, full dark, his servant tapped him gently and said, "The Master's compliments, sir. The sun has just risen."

That is the manner. In America, of course, we would have sent the boy to a student counselor and made him fill out a questionnaire. We are a solemn people except in spots.

The second is the tale of a youth who vainly defied the seats of power but kept his aplomb to the end. He fell foul of the University proctors. The progs are young dons who stalk through the town several hours a day in mortarboards, gowns, and white tabs at their clavicles looking for student misdemeanants. They are each accompanied by two "bull-ers," servants in bowlers, wing collars, double-breasted black jackets, gray-striped trousers, and patent-leather shoes. In my time, although it has changed now, students were for-

bidden to drink in public houses. Drink itself was not forbidden—you could have all you wanted in your rooms—but
public houses offered the contamination of low company:
clerks from banks and stores, college servants, factory work-
ers from the Morris plant and such. You might be enjoying
a quiet can of beer, look up and find the Marshal Buller
courteously tipping his hat and asking the old question,
"Beg pardon, sir, are you a member of this university?" He
knew you were, of course. There was no danger of anyone
mistaking a young gentleman for a townee. At this point,
theoretically, you had three choices, hit him, run, or answer
and go with him. Hit him and he would hit you back, probably harder. Run and he would chase you and he knew the
lanes and back alleys of the town better than you did. If
you said, "Yes, I am," he would say, "Will you speak to the
Senior (or Junior) Proctor, please?"

The prog woud be waiting outside. He did not deign to
enter a pub himself. He would tip his cap and say, "Ah, good
evening. Will you give me your name and college, please?"

When you had, he would say, "Will you return to your
college at once, please?" That was the formula. It never
varied.

The next morning your scout woud bring you an engraved card which read,

The Senior Proctor will be pleased if
Mr Insertnameof
will wait upon him today at two o'clock
at the Old Clarendon Buildings

Whenever you had dealings with officers of the university,
as distinguished from those of the college, you had to dress
for it. You put on a dark suit, called *sub fusc*, wing collar,
and white dress tie, your mortarboard (which is not at
Oxford a kind of award for getting a degree but part of the

costume) and your gown. When you saw the prog, he would blandly fine you a pound if it was your first offense, thirty shillings for your second, two pounds for the third and so on. After three or four appearances, he might notify your college and your dean would fine you some more. No moral lectures, no promises of amendment extracted, just a steady belting of your pocketbook, wholly comprehensible, thoroughly English.

The young man of the story was caught by a proctor one night as he was seeing a beautiful barmaid home. It is, I believe, a university rule that an undergraduate must not be seen in public with a female who is not a lady. Barmaids, however lovely, are not ladies. The traditional question the prog asks is, "Will you introduce your companion?" Your true-born English gent cannot introduce a nonlady to another gent and properly he says "I'm sorry. I cannot," and the girl stands there and takes it.

On this occasion, when the prog asked the question, the young man did not crumble. He said, "Why, yes. This is my sister. The Senior Proctor."

The prog said, "Will you give me your name and college, please?"

The young man did.

"Will you see your uh–sister home and return to the college at once, please?"

The next day in the Old Clarendon Buildings, the prog said, "You were apprehended last evening in the company of a woman who you surely must know is one of the most notorious in Oxford and yet you introduce her as your sister."

"Yes, yes, I know. The family are frightfully cut up about it."

The prog laughed loud and long and said, "Very good. That will be ten pounds, please."

Is it worth fifty bucks to start an immortal story? Probably. It is this confidence, this aplomb, this perfect self-possession that irks Americans who don't have it, but it also informed the officers of the Coldstream Guards—the last regiment off at Dunkirk.

In my first fifteen minutes contending with Mr. Simpson's manner, he gently and blandly dealt me a stunning blow. He showed me what it was like to be treated as an intellectual adult, something that had never happened to me at Ann Arbor, where they were officially anxious and still are. As if it were as simple as shaving, he told me he would expect me to visit him once a week with a three-thousand-word paper on the author he had assigned. His primary assumption was that I had long since read all of English literature and the work of each week would be merely to read the principal critics, sift their opinions, and come up with my own.

"Perhaps you will care to go to some of the lectures," he murmured. He didn't tell me where they were, who was lecturing, or their subjects. He did, however, warn me away from a lady lecturer from one of the women's colleges. "Don't go near her. She's mad," he said fretfully.

It was Haines who showed me the lecture list in the porter's lodge. He told me how to get books out of the Bodleian Library and explained how, if I had sound feet, I could go to Blackwell's, lean against a wall, and read any book I was likely to need without being plagued to buy it by a clerk. I was so scared that I holed up and read about fourteen hours a day before I learned to pace myself. I had suffered a revelation: I was supposed to know all of English Literature, the whole damned shooting match.

During my tutorials, Mr. Simpson would doze comfortably in a big armchair before the fire while I read my paper aloud, but he woke up sharply to correct any mistakes and when I finished, he would criticise my critique with great good nature. For a long time I thought he thought I was an

idiot and an anecdote he told me about Huxley didn't help
me much, either. He said, "As you know, I begin somewhat
pompously, and I said to Huxley, 'Now, Mr. Huxley, we
will begin our study of English literature. . . .' He cut me off.
He said, 'Oh, I don't intend to *study* English literature. I
know it all already.' " Mr. Simpson laughed a silent laugh
that made him quiver. "And you know," he said, "he was
right."

During the first two weeks I was settling in, I didn't say
"Boo" to any undergraduate Englishman. I knew a couple
of Americans who had been on the *Aquitania* with me and
when I wanted to talk to someone, I went to their colleges
and talked to them. One, a figure in campus politics at his
university in the States, said the English were hard to "get
to know." He had been trying to make friends with them
by passing loud remarks on the weather or the food in hall
whenever he found two or three gathered together, but they
had only stared at him and he was hurt. I did not share
this eagerness or his disappointment. I was damned if I was
going to speak first, that was all.

One day early in the term the college freshmen were in-
vited to tea with the Dean in the Senior Common Room.
The Dean of Oriel was a clergyman, the Rev. J. W. C.
Wand, later Archbishop of Brisbane in a purple dickey, then
Bath and Wells, and when I watched the Queen's corona-
tion, there was the Dean in cope and mitre, Bishop of
London. He was very light on his feet—not just for a parson, for anyone. He lived on my staircase and on Saturday
nights when the drunks were baying in the quad and breaking things in people's rooms, the Dean would skip down the
stairs, seize the first student he saw and fine him ten pounds.
"But I didn't do anything," he would always wail. "Of
course not," the Dean would say, "but you know who did.
Get the money from them."

On the day we were his guests he wore a black dickey,

white dogcollar, and he was smoking a pipe. I got there early along with a couple of other freshmen before the S.C.R. was open. We just stood there. At last one of the Englishmen said to me, "Would you have a match?" I gave him one and we started to talk in much the same way we would have at home. That night coming out of hall after dinner he said, "Come along and have some beer." His name was Dick Gorton and while I now realize it was rather daring of him to entertain an American, he dared it and we became friends, no sweat.

We became friends in the American sense, that is. Sit next to an American in a plane, train, or bus and he is apt to tell you the story of his life pretty candidly and with enough detail to last the journey. Is this a hangover from the frontier where every man appeared as a free-standing individual unencumbered by a personal history and so had to identify himself, sometimes by bragging? Hear an Englishman speak and you will know his class. Look at his necktie, and if you know how to read it it will tell you his school, college, or regiment. In England these two things are enough to establish normal personal relations. Friendship, I discovered, takes time.

Nobody believes this because they erect a façade to hide it, but the English are a boilingly emotional people—much more so than the Italians, who throw joy and anger around casually, more so than the French, who use emotion judiciously, equally with the Spaniards but with greater variety since they are not a Catholic people. If proof is wanted, look at their poetry. Reach the point of genuine friendship with an Englishman and you become emotionally engaged. He will expect you to hate the things he hates, love the things he loves, and the whole spectrum in between. Once an Englishman told me his sister had married a Chinaman. As he said it, he burst into tears. Mentally I shrugged and thought, "So she married a Chinaman." At once I could see that although he was my friend, I was not really his. I couldn't feel as he did. He had admitted me to this intimacy but I had not reciprocated. We are drier than they.

My relations with Dick Gorton were genial and offhand. He didn't tell me where he lived or what his father did, but we talked nearly every day and went to pubs together. He introduced me to such friends of his as he thought would like me. (They do not introduce casually. I have gone to tea in a man's rooms with two or three others, not been introduced, talked volubly to everyone the whole afternoon, and next day had one of the guests pass me without speaking. This takes some getting used to.)

One of Dick's friends was a tall youth he had been at school with, a rather hearty type named Michael Horner. He was never hearty with me and we didn't really hit it off, but he was kind enough to ask me up to his rooms for a Saturday night near the first of November; said his brother was coming up from London.

I couldn't give either Michael or his brother much thought. I was too busy frantically trying to learn to handle Number Six oar in an eight-oared shell, and I had a problem that was simultaneously moral and financial. Early in the term the College had informed me that I owed them fifty pounds Caution Money, payable forthwith. Caution Money was a deposit against anything I might break. I had been told that my term battel (room and board) would come to about fifty pounds, payable at the end of the Christmas holidays. I had received a stipend from the Scholarship of a hundred pounds. These two bites would leave me exactly nothing on which to get to Paris during Christmas—we had six weeks' vacation. I was in despair and I wrote a despairing letter to a lovely girl back home. Her answer had just come, containing a hundred-dollar bill, a yellow-back. This bill burning in my wallet seemed to pose a moral problem. It is hard to remember what the terms of the problem were that troubled me so. The girl's family was rich and sending me the money was no hardship. However, the phrase *kept man* drifts back. I wrestled with it for days and at last reluctantly sent the money back to her. I took the letter to the lodge for Bough to give to the postman. I felt smug immediately.

Coming out of the lodge, I met Gorton.

"You're coming to Michael's tonight," he said.

"Yes. He said his brother was coming up from town."

"Hell of a man, Peter Horner. He's in The Blues," Gorton said.

I didn't know what that meant. I was continually picking up bits of information about English life and if their meaning was not obvious, I kept quiet. If I thought anything, it was not that Peter Horner was melancholic in some odd British way, rather that he was a professional football player. Actually, he was a lieutenant in His Majesty's Royal Horse Guards (The Blues).

After dinner Gorton and I climbed two flights of stairs to Michael's rooms. They *were* paneled and he had a big fire going. He was just opening some beer for four other men when we came in. It was easy to spot Peter Horner. Shorter than his brother, he had a mustache, red; hair, red; face, red. He was in what Guardsmen call plain clothes, a tweed jacket and flannel bags, and he wore his handkerchief up his sleeve as Guardsmen have done since the Regency, when trousers were too tight for pockets, but of course I didn't know he was a soldier then. Michael introduced me. "Peter? Allan Seager. My brother."

We both nodded and muttered. I had learned that much— never try to shake hands.

We all sat down and attacked the beer in almost unflawed silence. The Oxonians were clearly scared to death of Peter Horner because of his great age—which was about the same as my own, twenty-three. They put back the beer steadily, perhaps in the hope it would do their talking for them.

Desperately Gorton said, "See many girls in town, Peter?"

Peter gave a lieutenant's snort, a noise that would acquire greater resonance and contempt when he became a colonel. It conveyed that Gorton's question was unacceptable and preposterous. Later when I knew some London debutantes I learned that they seldom had escorts other than Guards officers. The snort crushed Dick, however.

Michael Horner kept saying gamely, "Beer anyone? Beer?" And eventually little conversations broke out, conversations that did not include Peter Horner. He took a stance with an elbow on the chimneypiece and smiled a choleric condescending smile at the children playing.

About the time they began to sing "The Ram of Derbyshire" (this didn't take long because they were all learning to drink) I found myself standing at the other end of the mantel facing Peter Horner. The wrong terrain, as it turned out.

Vaguely I remember one of the guests leaving and returning a few minutes later with a bottle of Scotch. Michael opened it and placed it, two glasses, and a siphon of soda between us. "Perhaps you'd like some whisky," he said. To this day I believe he got it mainly for his brother, who seemed bored. Anyhow Peter and I each took a drink. We began to talk.

After about the third drink I realized that the others had ranged themselves in chairs and sofas to watch. I was in a drinking contest with Peter Horner. I don't think it was prearranged, but there was no doubt it was a contest. I could tell by the way Peter evened up the drinks.

I forget what we talked about but it came out smooth and polite with no overt acknowledgment that we were competing at all. Over the edge of my glass I gauged my man. He was about five-nine and a hundred and fifty pounds. Other things being equal, I could hold more than he could. Also he had been reared on the soft true tender whiskies of the Highlands, the mild metropolitan gins. He had never drunk sheep-dip or beer that made your lips numb. I figured I had the edge.

I made every other round of drinks and I made the rounds deeper than his to show my confidence and depress his. Our talk flowed very easily and the others listened, perhaps for signs. The first bottle of Scotch went down quickly but when I saw Michael approaching with a fresh bottle and a new siphon, I began to see that this was serious. True, there were beads of sweat glistening above Peter Horner's eyebrows, but there were probably beads of sweat above my own and anyhow we were standing by an open fire, a grave mistake. Had I been handicapping the event I wouldn't have bet either one of us would finish.

It didn't occur to us to move. Although we had agreed on none, rules seemed to be growing up. We could not sit down. We could not stop talking. We could not even change our positions, weight on one leg, one elbow on the mantel, and the pace of our drinking had to appear to be regulated by our conversation as if we had met to talk, not to drink. The way to learn the Oxford manner is to act it out.

The paneled walls were the first to go. I seemed to be standing in the middle of a blasted heath but a hot heath. The room got a lot darker and when a hand took the empty Scotch bottle off the mantel and set a bottle of Drambuie in its place, I got tunnel vision. I could see only what I was looking dead at, chiefly Peter Horner. His flush had waned. His face was as white as paper enlivened by two little angry red eyes.

I like Drambuie in its place, but its place is not to sweeten the rear of a flood of Scotch. It was hell and I foresaw that the one who survived it would probably win. One foot, according to the rules, was still nonchalantly on the fender (the fire was dying now), but I had the other knee locked to keep from falling down. The spectators when I looked square at them seemed to be a row of balloons with faces painted on them, gently floating up and down, their voices the giggly gibber of a record played too fast. Mentally I had dwindled. Peter and I didn't talk much now, it was too hard. I had one sedimentary thought, "Stick with it." Long since I had seemed to feel a flagstaff in my skull with the Stars and Stripes floating from it and I could almost see the Union Jack hanging limp on its pole above Peter. I was fighting for my country.

After a long time, peering and cocking my head sideways, I made out a single bottle of beer standing where the Drambuie had been. As if from down in a valley a voice hallooed, "That's all there is."

I swung my head in the direction of the voice. "There isn't any more?" I said, echoing Ethel Barrymore.

"It's all we can find."

At once I began to think jerkily and briskly. I knew what I had to do. I had to shake hands with Peter, thank Michael and tell him what a hell of a lot of fun it had been, get to the doorway, go down two perilous flights of stairs upright and unsupported across two quads, penetrate the blackness of my corridor, hang up my clothes and get to bed. I did this with the feeling that I was on a high wire where one slip—the abyss. I also felt idiotically that there should be applause somewhere.

The next morning after Haines woke me, I stumbled into my sitting room and stared at my breakfast. I didn't feel too bad. The hangover hadn't started yet. I was sitting there blankly when Dick Gorton scampered in.

"You won! You won! You know where Peter Horner spent the night?" he asked.

"Where?"

"In a stall in the lats, his head right down on his bloody knees. Michael and I just now forked him out of there and put him to bed. Bloody good show!"

I didn't feel any triumph but, then, I didn't feel anything

else either. I went on sitting there. The liquor gradually wore off. The hangover began. By teatime I was intellectually convinced I couldn't live out the day, but after a night's sleep I felt all right.

When I went back into society, the word had gotten around. I was accepted in the college. Even the Dean nodded as we passed in the quad. While my grandfather might have overcome his Victorian scruples so far as to applaud my victory over an officer of the Brigade of Guards, it was not his ghostly pleasure that pleased me. It was rather that my eyes were opened. England was not the old home after all. It was a foreign country where you lived among strangers. You couldn't count on the family affection of cousins once removed. Respect had to be worked for even if you had to drink them bowlegged to get it.

* XI *

The Joys of Sport at Oxford

During my first week at Oxford I decided not to go out for any sports in the fall, or Michaelmas, term. My college offered Rugby, soccer, field hockey, and something referred to as "the boats." I had never done any of these. They were all outdoor sports, and outdoors was where it was raining. For a fee I could also have joined a team of chaps who trotted informally through the dripping countryside in mild competition with a group from another college. Or I could have subscribed to a beagling club and worn a green coat, stout laced boots, and a hemispheric little green velvet cap and legged it over the fields behind the dogs in search of hares and perhaps gotten a furry paw glued to a wooden shield as a trophy to hang in my room. The rain discouraged me, however; I got soggy enough walking to lectures. After my first visit to Mr. Simpson the fall term seemed a good time to lie up in front of a fire and get a good start on my reading.

I did this. I read heavily, but after three weeks I noticed a nervousness coming over me. And after the fourth week I knew what it was. I had been getting up every half-hour to look out the window. Now, there was nothing to look at out of my window but the college coal pile and beyond it a fifteen-foot wall topped with broken glass to keep students from climbing in after midnight. I was looking for a girl. I had got used to having dates at home but, after a day or two of scrutiny, I could tell that I was not likely to see one poised like a mountain goat on top of the coal.

I had won my Rhodes scholarship because I was the only man at the state examination who had worn a stiff collar. I did not wear it to Oxford. Instead, to help things along, I got some new clothes. I bought shirts with what we used to call bootlegger (tab) collars, a tweed jacket, and gray flannel "bags." Not knowing that Americans move differently from the English—looser, somehow—and that you can identify one as far as you can see him, I believed my attire made me indistinguishable from an Old Etonian, and I had peeped at the English girls in the lecture halls, thinking that I had at least an even start with the Englishmen. I was appalled at what I saw.

There are four women's colleges at Oxford. Most of their undergraduates were going to be schoolmistresses and looked it. They wore rugged tweeds full of sticks of heather and twigs of gorse that stank in the wet weather, and they had big frightening muscles in their legs from bike riding. A beautiful American girl would, I thought, be glad to make the acquaintance of a compatriot because of her loneliness.

I spotted an American girl in one of my lectures and she was beautiful. By asking around among other Americans I learned her name, which I have forgotten, and her address. I called. A maid let me in and went to fetch her. When she came in I said, "I wonder if you would care to drink some sherry with me this afternoon and bring a friend." I didn't want her friend but the university had ruled that young women could visit young men's rooms only in pairs.

"I don't think so," she said coldly.

"Tea, perhaps?"

"No."

"Ah, milk?"

She walked out.

I didn't know then, as I came to later, that American girls in Oxford don't want to meet Americans; they want to meet Englishmen.

After this rebuff I might have lingered before my fire until spring in a dangerous inertia, dangerous because the elements of English diet are extremely reluctant to move without help after you have ingested them. But I was asked to go on the river. I was flattered to be asked, and I went.

The river is the Thames, but it is mysteriously called the Isis where it flows through Oxford, and the way to it is past the walled garden where Lewis Carroll, himself an admirer of girls—but girls rather younger than those who interested me—wrote *Alice in Wonderland* while he was a don at Christ Church. Then you go down a long alley under tremendous elms and you come to the college barges. They are, or were, houseboats and they never go anyplace. They are moored tight to the bank and are used as dressing rooms. They are painted white, highly ornamented with colored moldings, and they made a pretty sight lined up along the riverbank.

The only rowing I had done was to pull a flat-bottomed rowboat over the weedbeds of small lakes after bass. I was not the only novice, however, and we all had to put up with two or three days of "we call this an oar" kind of instruction before they let us sit down and try to put our backs into it. The president of the Boat Club, Tom Smith, was the coach. There was no professional coaching in any sport (there still isn't) except that the varsity cricketers and swimmers had professionals come to look at them occasionally, during the season. Tom Smith told me I might make a No. 6, and he gave me politely to know that Six was supposed to move a lot of water. At 12 stone 9 (177 pounds) I was the biggest man in the boat and, as I found out later, in the college. The English had been children during World War I.

They had grown up on rationed food and I think this is why they were not very big.

At my college we were lucky. We began the season in a proper shell no thicker than a cigar box. I saw an unfortunate youth step right through it into the river because he had not set his foot exactly on the keel when he climbed in. We also had movable seats on little wheels and swivel row-locks (pronounced *rollocks*). I kept hearing a saying, "English rowing is ten years behind the times; Cambridge rowing is twenty years behind the times; Oxford rowing is forty years behind the times."

The varsity boat and those of some of the colleges began training exactly as their forefathers had done when Victoria was a young queen. In the first weeks of the season the varsity eight swung grandly down the river in a craft that resembled the war canoe of some obscure tribe. It was heavy enough for the open sea. It had board seats and the rowlocks were merely two straight pegs you laid the oars between. A month's workouts in this scow certainly preserved tradition, but they also gave a man a set of boils as big as walnuts. A varsity oarsman spent more time on his feet than a cop, and when he sat down he bellowed. With such a fine start, the boils lasted all season, even after the varsity shifted to the shell they would use against Cambridge. At my college, Oriel, we avoided all this pain. Daringly unorthodox, we rowed the Jesus style.

This was not blasphemy and we did not kneel in prayer before taking to the water. The Jesus style was developed at Jesus College, Cambridge, by a man named Steve Fairbairn. Succinctly put, it was "blade form." This meant that if your oar blade was right, nothing else mattered. Opposed to this was the practice of the varsity, all the other colleges and, I believe, American crews, called "body form," which meant that if your body was correctly poised, the blade had to be right.

A body-form crew was coached right down to its fingertips. You were supposed to keep a straight back, stare perpetually at the fifth or sixth cervical vertebra of the man in front of you, and never move your head. The head, it was explained, is a big knob weighing sixteen or eighteen pounds and any loose, unexpected movement with it might upset the boat. A body-form crew is impressive to watch. The muscular decorum makes its members look virtuous and clean-limbed. Perhaps this is its own reward, for a blade-form crew, rowing with backs bending comfortably and gandering around at the blades, may look raffish and sloppy but probably is going as fast as the body-form boys.

We trained all the fall into December. It was mostly just rowing. The Thames is a canal with locks all the way to London and, if we were taking a long paddle, eight or ten miles, we had to pass Iffley lock when we went one way and Osney lock when we went the other. I can remember sitting in Osney lock one dark afternoon, waiting for it to fill, with ice forming on the oars and flakes of snow as big as goosefeathers wetting the back of my skimpy little Jaeger shirt, and it was no consolation to remember that the Miller's Wife in *The Canterbury Tales* had probably lived within a furlong.

On short days when we stayed within Iffley lock we were coached by Tom Smith riding a bicycle beside us on the towpath. I doubt if we rowed as much as Washington or Yale. There was no other training. Beer was believed strengthening; gin would keep coxswains small. No one spoke of cigarettes at all. Green as I was, I didn't know whether I was in shape or not, but it didn't make much difference, because term ended about the middle of December and I took off for six weeks in Paris.

The Bump Races come in two sets, late in January and early in May. They are rowed for six days, Thursday through Saturday and Monday through Wednesday. The colloquial name for the January races is Toggers, the formal

one Torpids, but no one could tell me why. The May races
are called Eights, and they are quite social. If you have a
girl, you bring her, give her luncheons of hock and lobster
mayonnaise and she sits on the top of your barge to watch
you sweat. Toggers are grimmer because January is grimmer.

Bump races are examples of much made of little. The
Thames is a small river at Oxford; in fact, I think Ralph
Boston could jump over it at a place called the Gut if he
took a good run. There were about twenty-five rowing
colleges at Oxford, and each college put two boats in the
river, the larger colleges, like Balliol, three, sometimes four,
so there were perhaps sixty in all. I doubt if you could row
sixty eight-oared shells abreast at Poughkeepsie, and you
certainly can't on the Isis, so they start one behind another
and chase the one in front.

Small stakes are driven into the bank sixty feet apart. To
each stake a rope sixty feet long is fixed. The cox holds
the other end and lets the boat drift until it is taut. Each
boat has a starter. Five minutes before time all the starters
gather at a little brass cannon in a hayfield to synchronize
their stopwatches with a chronometer. Then they come
back and stand on the bank beside their boats, saying "Two
minutes gone. Three minutes gone" to the yawning oars-
men in the river below. In the last minute they count off
the quarters, and finally "Ten, nine, eight, seven, six, five,
four, come forward, are you ready?" and "Bang!" goes
the little brass cannon. The college bargeman gives you a
hell of a shove with a boathook and away you go, the cox
howling the beat at about fifty strokes a minute. It is very
common to black out during the first thirty seconds. As
soon as you are under way, the stroke drops to about forty,
but not much less, because the course from Iffley lock to
the top of the barges is only about a mile and a half.

Most of the members of your college are scrambling along

the towpath beside you, yelling and shooting off guns. You can't tell whether the boat behind you is gaining, because you are watching stroke's oar or your own, but if the cox's voice rises to a scream and he starts counting to raise the beat you know you are overtaking the boat ahead. When your bow overlaps his stern, the cox turns the rudder sharply. Bow touches stern. This is the bump.

When you make a bump, the next day your boat starts in the place of the bumped boat. You go up or down each day according to your prowess. The final aim, which may take several years to achieve, is to become Head of the River, the first boat in line.

I came back from Paris not in the best of shape. A wisdom tooth had started acting up. It ached and swelled monotonously. I made my apologies to Tom Smith, and he found another Six. For a week I tried to ignore it, hoping the swelling would go away. It didn't and I asked the Dean to recommend a dentist. I found this man in what I took to be a large bedroom with the bed moved out. The walls were covered with flowered wallpaper, and a chromo of Watts' *Hope* hung on the wall. He sat me down in a chair with four legs. He took a look and, as God is my judge, he prescribed an infusion of camomile and poppyhead—not opium, poppyhead—with which to bathe the afflicted parts. I was not sleeping much and I was smoking about fifty Players a day, but I bathed away conscientiously. It didn't do any good. The swelling went gruesomely on. When I looked as if I were trying to conceal a scarlet pippin in my cheek I went back to the dentist and said, "Lance this, will you?" He bumbled and said at last, "I can't. I'm not a dental surgeon." So he took me to a real surgeon, who had his learning son in the office, and there before a blazing coal fire, the three together gave me gas and lanced it. Afterward I didn't feel good, but at least I didn't feel like a bomb about to go off.

That night I was sitting in front of my fire, reading and bathing my wound with a little neat whisky when Tom Smith knocked at my door. He said that his No. 6 had just come down with a bad case of flu. Toggers started the next day. Would I care to fill in? It was so casual and the honor of the U.S.A. depended so heavily on it that I said I would be delighted—which was a lie.

On the first day of Toggers I was personally lucky. I had to row only the first six strokes. When the little brass cannon went off, we laid into the first strokes hard. The cox had just shouted, "Six!" when No. 7 in front of me caught a crab. If you are quick you can sometimes lie flat and let the oar pass over your head. Seven was not quick. He was probably blacked out, and the butt of the oar caught him in the belly and jackknifed him out of the boat. Falling, he broke his oar smack off at the rowlock. The boat staggered. There were cries of "Man overboard!" and Dawson-Grove, the cox, was yelling oaths like a banshee. I don't believe it is possible to overturn an eight-oared boat, but we nearly made it. In the confusion, Exeter came tearing into us from behind and sheared off all the oars on the starboard side. It was a mess. No. 7 avoided having Exeter's keel bash his head in by cannily staying under water until after the collision; then he swam soggily ashore. Our race was over for that day and I was barely winded.

The next day, with new oars, we caught St John's on the Green Bank and made a bump. In fact, we made five bumps in all during Toggers. If a boat makes five bumps in Toggers or four in Eights the college is required by custom to stand its members a Bump Supper, a big jollification in honor of the Boat Club. The Maunciple outdoes himself and provides a really good meal with fresh soup (I think) and champagne at will. Alumni gather and there are sherry parties. Since many Oriel undergraduates study theology, many of its graduates are parsons, but Church of England clergy are not stuffy. They go to sherry parties, and they don't stand around with a glass in their hands for the look of the thing, either.

At our Bump Supper the hall was in an uproar because of the sherry parties beforehand. Cheers were started but forgotten. Boating songs were begun, broken off, and begun again. A stately portrait of Matthew Arnold, once an Oriel don, hung on the wall. A swaying youth, his boiled shirt coming out in welts from spilled champagne, pegged an orange clean through Matthew's jaw just at the mutton-chop. A bonfire sprang up in the front quad, fed by side tables, chairs, and Van Gogh reproductions. The son of a Scottish laird broke into the Provost's lodgings, stole all the shoes belonging to that good old man (now knighted for his translations of Aristotle), and hurled them all into the flames.

High above the quad in a third-floor bedroom a man named Antony Henley crouched, waiting for the supper to finish. Tony had collected half the chamber pots in the college. (They used them then, and it is no more than even money they use them now.) In a room directly op-posite, another man had collected the other half. A rope hung in a curve from one window to the other. At last the dons appeared under the porch of the hall, chatting only less than boisterously from the champagne. They were in full fig—dinner jackets, long M.A. gowns, and mortar-boards. They walked down the steps in the wavering light of the bonfire. At that moment a shower of broken crockery fell on their heads. Tony and his friend were sticking the rope ends through the pot handles and letting them slide down the rope two at a time. When they met they broke and fell on the Dean, the Provost, the Bursar, the Gold-smith's Reader, a bishop or two, and other dignitaries. Big joke.

The party went on all night, consuming untold bottles

of Pommery and Piper-Heidsieck and much of the movable furniture of the college. At one point, I was told, seven drunken archdeacons danced around the bonfire, a spectacle very likely unmatched since the martyrdom of Ridley and Latimer, who had been burned some years earlier in Broad Street and from the top of whose monument the Oxford Alpine Club hangs a chamber pot each year.

The next morning the groans of hangover were decently stifled by the mists in the quad. The scouts were out with rakes and shovels, cleaning away the empties, the shards of crockery, and the ashes of the bonfire strewn with the nails and eyelets of the Provost's shoes. Antony Henley was haled before the Dean, presented with a bill for upward of a hundred and fifty chamber pots and laughingly fined ten pounds. Toggers were over. I have never rowed since, nor drunk so much champagne.

I was not, so to speak, an oarsman by trade, I was a swimmer. The rowing I had done, while exhausting and in some ways amusing, merely passed the time until the swimming season opened in the third, or Hilary, term. The trouble was, I couldn't find any place to "go out" for swimming. There was no varsity pool, I discovered, but I heard somewhere that the swimmers used the Merton Street Baths.

The Baths were in a grubby brick building, built long before with what seemed an ecclesiastical intent, for they had long Gothic windows in front. The pool itself, gently steaming in the cold of the building, was a gloomy trapezoidal tank, and I learned later that it was exactly twenty-five yards long on one side and twenty-two and a half yards on the other—which made for some tricky finishes in a race. The bathing master said there hadn't been any gentlemen from the varsity near the place in months. He suggested that I see Mr. Pace in Merton College, the club president.

After I had knocked, Pace opened his door six inches, no more.

"Yes?" he said.

"Mr. Pace?"

"Yes," he said.

"My name is Seager."

"Yes?" he said.

"I wanted to ask you about the swimming."

"Oh. Ah," he said. Then he opened his door. "Do come in."

I went in.

"Seager? Oh, yes. Someone mentioned your name. From the States, aren't you? Mitchigan? A good club, I believe."

"We were national champions last year."

"Really? Just what did you want to know?"

"When do you start training?"

"Oh, I'll let you know. I'll send you a note round the week before we begin. Will that do?"

It was the Oxford manner again. He was effortlessly making my enthusiasm seem not merely comic but childishly comic. However, it is just as well to be candid. I was after their records, and I didn't know then that he was Oxford's best sprinter. "I'd like to start now," I said. "I'm not in very good shape."

"I daresay you could use the Baths. Cost you a bob a time until we start meeting."

He waved his hand nonchalantly.

"Cheers," he said, and I left.

It was only later that I learned I had committed a *faux pas*. I was always finding out things later. You did not "go out" for the varsity. College sports, OK—you could turn up whenever you liked. But the varsity was strictly invitational, so much so that in my day the varsity Boat Club had never used an American oar. There was a faint general resentment of Americans and Colonials taking over Oxford sports. However, I paid my shilling and trundled a slow half-mile every day up and down the Bath. It was like swimming in church.

In a couple of weeks Pace sent his note round and the season opened. I was astounded. It was not so much that they swam badly (I had more or less expected that from their record times) it was that they worked so little. In fact, they didn't *work* at all. They swam until they felt tired and quit for the day, refreshed. Where was the old pepper, the old fight? Slowly I began to comprehend the English attitude toward sports, which, unless Dr. Bannister changed it drastically with his great meticulous mile, is this: sports are for fun. If you are good at one or two of them, it is somewhat in the nature of a divine gift. Since the gift is perpetual, it is there every day and you can pull out a performance very near your best any time. With a little practice to loosen the muscles and clear the pipes, you are ready for the severest tests.

I was drinking beer one night in Balliol College with several men, one of them an Olympic runner, a fifteen-hundred-meter man. It is rare that a subject so trivial as sports would come up in Balliol, the intellectual center of England, but it came up and eventually came down to the question of how fast could this Olympic man run fifteen hundred meters at the moment? We all piled into a couple of taxis and drove out to the Oxford Sports Ground, where there was a cinder track. The runner, full of confidence and beer, supplied a stopwatch and a flashlight, and there in his street clothes, in the rain, in the dead of night, this man took off and ran fifteen hundred meters in just over four minutes. This proved to me that the English were right but it did not prove to me that I was wrong. I knew I could not swim a hundred yards in less than a minute, untrained.

But I stayed untrained. It seemed overly zealous to go on chugging up and down after all the other members of the club had showered, dressed, and come to stand at the edge of the Bath to watch me as if I were a marine curiosity, like a dugong. I tried it a couple of times and quit. I swam as little as they did, no more. Then there was the problem of entertainment after the matches—they didn't call them meets. There was little university swimming in England, so our competition was usually a town club whose members might be aquatic plumbers and carpenters—not gentlemen, you see. With a splendid condescension, we set out a table loaded with whisky, beer, and wine after each match, and we had to drink to make our guests feel at home so that caste differences would be concealed and we could pretend to be all jolly good sportsmen together. After a match, say, in London with the Paddington police, the coppers would set out a table of whisky, beer, and wine, and we had to drink to show our appreciation of their hospitality. This drinking was not a detestable chore, but it meant that, with two matches a week, we were getting mildly stoned just in the way of business. This was not how I had been taught to train, and it came over me suddenly how far morality had invaded sports in the U.S.

I won all my races except one, but the times were shamefully slow and I was chased right down to the wire in all of them. In May, John Pace had the whole club to tea in his rooms. There was an hour of conversation interspersed with tomato and cucumber sandwiches. Then Pace stood up by the chimneypiece. "Now, chaps," he began facetiously (I never heard anyone use *chaps* except facetiously). "You know we swim the Tabs two weeks from now. *Tabs* meant Cambridge, from the Latin *Cantabrigia*. "Please smoke only after meals and cut down your beer to a pint a day. And do try to swim every day between now and then."

People clapped and cried "Hear! Hear!" as if Pace had been in the House of Commons. I gathered we were in hard training from then on. I had not gone under sixty-one seconds for a hundred yards yet, and I had heard that Cambridge had a fancy dan named Hill who had done fifty-eight. I was scared.

Someone said, "This rationing of beer, John. What if we're sconced?"

"Behave yourselves and you won't be," Pace said.

In Oxford dining halls a sconce is a penalty exacted in the spring of the year. It is a welcome penalty, eagerly exacted. If you showed up late for dinner or wearing something odd like a turtleneck sweater or if you said something that could be remotely construed as offensive, you were sconced. Once I defined a mistress as something between a mister and a mattress.

"We'll have a sconce on you for that," the man next to me said. He wrote my offense in Latin on the back of a menu, *Seager dixit obscenissime,* and had a waiter take it up to high table to be approved by the Dean. It was a formality. The Dean always approved sconces. "What will you take it in?" I was asked. In theory you had to drink a silver quart pot of some liquid, bottoms up. In practice you had no choice; custom said old beer. Once I saw a man take it in fresh cow's milk and he never lived it down. It is the sort of thing planters discuss in Kenya and Borneo twenty years later.

The strength of English beer is indicated by the number of Xs on the barrel. Ale is the weakest, one X. Bitter beer is two Xs. Old beer is five Xs, about as strong as sherry. It is never iced, but in college it comes from the cellars and it might as well be. It looks almost coal-black and it is as thick as stout. It is hard but not impossible to drink it all down at one go. If you do, the man who sconced you has to pay for it. If you fail, it is passed around the table like a loving cup. But the minute you set the pot down empty, you're drunk.

The Cambridge match was held at the Bath Club, then

in Dover Street, London. It was a posh club. (I like the origin of *posh*. When people used to tour the Orient from England, the most expensive cabins on the P & O boats, those that made the most of the prevailing winds and the least of the sun, were on the port side going and the starboard side returning, so the luggage for those cabins was marked *P.O.S.H.*, that is, "port out, starboard home.") We took an afternoon train down to London already dressed in white ties, black trousers, and our blazers, and with an affectation of gaiety we sauntered up Piccadilly in the early evening and into the Bath Club. I knew I had to fear this Cambridge speedster, Hill, who had done fifty-eight seconds because I had done only sixty-one that season. (I had done sixty-one when I was a long whey-faced boy of fifteen in high school in Tennessee.) My fear was degrading. That's why I was mad; it was a real fear. And I felt that my teammates had begun to wonder when I was going to demonstrate that I didn't fit one of the stock British images of the American, all piss and wind.

I figured I could take Hill in the fifty if I scrambled, but in the hundred I knew I would have to swim and I figured I could swim about seventy-five yards before I blew up. Since the English started slow and finished fast, I figured I would start fast, get a big lead, frighten him, and finish on whatever I had left.

The Bath Club looked like a court levee, the ladies in those English evening gowns, the men in white ties and tail coats, and the Old Blues wore their blazers. Diamonds glittered. I detected dowagers with lorgnons, a colorful throng. *Posh.* The club pool was twenty-five yards long on both sides but it was dark at one end. Since you can bump your head into a goose egg or even oblivion if you slam into a turn you can't see, I wet a towel and hung it over the far end in my lane to make a white spot. As I walked back I heard resentful murmurs from the spectators. "He's an Ameddican," as if what I had done were cunning or illicit.

The fifty-yard race went as I had expected. I scrambled. I won in a record time of twenty-five seconds. I went back to the dressing room to worry about the hundred. Hill was a fleshy little fellow whose fat might hide more stamina than I had.

I swam the first two lengths of the hundred in twenty-five seconds, and after the third length, I looked back at Hill. He was thirty feet behind, but I was not encouraged because I could tell I was going to blow up. I blew and finished the last twenty-five yards with a frantic overhand, dazzled by fatigue, my head out all the way so I could breathe. But I won by a yard and they said it was a new record, fifty-seven seconds. My teammates shouted and pounded me on the back as if I had done well. My shabby little victories gave Oxford the match.

The adulation of the English for sports figures is greater than that in this country, possibly because a sound sports records keeps a chap from being too clever—which is repugnant. (Churchill was too clever by half right up until the blitz.) Let a man die who has not specially distinguished himself as an admiral, a cabinet member, or a press lord, and if he has been a Blue, Oxon or Cantab, the obituary will very likely be headed OLD BLUE'S DEMISE. That is what is important. A few months after my victories I was having tea with some people at a public tearoom in Oxford.

A man came up to the table, a student, and said to me, "Is this Mr. Seager, the famous swimmer?"

I looked him straight in the eye for maybe three seconds. He seemed perfectly serious. "I'm Seager," I answered finally.

"May I shake your hand?" he said.

I shook hands and he went away, pleased apparently. Nobody at my table seemed to think any of this strange, and
I let my self-esteem expand a little.

It didn't get punctured for two years. I was back in Ann
Arbor then and I happened to run into Matt Mann, my
former coach.

"Say, I hear you got a couple of English records," he
said. Matt had been born in Yorkshire and he had held English records himself.

"Yes," I said. I couldn't look at him.

"What were your times?"

"Twenty-five. Fifty-seven," I mumbled. I had been a
bad boy.

"Fifty-seven! Were you dragging something?" he said
jovially.

Surprising myself, I said defiantly, "Matt, it was fun."

And it had been, all of it, the massive courtesy of the
swimming policemen, the singing in the pub afterward, the
soirée at the Bath Club—not real glory, which means work,
but a hell of a lot of fun.

* XII *

The Cure

One grim March morning I decided not to get up. It was not the soft implacable discouragement the day offered that held me bedfast, for it was a day like any other at this season. A cold fog would hang in the quads until noon when perhaps the gloom would weaken and you could spot the quarter-hearted sun, pale, remote, fuzzy. I never wanted to get up on days like this but unless I did and by nine, my servant was empowered by the rules of the college to call a doctor. It seemed a good idea.

When he came into my sitting room and found my breakfast uneaten, I could feel his disapproval seeping through the wall. Thought I had a hangover, probably. He knocked at the bedroom door.

"Come in, Haines," I called.

He came in, clucked like an old hen, and said reproachfully, "A long lie, sir."

"Yes."

"You didn't eat your breakfast."

"I think you'd better call a doctor. I'm not well." In any dialogue with Haines, I had long since cast myself in the role of the young master because it impressed him and squeezed from him phrases I had seen only in novels.

"Very good, sir. Touch of flu?"

"Probably." I felt hot and languid.

The doctor agreed. He was a red-faced little man with a bushy mustache and a D.S.O. ribbon in his lapel. He examined me deftly and quickly. "Touch of flu," he said. "Stay in bed over the week end." He put his stethoscope in his bag, snapped it to, and was on his way out the door. I coughed once.

As if I had shot at him he whirled and performed what every doctor has told me since was a brilliant piece of diagnosis. "Any sputum?"

"Yes," I said.

He whipped two little oblong pieces of glass out of his bag and took a sample. As one knows vague disconnected facts like the capital of Iceland (Reykavik), I knew that sputum samples were connected with the diagnosis of tuberculosis—but cases of TB, like arson and heartbreak, were things that happened to other people, not to me, and I turned over and went back to sleep.

An hour later the doctor came stamping back into my room. "You've got tuberculosis. Where do you want to go, Switzerland or the States?"

Half-asleep and feverish I sat up. "How bad is it?"

"I can't tell yet. Take a taxi this afternoon, come to my office, and I'll take an X ray of your chest."

"Oh, I can walk."

"You won't be walking much from now on."

"Can't you give me some idea, just a conjecture?"

"I can't be sure, but from the look of those slides I'd say a year and a half in bed."

I did not believe this. I had once been flung sixty feet through the air from an auto wreck, landed on my head, knocked my upper teeth horizontal, and I had not gone to bed at all. "I think I'd better go home."

"I'll just stop in and tell your dean. Two o'clock, don't forget," he said and went out.

After the X ray the doctor informed me that I was a far-advanced case and I could very probably look forward to a cure lasting two years if everything went well. This still did not make sense. Lie down for two years?

Back in bed I became pretty gloomy. I seemed to have been betrayed—but by whom? Properly put, the question would split me in two. I should have to ask my body, "Why didn't you let me know?" But of course, it (I) had let me know. In December I had swum in a meet and afterward in the Junior Common Room I couldn't get warm in front of a roaring fire. For weeks I had been so tired that if my cigarettes were across the room, instead of getting up automatically and getting them, I would become conscious of their location as a problem and ask myself, "Do you really want a cigarette badly enough to go all that way to get them?" And I had this cough, infrequent but persistent.

I also resented what I took to be the doctor's jaunty attitude. Where did I want to go, Switzerland or the States? I had no choice. I had fourteen pounds in the bank. If I were going anywhere it would have to be home. This was 1931. I was certain my father couldn't pay for two years in a sanitarium. I couldn't see what I was going to do. It was degrading to throw myself on charity and I didn't know how to make the throw in any case. What did you do, sit down in the street and wait?

I lay on my sofa drowsily worrying. Every now and then the coal would clink as it shifted in the fireplace. Fourteen pounds would take me about two-thirds of the way across the Atlantic. Although I didn't really think they would let me board in the first place, I could see the ship putting me off in a jolly-boat about seven hundred miles east of Ambrose Light with some iron rations and a flask of water so I could row myself in, the water black, the ice forming on the oars, my cough stifled in the bitter wind. The picture was a nineteenth-century engraving of a pitiful subject, but it seemed to symbolize my plight and I rowed away most of the afternoon.

The next day I was the beneficiary of a gratuitously kind act. This is rare and I have never forgotten it. John Philips from West Virginia, who was at Christchurch across the street, came in to see me. He had heard rumors. I corrected them.

"I'm going to see the Rhodes Trust. They've got a lot of money," he said. "They own De Beers."

John's mind worked with a beautiful, simple directness. There was money there. He went and asked them for some. It would never have occurred to me, but he came back with a check for two hundred pounds made out in my name. For an hour it was incredible.

With nearly a thousand dollars in hand I grew more cheerful. I knew next to nothing about tuberculosis. I had the childlike faith of the uninitiated in all doctors. Now that I had some money to pay them with, I was sure they would cure me if I were obedient. There was nothing complicated about it.

My English friends very kindly packed me up and bought me passage on the *Olympic*, an old Cunarder now long out of service. I had stopped worrying because I was filled with the excitement of going on a journey. In my room I held an auction of personal effects. I received a note from my tutor, Mr. Percy Simpson, saying that my work was "sound and promising." *Sound* was his highest accolade. Any lurking notion that I had a mortal disease was smothered by these preparations, and when an ambulance came and the bearers got stuck going down the winding staircase from my room, it all seemed hilarious. The Dean came out of his rooms, shook hands, and wished me luck while the bearers were pulling and hauling. At last it came free.

I was carried across the quadrangles in the mist. I made
my last good-bys. They shoved me into the ambulance and
away we went to Southampton.

A friend of mine, John Durkin of Queen's, had volunteered to accompany me and see me aboard the *Olympic*.
He knew no more of tuberculosis than I, but the ambulance
made it seem serious and he courteously made bright conversation to cheer me up. He stopped the ambulance two
or three times at pubs and brought me sustaining pints of
mild and bitter. The doctor had forbidden me cigarettes
but he said nothing about beer, which is well-known to
be nourishing. Once when we passed a clump of people at
a narrow turn in a village street, John stuck his head out
the back door of the ambulance and yelled, "Take off your
hats, damn you. We've got a dead man in here." They took
off their hats. On the whole it was a pleasant journey.

I remember nothing of going aboard but I can remember
waking up in the ship's hospital. It was clean but there were
so few amenities that it suggested the Cunard Line frowned
on sickness as a willful refusal to come to grips with life,
and that if you went sick at sea, you deserved nothing better. The wall was the simple hull of the ship, studded with
lines of heavy rivets, and while I knew that the North Atlantic was only an inch or two away from my hand when
I touched it, I felt safe and snug and it did not seem to be
a spurious safety. The ship's surgeon, a Mr. Somebody,
visited me, an Irishman with a shattered face, knobbed and
seamed in a sullen red. He was very kind, brought me
cigarettes after meals, and spent literally hours beside my
berth talking about everything under the sun. Only later
did it occur to me that he had nothing else to do. I was
the only person in hospital and it must have been dull for
him to sit alone in his surgery, reading. It was also later
that someone told me ship's surgeons were men under clouds,
chronic drunks, unfortunates who had inadvertently re-

moved both kidneys, mistaken cyanide for aspirin. From
his color and his unfailing garrulity I think Mr. Somebody
was the first of these.

Another pleasant feature of the voyage was the food.
True, it was English food, but it was English food striv-
ing to impress foreigners, the tourists, and while I doubt
if the Line was so slack as to hire an actual Frenchman as
chef, somebody in the galley had heard about French cuisine
and the food tasted good. I ate like a wolf. Before each meal
they would bring me a vast chart to select from and I remember breakfasts of bacon and eggs, York ham, creamed
codfish, grilled kidneys, small steak, two-rib mutton chops
and other kickshaws. I would eat them all, turn over and go
to sleep until the steward shook me gently and offered me
the program for lunch. Mr. Somebody was assiduous at
taking my temperature and weighing me. During the seven
days, my temperature went down to normal and I gained a
pound a day. I knew enough to know that these were very
good signs. It was a rough crossing, March, and Mr. Somebody told me that most of the passengers kept to their berths,
felled by seasickness. It didn't affect me. I felt fine.

We docked late at night in a blizzard. I had cabled my
friend Frank Adams, and he met me. I dressed and I felt
so good I walked off the ship. We took a taxi to the Bilt-
more and I went to bed. I had barely waked the next morning when Frank was back. He had half a dozen nickel hamburgers in a sack, with onion. "I knew this place was too
expensive for you to eat and sleep here both," he said. There
is nothing like sickness to bring out the kindness of friends.

At the University Hospital in Ann Arbor I was checked,
examined, and tested all over again. I weighed on entry 147
pounds at six feet, one and a half inches. I had cavitation,
two holes in my left lung, and infiltration, a spot as big
as a half-dollar on my right. My fever had begun again, a
low nagging heat that made it tiring to read for more than

a quarter-hour at a time because my eyes got so hot. An affair with needles, not acupuncture but artificial pneumothorax, was successfully begun to collapse my left lung and I was ordered complete rest. I was bored nearly out of my mind.

I had some cards engraved and sent them out to my friends:

Mr. Allan Seager

At Home

University Hospital

No cocktails　　　　　　　　　　　　　*No dancing*

This brought me a great many visitors, some of whom generously tried to smuggle me drinks of bad whisky. The nurses didn't like them. They forbade these simple corporal works of mercy and for the next four months I lay there, making what I could out of the cracks in the ceiling. At night I got up and walked around the room a little so I wouldn't lose the use of my legs.

Toward the first of July the doctors told me there was a vacancy coming up at Trudeau Sanitarium at Saranac. At Trudeau you had to be ambulant. The doctors said I could start sitting up on the edge of the bed with my feet hanging for twenty minutes a day. Next would be sitting in a chair, then, presumably, a few tottering steps around the room. I didn't dare tell them I could walk all right so I went through their routine for three days. The first day I was allowed to walk, I decided to take a tub bath. I left my room and walked down the middle of the corridor without hanging on to anything. The nurses came like a flight of birds. They settled on me, twittering and clucking, trying to get me to let them bear me up but I said, "Beat it, ladies. I'm all right." I walked on to the bathroom, drew

my bath and lay in it. It felt good after all those months
of wet washrags.

The day I left, the head nurse told me that the Travelers
Aid would meet me at the train in Detroit to see that I
was wheeled safely to the train for Saranac. I said I didn't
need a wheelchair but the head nurse, wrinkled by duty,
said that I must have one. A friend of mine, a girl, came
with me as far as Detroit. She had thoughtfully brought
along a pint of Golden Wedding, the favored label among
the local bootleggers. I took a compartment for privacy
and we drank the frightful whisky with water from paper
cups and laughed the whole way. The countryside looked
fresh and new and so did the girl. We had a wonderful
time.

As the train slowed down in the Detroit station I saw
a tiny little old lady pushing one of those high wooden
wheelchairs alongside the train. She wore a cloth hat with
a label sewn on the front with TRAVELERS AID on it. If I
didn't get in that wheelchair, nobody would and she would
have come all that way for nothing. But if I did get into
it, could she push me? I had shot up to a hundred and eighty
pounds. The train stopped. I had to face the problem. If
I seemed to stagger as I got off, it was not the weakness of
my malady. I said good-by to the girl and walked as cir-
cumspectly as I could over to the old lady. "Were you expecting a TB patient from Ann Arbor, madam?"

"Yes, I was," she said. I could tell she was tough and conscientious.

"I really don't need the wheelchair."

"It was ordered for you. Get in," she commanded.

I got in. It was embarrassing enough as it was, this little
woman bending to the task of rolling a big healthy-looking
guy around a railroad station (Most TB patients look
healthy. They eat so much), but I must have assumed what

I can only describe as a roistering pose in the chair because a well-dressed woman passed and I heard her say to her escort, "I didn't know they did that for lushes."

The Trudeau Sanitarium is now obsolete, its services discontinued, and its buildings house a high-level project having to do, I believe, with the Theory of Games. In my day it was rather like living in a fraternity again. The men and women were separated and assigned to cottages each with space for twelve or fifteen people. You had a dressing room and a screened porch where you slept.

My porchmate was a Swiss who said he was a "mechanical" dentist. This seemed to mean that his trade was making dentures and, apparently to keep his hand in, there were always a few loose teeth scattered on the table in his dressing room. Meals were served in a central dining hall and after each one you returned to your porch to cure. Curing was lying still, breathing the fresh mountain air, and sleeping if possible. I couldn't do this because of Karl's problem. He had not only chest TB but also some kind of hyperthyroidism and he couldn't sit still. He paced up and down ceaselessly and meaninglessly all day like a big cat in a zoo.

In October when the snow came he nearly prevented me from sleeping at night, too. I was persuaded to buy one of the early electric blankets, warm but fairly primitive affairs which shorted on a couple of my friends who were wakened in the dead of night by little rings of flame dancing on the bedclothes. Karl, however, although he had plenty, was close with his money. He had so many wool blankets on his bed that he used a bookmark pinched from the library to tell where to insert himself. About eight o'clock at night he would start to prepare for bed. He would pull on the pants to a sweatsuit over a pair of flannel pajamas, tie the ankles, crumple *The New York Times* and *Herald Tribune* and stuff them down the legs until he looked like a tackling dummy; then he would tie the waist and stuff the top, put on a knitted cap, two pair of wool socks, a pair of gauntlets, and he would into bed and rustle. This is enough to deter if not prevent sleep entirely. It got very cold there and these precautions, wool or electric, were necessary. It was often forty below at night and for two weeks it didn't get above twelve below at noon. Usually you slept on your back with two pillows criscrossed over your face, the Adirondack Pack. You pulled the blankets up to the base of the nose, leaving only it exposed and greasing it beforehand so it wouldn't freeze to the pillow. It was Karl who challenged George Kelly to a duel, implementing the challenge with a case of pistols with beautiful long blue barrels. I knew by this time that worry and confinement could make people strange, but when I heard that Karl wanted George to go up the mountain with seconds, stand back to back, and each take ten paces forward, turn and fire, all like a novel, I didn't believe it. I asked Karl to show me the pistols and he did but he wouldn't say how George had insulted him.

It was a sure thing that George had done something or said something that he could take as an insult. George was a big, shrewd, red-faced, knowledgeable Irishman. The year before he had been playing tackle for Manhattan College. Somebody threw a block on him and he coughed half a pint of blood on the field. They tried to get him to a doctor but he waved them away, "I'll just finish the season." He played four more games, let a doctor examine him, and was sent posthaste to Saranac. He knew what he had all the time. His parents had died of it.

He was a bad patient because he treated the disease with scorn. It was ridiculous to be felled by Lilliputian bugs fifty thousand of which, we were told, could pass through the eye of a needle without touching the sides or one another and he made elaborate jokes about it that set the whole sanitarium laughing. He took our common plight, contemptuously turned it upside down, inside out, and for all but the butts of them, his jokes wore away the endemic fear that seemed to hover in the spruce trees at night when the wind kept you awake. In a sanitarium everyone is passive, waiting hopefully. George was active.

There was a man there from the Long Island City fire department. I forget his name because we called him Chief. The Chief was a friendly round little guy and he was just short of what they call in the South blood simple. He didn't have TB. He had osteomyelitis on his ribs—"Sorta like moss," he said. He had to have an operation to remove the affected parts. Since it was similar, perhaps identical to the operation for removal of ribs in TB, the thoracoplasty, he had been sent up here. He did not have to cure and had the run of the place at all hours. One day George Kelly got hold of him.

"How long before they give you the rib, Chief?"

"Oh, three, four days. Thursday, I guess."

George, elbows on knees, looked at the floor and said, "Uh-*huh*." Then he said, "Feeling pretty good?"

"Oh, yeah, George. Nothing to do. Eat good. Sleep. You know."

"Yeah, yeah, yeah," George said frowning. "I mean, mentally."

"Mentally?" An expression of wonder came over the Chief's face. Nobody had ever asked him that before, apparently. "How do I feel in my mind? Wonderful. Never better."

"You sound as though you're looking forward to it." This sourly.

"It's coming. I gotta. What else?"

"Yeah, sure." George looked at him now. "Back in Long Island City when the fire bell rings, you slide down the pole . . ."

"I ain't always in bed when the bell rings. Sometimes I'm playing checkers."

"Okay, okay. So you jump up or slide down and get on the truck and you zoom off to the fire and you run up ladders and wrestle the hose. . . ."

"Oh, it's more tetnical than that, George."

"But, goddam it, that's what you *do*, isn't it?" George roared.

"Well, gee, yeah, but . . ."

"All I'm asking you is, do you think you'll be able to do it *after* the operation?"

"Sure. They said . . ."

"They said." George spat right on the floor, a grave offense here. "Look, Chief, you know Doc Speidel, first assistant surgeon."

"Sure."

"You know how he limps when he walks, kind of pushes with his right leg?"

"Bone TB," the Chief said confidently. "He had his knee scraped, they said."

"They said."

"Well . . ."

"Speidel had the rib, too, didn't he?"

"Yeah."

"Well, the reason he keeps pushing with that right leg when he walks is to keep him going in a straight line. See, Chief, what they don't tell you when you get the rib, it destroys your sense of direction. You walk round in circles."

The Chief stared at George maybe ten seconds. "Honest?" he said.

"Look at Speidel. He's smart. He worked it out. He pushes. But I don't know about you getting up on a ladder. How do you walk in circles on a ladder?"

The Chief listened no more. He spun around and ran out of the cottage. You were supposed to walk no faster than two and a half miles an hour but the Chief ran like a white-head. Dr. Speidel was with a patient but the Chief burst into his office, waving his arms and shouting, "Oh, no. You can't do this to me. Oh, no. I know all about you, Doc. No, sir. You can't do this. I ain't gonna letcha."

"What's the matter, Chief?" Doc Speidel said.

"You cut out my ribs? No, sir. Take away my job? No. I know all about you, Doc. No, sir, you can't do it," the Chief babbled. "The rest of my life walking around in circles? Nix."

Patients blow their tops not infrequently and Speidel was used to this, the confinement and the strict regimen, worry about money, worry about death, but he also recognized a sinister foreign richness of invention in the Chief's outburst. "Who've you been talking to, George Kelly?"

"You bet. He's the only friend I got here."

Wearily Dr. Speidel went to work cleaning up after George. It took about an hour to calm the Chief down and settle him for the operation. Later he chewed George out, but half-heartedly, because I think he obscurely realized that George was on his side, deviously, obliquely, on the side of life.

The sanitarium's conscientious efforts to inform its ignorant population about their disease spread misconceptions that floated like thistledown at random among the patients. One day after a lecture Jake, the upholsterer, sidled up to George and asked, "George, have I got a lesion? What the hell's a lesion?"

George was always ready to go. "You get downtown to the movies once a week."

"Yeah."

"You see these kids playing in the alley beside the theater, huh?" George always assumed his hearer's diction, a gambit to solicit plausibility.

"Sure. Playing marbles."

"Uh-huh. You're sure it's marbles they're playing?"

"Sure I'm sure. I used to play when I was a kid. We drew a big ring and . . ."

"But you never went and picked up one of them marbles."

"Kids don't like you to bother 'em when . . ."

"Those things ain't marbles, Jake. Them're little round stones, not perfectly round but round enough to play with. Them're your lesions."

Jake was a little smarter than the Chief, and he knew George. "Okay. So these are the lesions of tuberculosis. How come the kids're playing marbles with 'em?"

In a wonderfully *négligé* manner George shrugged and said, "You've heard of gallstones. Calcium."

Conviction began to cramp Jake's hamlike face. "Yeah, but how do the kids . . ."

"How many sanitariums are there in Saranac, fifteen, twenty? I dunno. Somebody must be getting the rib every day. Every time they open you up, they find lesions. Why, hell, they took about a pint of 'em out of old Mrs. Underwood."

"But how do the kids . . ."

"Out of the trash barrels."

"You mean they throw out our lesions into trash barrels?"

"So they're pearls? What you want they should do with 'em? Put 'em in a golden box and give 'em to you? Let the kids have some fun, Jake."

"But these are colored. They look like marbles."

"So you never had any colored crayons when you were a kid? Where'd you come from—Green Point? Red Hook?"

Time had taught the authorities that the Puritanic regimen so beneficial to the disease could not be maintained without any breaks. It sent people up the wall. With no official announcement, merely by the seepage of custom, new patients learned that the week between Christmas and

New Year's was a licensed saturnalia. If you didn't fall on your face before the Head, you could carouse, and visiting between the men's and women's cottages was winked at.

Preparations began as early as October. With childlike glee as if they were breaking the rules at a boarding school, the men began to make dates with the women for the Christmas holiday. The marriage tie did not seem to hold. It was a saying that you left your spouse behind at Utica. There were half a dozen patients who had been divorced by their husbands or wives as soon as the TB was diagnosed. The staff lectures taught us to be selfish, to watch ourselves, to take care of ourselves, to listen to ourselves. We were selfish.

I had done very well eating, lying in the open air, walking a little. My fever had gone. My weight stayed put. I was cheerful. About the first of December I was allowed full exercise, two hours walking a day, the caloric equivalent, they said, of eight hours' sedentary work. One hour was to be walked in the morning, another in the afternoon with rest between. Conscientious people owned pedometers and paced off their miles exactly. I did my walking with George Kelly and we were more casual. (It was better to walk in pairs. One could watch the other's cheeks and warn him if they began to freeze. It was cold.) George had heard it was exactly two and a half miles to Peck's Corners, a grocery store under a big oak tree, and we began to walk our five miles in one whack, there and back. Then we timed ourselves, two hours at first, then an hour and a half, and finally we did our best time, mostly at a dog-trot, forty-eight minutes. After a fortnight of this, my fluoroscopes and X rays looked so good that Dr. Speidel told me I could leave after the first of the year. Let me hasten to add that I think the improvement ran parallel to me on those long stumbling runs across the mountains and was not necessarily caused by them although it may have been. We breathed a lot of fresh air.

Somebody went up the mountain, cut down a spruce and fitted it into a tub in the living room of our cottage. Nobody could remember to buy any decorations when he went downtown into Saranac. A few people tossed cigarette foil into the branches and that was all our Christmas decoration. What people did remember when they went into Saranac was to dicker with bootleggers. After long bargaining, all the men in the cottage made up a pot and sent Jake the upholsterer to buy a five-gallon can of alcohol from the man who had set the best price.

Christmas Eve I went to a party in another cottage and I didn't drink any of this alcohol. As I was dressing late Christmas morning, three men came into my room and said "Can you do this?" They lifted their arms from the elbows.

"Sure," I said and did it.

"We can hardly do it," they said.

"What do you mean?"

"It's hard. We think there was something in the alcohol."

"Can you see all right?"

"Yes, but it's hard to lift our arms."

"Is everybody like this?"

"All but Pops." Pops was a Latvian shoemaker. All he did was play checkers. He had told us Christmas Eve we were swine to drink.

I looked around the cottage. Everybody but Pops was trying to lift his arms and Pops was laughing. It is rare to see an occasion when clean living clearly pays off and he was enjoying it. At last someone went and pulled a resident chemist away from his tree and his gifts and persuaded him to throw an analysis on the alcohol. A deputation from our cottage stood and watched.

"It's full of pyridine," he said finally. "You go on drinking that stuff and you'll be paralyzed."

It was then that McGinley took over. He was a young lawyer from the Bronx, a protégé of Ed Flynn's. He was often visited by the bishop of the diocese and that good old man always left him a bottle of fine Episcopal rye whisky. McGinley was a light case and he looked a little like Adolphe Menjou, a sinister way to look in those days. In a snap-brim hat and a camel's-hair overcoat, he went downtown to see the bootlegger who had sold us the liquor.

In a side pocket of his overcoat, McGinley clenched his fist and extended a stiff forefinger. He said, "Look, Mac, I come up from the city for Christmas to see some friends of mine. They're up at the Trudeau Sanitarium, you know?"

"Yeah."

"These friends of mine, they're old buddies, they got the con, see? They're sick."

"They all got the con at Trudeau."

"That's right. Now these friends of mine, they're sick, it's Christmas. Maybe they don't see another Christmas. I want 'em to have a good time, see?" As he spoke, McGinley would frequently thrust the muzzle of his forefinger against the cloth of his pocket. "So I give 'em a little dough to buy some alcohol. A little Christmas cheer, you unnastand."

"Yeah."

"They bought that alcohol from you, Mac."

"So?"

"So this: They're lying up there half-paralyzed."

"So it's my fault they get stinko and . . ."

Softly McGinley said, "This ain't stinko paralyzed. This is nerve paralyzed. That alcohol was full of pyridine, Mac. That's poison. They had it analyzed by a chemist in a laboratory. These guys, they ain't got enough trouble being eaten away with the tuberculosis, no. You got to sell 'em some pyridine so they can be paralyzed, too."

By this time the bootlegger had begun to sweat the big drop. "Honest to God, I didn't know. I just get the stuff off a truck that comes through. I didn't . . ."

"Now how's it going to be, Mac? You want to make it

right with my friends? Or"—McGinley let it hang a moment and then finished in a low, slow ominous voice—"maybe you want a little trouble for y'self." He gave the side of his pocket a last poke.

Fluttering with terror the bootlegger pressed the original purchase price, seventy-five dollars, on McGinley and gave him a new five-gallon can of alcohol he swore was pure. He would drink it himself. McGinley grudgingly accepted the money and the can, leaped into a taxi, and came back up the mountain. It was a nice stroke of work.

On the day I left, George Kelly, McGinley, and Jake the upholsterer came down to the station to see me off. The Rhodes Trust had told me I could resume my scholarship and I was going to stay with a friend in Virginia until I sailed for England. I felt there was a certain arrogance in my departure, in having plans beyond these mountains, in leaving at all because I left these friends behind. As we waited on the station platform for the train, feeling the involved ironies of each other's good wishes, it was George who loosened us up. "Well, you won't be going alone," he said. I seemed to be. No other passengers were waiting. George pointed to two long pine boxes stacked one on top of the other at the end of the platform. It was funny then, desperate but funny, but only now do I see how courteous it was.

* XIII *

The Last Return

I sailed for England late in March to return to Oxford for my examinations and I was pumped up hard. A rap on the ribs and I gave off a taut sharp sound like a well-tuned kettledrum. It was my artificial pneumothorax and my doctor had injected enough air to last me until I could be refilled in England. I was taking a small ship that divided its burden between cargo and passengers. It was not in a hurry and after sixteen days at sea, a day out from Gravesend, I tapped myself on the chest. I had gone slack, lost tone, and I became mildly alarmed. The good feature of the voyage had been its monotony because it let me read without distraction. I needed that. In June I was to be examined on the whole corpus of English language and literature.

Once ashore I headed for the Brompton Chest Hospital. My doctor had recommended it and had written me a letter to go with the little blue book I carried, a record of all the air injections I had had. When I got to the hospital, there was a long queue of people attached to its front door. I remembered that hospitals were charity institutions in England. Perhaps all these people were waiting for pneumothorax injections, too. I wanted to catch a train to Oxford before noon so I went into the hospital to find someone who might allow me to pay for what I wanted. I was sent to the office of the Lady Almoner, a woman in a vaguely conventual garb like a Mother Superior's. In England some medieval traditions cling like leeches, and as I knew that nurses were called Sisters as a gesture toward a time when hospitals were church foundations I surmised that the Lady Almoner handled the money. I asked her if I could pay. I had a train to catch.

She said it would be impossible. Brompton was a charity institution.

I had an idea. "Perhaps if I made a small gift to the foundation?"

She said that would be satisfactory and I made out a check for thirty shillings.

I was shown into what seemed to be a small bare Victorian sitting room. A cheerful fire blazed in a fireplace. There was a kind of operating table covered with a horse-blanket, a wooden cabinet, and a couple of chairs. I waited a quarter of an hour smoking a cigarette. At last a doctor entered. He looked at my little blue book and I gave him the necessary information. To shorten the proceedings I said, "I don't take an anesthetic."

"Oh, you tough Americans," he said.

I had no thought of impressing him. The form for these injections is to anesthetize the rib area, then to insert the hollow needle to let the air in. At Saranac, however, very sharp hollow needles were used and no anesthetic. There was always a nurse rubbing a needle on an oilstone.

I lay down. The doctor didn't do any sharpening. He put the point of the needle on one of the intercostal spaces and began to shove. I thought maybe he was using a knitting needle. The pain was intense but I was a tough and therefore silent American. At last the point went through the skin with a loud pop and I nearly jumped off the table. The rest of the operation went on normally but my ribs were sore for days.

At Oxford I found some digs near my college in the house of a medieval scholar. He was not English, nor was his mistress. She was a Slav, I think. At least she played Chopin loudly on the piano through most of the daylight hours; evenings they seemed to quarrel, but of course cats seem to quarrel when they are making love. It was not an atmosphere for quiet study and I spent a lot of time in the Bodleian Library and begging the use of other people's digs while they were out.

I had not done much reading during my illness. I had eight weeks to revise, as the English say, my study of the literature from the Venerable Bede down to 1828, a seemingly arbitrary date. All that anyone had been able to discover of its importance was that 1828 was the year Thackeray went down from Cambridge. I began with Chaucer. Two of my eight weeks passed and I had thirty-eight pages of typewritten notes, single-spaced. It was ominously plain that I would never get through at that pace. I panicked and spent a whole evening drinking beer with some ne'er-do-wells who had already given up and were drifting fatalistically toward the examinations like canoes on the Niagara.

The evening did me good for someone told me that Blackwell's sold booklets containing all the examinations ever given. I bought the ones for the last ten years. Nine papers were always set, which would run mornings and afternoons for four and a half days. Fifteen questions were asked on each paper and we were generously expected to answer four or five. I scrutinized these old questions, trying to spot the ones that tended to recur—assuming, justly I still think, that the examiners no matter who would find certain poets, certain influences, certain periods of prime importance and would repeat questions about them. I found these questions and I made a list of four for each paper, thirty-six in all. From then on I didn't even try to study everything; I puzzled out the answers to these thirty-six questions. I didn't feel good about this. It was a makeshift but time was getting short.

It was, I remember faintly, a beautiful spring with copious sunlight and almost tropical scenery, but I ignored it. I did not go near the river where Eights were being performed. I didn't drink beer at the Trout, a stone inn where you could sit on a terrace and watch water flow soothingly over a weir. No, in my little cubby high above the Chopin and the quarrelling I spent my evenings swotting up the facts on Euphues, on Charles Diodati, friend of Milton, on the Battle of the Books (uncovering, incidentally, the fact that Shelley was six feet tall and would have towered over Byron as they walked beside Lake Geneva. It had not the slightest relevance to my problems but none of his poetry or his letters suggested that they were written by a tall man).

The week before examinations the tensions tightened themselves up. Mr. Boots, an Oxford apothecary, thoughtfully peddled bottles of a turgid mess called Mr. Boots's Schools Mixture. It was designed to keep you awake and was probably composed of caffein muddled in a syrup. I didn't buy any but most of my friends lived on it and whisky, hardly going to bed at all. The Oxford manner had all it could do to maintain its façade of *negligé* confidence, covering as it did patches of raw ignorance, short tempers, and lack of sleep.

I heard of an old rule which permitted a student if he felt faint or hungry during an examination to call for a pint of beer or a beefsteak, which would then be served to him on the spot. Such genial relaxations were not for me, for with any luck I would be writing hard all the time. On the first day I saw a beer lorry parked in front of the Examination Schools and a man carrying in cases of beer. No one in my room called for any, however.

I had the answers to my thirty-six questions pullulating

in my head but I felt overmatched, like a lightweight fighting a heavyweight and doing it with one hand tied behind
his back. And it was so. Frantically I seized the first list
of questions, scanning them to find out which one of my
four prepared answers I could use. None. I looked again.
None. It was the first blow, but one that was repeated every
morning and afternoon for four and a half days. Do you
know how many of my answers I got a chance to use? One.
Just one.

Grogginess set in about the second day and it flittered
through the back of my mind that the examiners were mad
or they had had me watched by agents who had craftily
determined how they could foil me. It seemed unlikely, but
since they had exploded the law of averages what other ex-
planation was there? Grimly, somnambulistically, I concocted answers out of untrustworthy general knowledge,
tossing in known facts with artificial relevance, bridging
pits of ignorance with half-truths and literary fakery and,
with the brassiness of despair, shoving in a few bald lies.
Toward the end, with exhaustion settling over my skull and
cramping the back of my neck, I didn't care what I got
the paper covered with as long as I got it covered. I was
not the only sufferer. Two women in my room fainted, one
sliding slyly to the floor, the other giving a long howl and
shooting up out of her seat like a rocket before she collapsed.
As far as anything could make me feel better, this did. The
women were removed by the invigilators.

The night after it was over, instead of going to drink
myself blind at the George Restaurant in celebration with
my friends, I crept upstairs to my room and lay there in
the darkness, panting. It was the hottest summer in seventy-
five years, a circumstance probably arranged by the examiners in collaboration with Greenwich Observatory. My
hand had stuck to the paper every day. The pearly tones
of the loathsome Bechstein below swarmed over me from

the open windows. I was dead tired and deeply ashamed of myself.

The *viva*, an oral examination, occurred some weeks later after the examiners had had time to judge the papers. Rule or custom decreed that you couldn't go down in your standing no matter how big a fool you looked. If they asked you only one question, it was perfunctory and meant you were safely lodged in whatever class you were going to get, First, Second, Third, or Fourth. If they kept at you, it meant that you were wavering between two classes and if you answered well, you would get into the higher. Depressed beyond measure, I got myself properly duded up for the occasion, dark suit, white wing collar, white tie, cap and gown. When my turn came, the examiners did not treat me with any special scorn. They asked me a question from my Old English paper and dismissed me. I was safe in whatever class it was. I hoped for a Fourth because I was sure I had been ploughed.

Ten days later the results were printed in the London *Times*. I had gotten a Second. At first I didn't believe it. The examiners seemed not only crafty but stupid. Why reward blatant ignorance, I thought. A few minutes later I got myself up to Rhodes House to apply for a third year on the scholarship. A Second was not a bad degree. I was granted the third year, but they turned down my request to do a B. Litt. They seemed to think I was too fragile.

I had the equivalent of about $165 to last me until October. Travel was out of the question. Also I was tied to Dr. Stobie, former Lord Mayor of Oxford. He had to pump me up every two weeks. I went out to a country pub I had visited before, the Crown, East Hanney, Berkshire. East Hanney was not a quaint village. It had no antiquities, no natural features worth looking at. The Crown was a square brick building erected some time in the later years of the nineteenth century. Mrs. Faulkner, the landlady, remembered me and said I could stay there for thirty shillings a week, about six dollars then. I jumped at it and moved in.

The summer stretched before me like a calm lake with no fish in it. I had nothing to do. I had brought no books with me, obviously, except a volume of Maupassant's short stories, French stuff, not English. I had no friends nearby. At first I slept a good deal, probably a good thing. Later I walked, a form of devotion much cried up by the English, but it bored me silly. Still later I tried my hand at the pub games—shove ha'penny, darts, and dominoes—but when I learned that each game was played for a half-pint of beer, costing threepence, I had to go slow. I liked the people, farmhands, carpenters, plasterers, ditchers, old women who had been in service in London. I practiced daily on the shove-ha'penny board until I could win as often as I lost, then I could get to know them better by playing with them evenings. Although I was an Oxford gentleman, I was also an American and they called me by my Christian name.

One of these old women who seemed to have no other name but Skinner did my laundry. She was about seventy, toothless, with black hair and a kind of glazed brown skin like a gypsy's. She lived all alone on the edge of a field in a hovel and she served in the bar evenings. "You know wot I'd do an I get a fortune? I'd build me a 'ouse but I wouldn't sleep in it. I'd sleep out in the fields with the cows and sheep and conies and birds. I likes animals," she said. She couldn't read or write but she could reckon up and she was never wrong on the laundry bill. One day, puzzled by her brown skin, I asked her, "Skinner, when was the last time you had a bath?" She was stunned and delighted me by replying, "Why, Ollin, they's just three times a girl 'as a bath—when she's born, bedded, and buried." Once I saw her take on her lap a poor man who had just lost his little son and rock him like a baby.

These friendly people worked during the day and I saw

them only at night after their teas and washups. Daytimes were still blank. For some time I had considered myself marked for a writing career but I had done nothing. I finished the Maupassant and it occurred to me to try to write a story as good as one of his. I had the story, based on an incident I had seen in the hospital, but I didn't know how to begin. Contemplating the writer's condition beforehand, how he did it had seemed quite simple. Now that I was at the brink, it was not. I lay on my back under the polled willows. I knew the changing cumuli of the summer skies from the time they formed until they blew away in wisps. I would sit poised over my typewriter with a beginning sentence in my head, mutter, "Ah, that's not it," and draw back. It seemed to me the right sentence was floating somewhere but to get it was like catching a rabbit with a hat, a quick move and it scuttled away. At last of course I got one and maybe two hundred more to follow it. I rewrote the story so often I knew it by heart and would have been glad to recite it had anyone asked me to.

At the summer's end I counted the pages I had written. There were a hundred and twenty-six. The final version was eight pages. It was the best I could do. I thought the *London Mercury* was the best magazine in England, and looking at the story with pride and loathing (for I was very sick of it by that time), I sent it off to Sir John Squire, the editor, under the initials J. B. A. Seager, the right ones, but I included the first two as more English to throw Sir John away from any inkling that I might be an American. The story was written in English, too. As soon as the postman took it from my hand, I began to wait.

Every two weeks during the summer I would borrow a push-bike and ride the eleven miles into Oxford to get a refill from Dr. Stobie at the Osler Pavilion. In the city I looked neither right nor left for fear I should see something I wanted to buy or, the very worst, run into someone from home whom courtesy would force me to take to lunch. Each time at the Pavilion I noticed a girl ahead of me, very pretty with that lush complexion you see only in England. Waiting, we used to talk. Talking and looking started furious computations. If I played no more public shove-ha'penny and smoked Woodbines, four a penny, instead of Players, I could see my way clear to asking her to tea, so I did.

She gave me her address. The next time I came in I ditched my bike in my college, which was full of tourists, and took a taxi. It was an address in east Oxford somewhere off the Cowley Road, an area of cheap semidetached villas with names like *Mon Repos* on the front gates. The taxi stopped before one which had *J. Andrews, Tailor* in gold on the front window. It was the right place. I rang the bell. A tired-looking woman answered it. I asked if I could see Miss Andrews. "She's only a little gel. She's not but fifteen," she said.

"Oh," I said. "I'm sorry," and I stumbled back to my taxi. With embarrassing clarity I saw what I had done, and I felt the mother's opinion of me come over me with a blush. A pretty girl has no caste. At the Pavilion I had paid no attention to her accent or even her dress. I should have, for then I would have seen that she was lower-class and avoided her mother's obvious conviction that I was a cad of a young Oxford gentleman out to ruin her daughter. The Middle Ages are hard to kill. I think her mother asked Dr. Stobie to change the time of her appointment; I didn't see her again.

At the end of summer I went back to Oxford to wait. I discerned that I was really doing nothing else. The *London Mercury* was as silent as the sky. I moved into digs in Wellington Square and sent a note to Mr. Edmund Blunden of Merton College asking if he would take me as a tutorial student.

He very kindly accepted me and I began to read in the nineteenth century. He was an excellent teacher. Information was conveyed by shrewdly formed questions and the molding of taste went on by oblique hints and minute clouds of surprise when I did not know something. Occasionally we would walk during the tutorial, sometimes to Morton-in-the Marsh, and heighten the discussion with a pint of beer. After one of these excursions he excused himself, went over to a typewriter in a corner and began to write. After ten minutes he handed me a sonnet celebrating our walk, slight but graceful and pointed. He could do things like that. He told me that after the war, he, Siegfried Sassoon, Robert Graves, and T. E. Lawrence had lived in chicken houses behind John Masefield's house on Boar's Hill. I saw Robert Graves a few years ago and asked him about it. He said it was true about the people but the houses were little sheds. They had all returned from the war more or less broke, at loose ends, and Masefield took them in. Something of a jump from Lawrence's entry into Damascus to a little shed on Boar's Hill.

As the autumn drew on into its fogs and mists, the wait got more prickly. I still had heard nothing from the *London Mercury* and when I heard his step, it was all I could do to keep from running out to strike at the postman. In rare calm moods I knew that my little story was not going to change the course of literature but its acceptance or rejection would, I believed, change my course and this justified my perturbation. At last I could wait no longer. I put together a wily letter, "Would you please return to me a story called 'The Street'? I have an opportunity to place it elsewhere." I felt that the word *opportunity* steered neatly between truth and lie—you always have an opportunity to place it elsewhere. As soon as I mailed this, I typed the story up fresh and sent it off to another magazine. With an almost electric promptness I had a note back from the *Mercury;* "We are sorry you must have this excellent story as we would like to print it."

Now two magazines had it. One had accepted it. What if the other did? What could I do then, tear it down the middle and offer each half? After the *Mercury*'s long torpor I was so pleased and astonished I couldn't think straight. It took me an hour of fidgeting to decide on the obvious thing to do. I fired off a letter to the other magazine asking them to return the story because I had an opportunity to place it elsewhere and I wrote the *Mercury*, "If you would like to print 'The Street,' please do." I felt less criminal immediately and when the *Mercury* sent me a check for three guineas, about $15.75 then, it seemed a fair reward for my summer's work—not the real reward, for I would happily have given them the story if they would print it. Since they were going to in the January issue, the three guineas were mere lagniappe. Shops where they sold magazines began to burn as brightly as jewels. I could not have been more sharply aware of them had they been beautiful girls standing there as I passed and by the middle of December I hung around them so much (and in a mackintosh, too) that the proprietors must have thought they were under surveillance.

Right up until the last I feared that the *Mercury*'s printing shop might burn to the ground or Sir John might write me, "It's all a joke. Of course we can't print this ridiculous story," but one day I saw the issue in a shop. Trembling I bought it. Trembling I opened it. The story was there. I was in print. It seemed to me that readers from Land's End to John o' Groat's ought to be dancing around bonfires shouting my name, that a throng should gather as I left the shop and bear me through the street cheering. It did not happen. In fact, I couldn't bring myself to mention it. I left the issue lying around the digs in hopes that my roommate might pick it up, but he didn't. The only person I told was Edmund Blunden. He seemed pleased but not enough. Modesty does a lot of forbidding. It was only then that I could begin another story.

I had a quiet roommate and this made working easier. I had asked a man named John Wotton to share my bed-sitter for economy. He had lived above me in college and we had often made coffee together when we were reading late. He was studying history but not very hard. He read only memoirs and biography and he had pieced together the backstairs gossip of half the courts of Europe. He was very handsome and tried to seem older than he was by walk-ing slowly with a stoop and never brushing a lock of hair out of his eyes. He talked slowly, too, but I think he did this to have time to think so he could say something clever, which he often did. He had very little money. This irritated him.

He kept a portable phonograph beside his bed and a bot-tle of Madeira under it. When he was coming alive in the morning he would turn on the phonograph, pull up the bottle of Madeira, and take a swig. The record on the turn-table was always Mozart. It was not a bad way to wake up in the morning. He spent fifty-five pounds on Mozart in one term, the most heartbreaking music in the world, he said. I asked him how he was going to pay the bill. He shrugged, "That man exists to supply me with Mozart rec-ords. He ought to be glad to do it." "I know, but will he be?" I asked. He only shrugged again. It occurs to me that this adolescent single-mindedness, when stuck to, has sup-plied Britain with some of her most glorious deeds.

The only time John made any disturbance was when he got a letter from his mother; he would tramp around the room cursing her. He said he hated her and I believed it for I have seen him turn a dark purplish red as he recog-nized her handwriting. He liked to discuss means of doing away with her and at one time he had a stack of books on poisons, one of which he said he was going to use, the one that was undetectable.

His tastes, while not spectacularly expensive, kept him broke. His wine merchant threatened to cut off his supply

unless something was occasionally paid him on account and
John got to London much less often than he liked. He lived
in London but he never went home. He liked Wren churches
and he spent his time there admiring them. It was in a Wren
church that he found a way if not to affluence at least to
a nice steady little income.

The verger was showing him around one of them, perhaps S. Lawrence Jewry or S. Swithin's, and the old man
said, "Like to see our manuscript collection, sir?" John said
he would. The verger took him to a row of little cupboards,
all unlocked, and started pulling out dozens of parchment
and vellum rolls, heaped carelessly inside, apparently un-
classified, of all dates and conditions. John was moderately
bored until the verger said, "Good job there ain't no thieves
about, sir. That's the only list we got." He pointed to a
couple of typed pages tacked to the inside of one of the
cupboard doors.

John pinched the list a few days later. From then on, he
said, it was money for old rope. He spent a day in London
every week and he would take a manuscript or two and
sell them in Charing Cross Road, where you can sell anything. I could always tell when he had struck. He would
leap into the room caroling and shouting and we would
eat a champagne dinner at the George. On fine spring days
he would hire an open victoria and we would be driven
down green country lanes, drinking beer. He even brought
one of the manuscripts to the digs, "To show the kind of
work I'm doing," a Henry VIII land grant with a whack-
ing great lead seal and the royal hen-tracks below.

Occasionally he would ask me courteously if I could spend
the day out as he was having a young widow up from London and I would courteously go away.

One afternoon I was lying on my bed reading and he
was sitting reading and yawning in front of the gas fire.
(We lived in modern digs.) I heard him murmur, "You're

a great man, Wotton. You're going to be rich. You're going to be famous." He said it loudly enough for me to hear.

He finished all his books on poisons and said they disappointed him, but one day he capered into the room shouting, "I've got it! I've got it!"

"Got what?"

"How to do her in!" he shouted.

"How?"

"Push her under a bus in Oxford Street!" In a hoarse agitated voice he described how, one foggy day, he would pause for traffic holding her elbow as if kindly, and as he saw the bus loom toward them, give her a big push under the wheels. When the crowd gathered he would curse and tear his hair in rage and sorrow at the accident. "That ought to do it," he said complacently.

I have made him seem more active than he was, given him a dark repellent brilliance perhaps. Actually he spent most of his time grumbling before the fire with a book face-down in his lap. He said once in a quiet voice, "Do you know what I'll be doing twenty years from now?"

"Ninety-nine years hard in Wormwood Scrubs," I said.

But he was serious. "I'll be a history master in some bloody little third-rate school." He believed this. The thievery and the plotting were a mere panache. I knew many like him, not so flamboyant but just as scared. The future seemed blocked somehow. It did not yet contain the war. His depression, although we didn't know it, was a nasty little tendril of The Depression. I got it in letters from home. It was all around us here. I gave a shilling to a decent-appearing man who had walked from Dover to Scotland and back looking for work. In the country I gave a shilling to a man who gave me a tip in return, the third race at Newmarket next day, Ginger Man, eight to one. I didn't have enough money to get a bet down, but Ginger Man won.

The President of the Swimming Club came to ask me if I would coach them during the late spring and John jeered at me for a hearty. A hearty was a jock. Students divided themselves into hearties and esthetes. John regarded himself as neutral and jeered at both. I told the President I would do it and one afternoon I went up to the Merton Street Baths.

The President said, "We'd like to put in an American system."

"Okay," I said. "All of you get in and swim a mile."

"Good God!" he said. He seemed shaken.

"All right. Swim a half-mile."

"See here, Allan, is all this—uh—churning up and down for vast distances really necessary?"

"What will you swim then?"

What they swam was their usual quarter-mile a day. I tinkered with the strokes of two or three of them and insisted that they swim a few sprints but when I tried some American fight-talk on them, first they gaped with astonishment, then they were fascinated. "What's the purpose of these absurd exhortations? D'you think we might actually swim faster if we believed them? But one can't believe them. Too ridiculous." I just did it as a gag. I had never believed in them much myself.

As the term and with it my scholarship drew to a close, I was reading the Victorians and showing Edmund Blunden whatever I wrote. He was steadfastly encouraging, a pedagogical technique I understand now, and I sold another story, to *Life & Letters* this time. Through the mails I placed a third with *Story* in New York but it was clear that I couldn't live on what I made even if I went on finding markets. I wrote letters to public and private schools at home asking for work. There was none. The high school in my home town said that I could by no means teach English with a mere Honours degree in English Language and Literature from Oxford—I would have to have a degree in Education. I knew how tough things were. I wasn't proud and I began to see myself in one of those green uniforms carrying Western Union telegrams. Unexpectedly Jonathan Cape offered me a job in publishing in London, seven guineas a week and long week ends from Friday to Monday noons but, standing in their offices looking out into the trees in Bedford Square, I said no at once, somewhat surprising myself. Much as I liked the English, I knew then I was not, despite my grandfather and a long stay in the country, an Englishman. I would deliver telegrams.

I wasn't able to wait to see how my charges did against Cambridge because I was sailing for home. The President, the last time I looked them over at the Baths, came out with a box and said, "We'd like you to have this." In the box was a beer mug engraved with the arms of the club, my name, and underneath, *In recognition of kind and valuable services.* Someone drove me out to the Crown at East Hanney where I said good-by. Les Herman, the plasterer, said, "Domn it, Ollin, we didn't know you was going. We wanted you to be captain of our shove-ha'penny team. We've this match going with the Seven Stars at Abingdon and we're going to hire a charabanc and make a night of it." I was sorry I couldn't make that one either.

In midocean a steward handed me a cable. It said WE BEAT CAMBRIDGE THANKS TO YOU.

About the Author

Allan Seager was born in Adrian, Michigan, in 1906. His father sold fence for the Peerless Wire and Fence Company and was a practiced teller of tales. Sherwood Anderson once observed that Seager's storytelling ability came from his father.

Upon graduating from the University of Michigan, Seager went to Oxford on a Rhodes Scholarship. Afterward he moved to New York, where he worked briefly as an editor at *Vanity Fair*, before returning to Michigan and joining the faculty of the University of Michigan. When asked why he had returned, Seager replied, "I hated the people I came from and I wanted to find out why." He married Barbara Warner, and the couple raised two daughters.

Primarily known as a short-story writer, Seager was also a best-selling novelist. All told, he published five novels, including *Equinox* and *Amos Berry*, as well as a collection of thumbnail biographies called *They Worked for a Better World*, a translation of Stendhal, and *The Glass House*, a biography of poet Theodore Roethke.

Seager died in 1968 in Tecumseh, Michigan, at the age of sixty-two. He is survived by his two daughters, Mary and Laura, and his second wife, the writer Joan Fry.